1283

THE CHINESE FIRE DRILL

MICHAEL WOLFE

A Critic's Choice paperback
from Lorevan Publishing, Inc.
New York, New York

For Marion, Ann and Ellen,
the Class A dependents

AUTHOR'S NOTE

This is fiction. If you want to believe it could or did happen, that's your own business. I say that all characters and situations came right out of my head.

A glossary of GInglish, Vietnam version, appears on pages 245–247.

◀ 1 ▶

Everyone knocks West Point. They disparage the curriculum, they smile tolerantly at the traditions and, most of all, they bad-mouth the graduates. That's especially true of the rest of the officer corps of the Army. To the average nongraduate serving officer, the rapid promotion and special treatment the trade-school boys get is an ever-present aggravation. Of course for a lot of the marginal types it's easy enough to blame the Academy and its sons. Still, there's something in the idea and you see it best when a couple of them spot each other's class ring and a silent signal passes between them.

Yet no matter how much one of the unblessed may gripe about it, there's still a special feeling in the Army for The Point. You go to the Army-Navy game and there's maybe a hundred thousand people there. Figure half rooting for each side. Out of the Army's fifty thousand, not more than a tiny fraction ever went to the place as cadets and the biggest majority never even visited. You wouldn't know it, though, when the long gray lines march into the stadium and the team comes trotting out on the field. There's a lot of choking up for the fight songs and if the cadets win, you can hear the cheering from Philly to the Thayer Gate.

If you've ever worn the uniform you get that same kind of feeling when you actually go up the Hudson to The Point. From the moment you pass the MP standing outside his stone sentry box and drive along past the rows of quarters, the feeling builds, and when you come around the bend and see the massive gray walls rising tier on tier up toward the chapel, even if you got your

1

commission from Sears, Roebuck, your chest goes out and you become a little mushy around the edges.

I've always figured myself for a no-nonsense type about that kind of thing, but it affected me. I'm strictly your ROTC product and, up to the day before, I'd felt sure that I wouldn't be sticking around the Army long enough to let the system bug me. I'd stay as long as it was fun and I didn't have something better to do. If anything that looked good stuck its little head up, then I'd put in for relief from active duty and put my uniforms in mothballs except for the annual two-week tour I'd be obligated for. That's what I told myself.

I'd told the same thing to Tiny a couple of dozen times, at least. They weren't going to hook me the way they got her. Anyway, she liked the life and she had a hell of a lot to offer. When she'd made lieutenant colonel she'd been the youngest in the whole WAC and you have to give good odds if you want to bet on her commanding the whole shebang before she packs it in. Her twenty years in harness were going to be over pretty soon and you knew without asking that she'd keep right on going until she'd made it thirty for the full retirement.

That wasn't my idea of how I wanted to spend my life. I'd just got my second bar in Vietnam and it looked like a long wait until I could think about making major. I'm a specialist in a small field and there are just so many slots for my kind of thing. That's why I'd never bought a set of full dress blues.

Some guys, the ones who can afford it, buy blues right off the bat. For the few times a year you get to put on the rig it's not worth it to most. They don't spend the money unless they plan to stay in for the full career. That was my excuse but I didn't have it anymore. The store had delivered the whole affair to the hotel early that morning just as they'd promised. I went in and shaved and then got myself dressed. I had to put the few decorations I'm entitled to on the jacket and they helped brighten things up. I got the cap out of its box and put it on and then stood in front of the mirror to get the full effect. It wasn't bad and even Tiny said so when she came through the door that connected my hotel room with hers.

2

She looked sensational. I'd never seen her in blues before and I had to admit it couldn't have looked any better if the designer had planned the thing just with her in mind. She had her dark auburn hair done up just right for the cap with its scrambled eggs along the visor. Just in case you missed her really monumental façade, there was a double line of decorations that hung just below her clavicle. If you knew anything about the subject, you could tell she hadn't got them just for attendance or deportment. There were some pretty good ones there, a number from foreign governments. Even her Vietnamese order was a step better than mine. The rest were the kind where the citation doesn't get any more specific than "meritorious service in a matter affecting our two countries."

Just in case you haven't figured it out for yourself, Tiny is a spook and I work for her. The big difference between us, beyond the rank, is that Tiny is right out there where everybody knows what she does. I sneak around trying to look like I'm just a harmless piece of the scenery.

It's not hard for her to stand out. In heels she's almost six foot, with a type of beauty that gets better and more exciting the longer you look at her. Believe me, Margaret Eriksen, Lieutenant Colonel, WAC, is a dish.

I guess I stand out a little in a crowd, too, but it's not my good looks. Michael J. Keefe, Captain, Signal Corps. Six one in my socks and with a red mop on top of my head that looks like a bunch of carrots past their prime. I've still got the freckles and I burn and don't tan. Tiny says it's my normal look of happy stupidity that takes people in. They figure I'm just not smart enough to be anything but what I say I am. It may not be flattering but it's useful.

She didn't comment on my having bought the blues instead of renting them. Luckily there wasn't much in the way of alteration and I had them the next day. Still, she knew that it meant I was beginning to think about staying with the flag long enough to make the investment worthwhile.

Anyway, we stood there admiring each other until the phone rang with word that a car was waiting for us at the door. In the

3

elevator Tiny got a lot of sidelong looks from the other passengers, and when I followed her across the lobby, people turned around and stared.

Out in front was a shiny staff car with West Point markings and an enlisted driver. I heard the doorman snort when I climbed into the back seat first. How was he supposed to know that the junior officer is the first in and last out of a car or boat, and that the senior officer sits on the right? Even without swords to worry about it's a good idea, and it keeps the low man from tromping on the top man's shins as he tries to get over them.

I guess neither one of us realized how used to switching roles we'd become. During duty hours and in uniform she ran the show just as she was supposed to do by Army Regulation and plain common sense, and I did as I was told.

Most of the time, that is. Sometimes I had to improvise without taking time to let her know what the hell I was doing. When I got myself into a concrete mixer and, maybe, looked pretty bad, she came to bat for me just the way I knew she would. It worked both ways.

After duty we had settled into something else. We must have been discreet enough because I never had a hint from anyone that they thought we were anything more than two officers who worked together.

It was a near thing once, though. We were meeting with some people and Tiny hadn't had enough time to brief me. In trying to shut me up she managed to push the wrong button and my Irish rose like a mortar round.

She knew it as soon as she saw my face and managed to go into reverse just before I was going to say, "Colonel, you've got a small birthmark on the left cheek of your ass."

I told her about it later and she said, "You would have, too, you skinny son of a bitch."

She didn't say any more but a couple of times in the next few days I caught her looking at me in that funny way of hers.

I still hadn't any idea of why I was sitting in a staff car with

4

her and both of us dressed to the nines but she waited until the driver had worked his way through the traffic and was out in the clear and heading up the East River Drive. Then it turned out she didn't know much more than I did.

◀ 2 ▶

I had been back in Hawaii only two days when the orders arrived. I'd been up in Alaska filming some sexy new piece of military hardware in field tests and that meant a long spell of forty below and no relief in sight. When we finished, some kind soul got us a SAC flight from Elmendorf in Anchorage right to Hickam in Honolulu and I was just beginning to thaw out when the alarm went off. I was directed "to take first available transportation to Washington and then to the United States Military Academy to report to the Superintendent for temporary duty."

That's how I found myself first in a New York hotel, with Tiny in the room next door, and then riding up the Hudson with her, looking like a recruiting poster.

Typically, she started with a question. "Mike, what do you know about the Bostwicks?"

"Not much. Old Army family. All West Pointers. One of them has a top slot in Germany and I seem to remember he has a son in service, too. Or did. Didn't he get captured or something?"

She nodded. "Missing in action. Not on any of the lists, though, and when the others were all home he was still missing. Still is, I suppose. He and his enlisted radio operator, a sergeant named Bailey."

"So what are we doing here?"

"Last week General Bostwick died in Europe. The funeral is today and that's why we're here."

"But I never knew any of the Bostwicks."

"No, but some of the people coming want to talk to us."

6

"Like who?"

"Well, there's young Bostwick's father-in-law, Senator Colville. In case you've forgotten, he's a top man in the field of military affairs. The services treat him with kid gloves. I guess his daughter Anne will be there, along with the old general's classmates. People like the top command in the Army."

"And there's no point in asking you what they want to talk about, is there?"

She tilted her head toward the driver and said, "Enjoy the ride, Mike."

There wasn't much else I could do. It wouldn't be long before I had something new to worry about, so I just took in the sights. The first part was a mess.

The drive wound its way along the Harlem River, a discouraging prospect of abandoned cars, cement plants, crummy-looking barges and the remains of last summer's weeds. Of all the countries I've ever been in, the United States is the only one that doesn't make use of its waterfront areas. Even in Saigon the stretches along the river have parks and cafés and floating restaurants like the famous My Canh, where people can get out and stretch their legs and their vision. The only sign I saw of anything like that was a Columbia University crew stroking their shell along the fouled water, getting ready for the spring rowing season. It was all pretty depressing.

Once we got across the George Washington Bridge it began to look a lot better and there were signs all along the way of things beginning to green up. The parkway ended at the Bear Mountain Bridge and we went through the small settlements that still mark where the outer fortifications of the West Point complex were built to deny the upper Hudson to the British down in New York.

At the Thayer Gate the sentry waved us through, saluting smartly at the sight of a staff car with passengers in the back seat. We entered the grounds, went past the Thayer Hotel and along the edge of the cliff to the Officers' Club. The driver said he'd be back to take us to the chapel in an hour and we went into the club and straight to the big dining room with its broad bow window that looked out over the river. We ate alone at a table for two that made the most of the view. I noticed a group at a

7

long table in the center of the room. There was a white-haired man even I recognized as Senator Colville seated beside a young woman I took to be Anne Bostwick. The rest of those at the table were in uniform, dress blues for the occasion, and the junior man aboard was a brigadier. Tiny saw me eying them and helped out with some identifications.

"The one at the end you probably recognize. He's the new Chief of Staff. Next to him is the Superintendent of the Academy and on his other side is the Chairman of the Joint Chiefs of Staff." She knew most of the rest by sight but they were just names to me. One seat was still empty when they began to eat but in a few minutes an aide entered the room, followed by a civilian in a plain dark suit. As he approached the table the men in uniform rose, waiting until he was seated before resuming their meal. Whoever he was, he had to draw a lot of water to rate a greeting like that. Tiny knew who he was, all right, but I could see that even she was surprised at his presence.

"Who is the wheel?" I asked.

"That, my friend, is Emerson Kenzie, Assistant Secretary of Defense for Personnel Affairs. He hates to travel and he loathes ceremonial. If he's here, then this business must be bigger than I'd thought."

"You mean even you don't know what we're up here for?"

She smiled. "Even the Sphinx missed out on a few things. All I do know, Mike, is that all this has to have something to do with the Bostwicks and you're welcome to guess for yourself what it might be."

We timed our meal to the one being served at the center table. When their coffee came we paid our checks and went out to the car so we'd be in our seats when the brass arrived. From that point the proceedings went strictly by Army Regulations: Ceremonies, funeral, general officer.

There was a service, a caisson, a riderless horse with reversed boots in the stirrups, a firing party, a bugler and a flag. The flag went to Anne Bostwick as the nearest of kin. She accepted it soberly and the ceremony was over. The guests left the grave site in descending order of rank. We were the last to leave and

8

without a word from us we were driven directly back toward The Plain.

We pulled up in front of an imposing house that looked directly out on the velvet green of the parade ground. I followed Tiny through the front door but not before I'd noticed the MPs stationed inconspicuously around the place. Even the hand-picked West Point MPs, accustomed to the great from all over the world, were on their toes.

I could see that we were expected. Without delay we were shown into a large sitting room. There was a table of drinks and a white-coated messman to serve them. Facing each other were a pair of comfortable-looking sofas in front of a big fireplace where Kenzie and Senator Colville were standing, talking quietly with the Chief of Staff and the Superintendent. Seated on one of the couches was Anne Bostwick, with a slim glass of sherry.

When he saw us come in the Superintendent pointed to the messman and as we ordered our drinks I heard him say, "If there's anything further you require, gentlemen, I'm sure you'll ask."

He watched as our drinks were mixed and then he and the messman left the room. It was pretty clear that whatever was going to be discussed even he had no "need to know."

I stood beside Tiny, trying to take my cue from her. She hadn't saluted or reported us so I just kept my mouth shut until Colville asked us to sit on the sofa across from his daughter. Kenzie and the Chief of Staff found seats and it looked like Senator Colville was going to carry the ball.

Standing in front of the fireplace, he took a moment to collect his thoughts and when he spoke it was to Tiny and me.

"I'd like you both to know that I've been told something of how you two and your organization handled the Forsberg matter. Those of us who were told about it consider that it was very well done. What might have been a major scandal and an embarrassment to the whole country was concluded very satisfactorily."

It's always nice to be appreciated but I was beginning to get the feeling that we were about to find ourselves with another prize stinker. Colville went on.

"That was the thing that finally convinced me it would be best

9

to let the Army handle this matter. There was some thought about turning it over to a civilian agency, but these gentlemen have persuaded me that you are better equipped."

He wasn't saying so but I got a strong feeling that the reason our own organization had been tapped was because it's about as leakproof as you can get, with a reputation for minding its own business. That just might have been the big factor in his decision. That "civilian agency" is full of people just waiting for their retirement to begin writing books about their covert operations, and some aren't even waiting that long. If the senator wanted to keep his affairs out of print he could do worse than do business with us.

The Chief of Staff spoke up. "I'm sure we won't disappoint the senator. Just to make it official, you are both directed to place yourselves at the senator's disposal and to give him every possible assistance the Army can supply."

Kenzie nodded and said, "Now, Senator, if you'd like to take it from there . . ."

Colville took a deep breath. "You probably know that Captain Bostwick, my daughter's husband, is still missing in Vietnam and is presumed captured."

He reached into the side pocket of his jacket and walked to the low coffee table between the two sofas. On its polished surface he placed a small cardboard box and lifted off the lid, revealing a square of grayish cotton. Carefully he drew it away and we saw a pair of gleaming gold rings. Tiny looked up at the senator and he nodded. She reached into the box and took the rings, placing them side by side on her palm so that we might see them in a better light.

One was a wide gold wedding band, a man's, the other a West Point class ring, the stone flanked by the Academy arms and a class date.

Colville said, "That was found in my mailbox at home in Washington a few days after Anne's father-in-law's death in Germany. It hadn't come in the regular mail delivery but had been placed in the box sometime later in the day. This was with it."

He handed Tiny an envelope with the name of a cheap Washington hotel in the corner. Handwritten was: "For Senator Colville only. Very Confidential."

Tiny took it from him but she didn't take out the contents. Instead she asked, "I take it these rings belong to Captain Bostwick?"

Colville turned to his daughter. "Suppose you answer that, Anne."

Pale and tired as she looked, her voice was steady enough as she spoke in a low tone. "Yes, those are Duke's. There's a nick in the class ring that always catches on the lining of his jackets. He keeps saying he's going to get it filed down but somehow he never gets time." She held up her left hand. "The wedding ring is the mate to mine."

If she said they were her husband's that was pretty conclusive. It wasn't any kind of proof that he was alive, though. The thing to do now was to see what the envelope contained.

It was a sheet of stationery from the same hotel. The message was short and to the point. It was ordinary cursive handwriting with no apparent effort to disguise it in any way. Tiny read it and passed it over to me.

Place classified ad in next Sunday New York Times offering 1957 Edsel sedan for sale. Give local telephone number to call. Recognition word, "radio." Response word, "photo."

That was all there was. For a moment the room was silent and then Emerson Kenzie asked, "What does all this mean to you, Colonel?"

Tiny took the note from me and looked it over before she answered.

"For one thing, sir, the man who wrote this—or the people he works for—knows his business. He's had some experience in skating close to the law."

"What makes you say that?"

"For one thing, he doesn't bother to disguise his handwriting. He doesn't do what an amateur might. You know—cut out letters

11

or words from a newspaper and paste them up. He doesn't care if we eventually find out who he is or not. He's only going to need his cover for a short time and then he doesn't give a damn.

"Then there's the message. No extra words, no bragging, no threats. He says what he has to and that's all. An amateur would take the chance to spread himself a little."

"Anything else?"

She looked carefully at the message, bringing it close to her eyes. "Well, he didn't go to school in this country. We don't make that kind of seven with a stroke."

"What do you think will happen next?"

"If we put the ad in the *Times* he'll make contact and give instructions for a meeting. He'll try to set it up with the least danger to himself and then we may hear what he has to say."

"Any idea of what that might be?"

Tiny shrugged her shoulders. "Any one of a number of things. If you'd like my favorite guess, it'll be a demand for some kind of ransom."

Colville broke in. "But that's preposterous. Forgive me, Colonel, but it just doesn't make sense. Duke's been a prisoner for almost three years. If it's ransom they want, why have they waited this long?"

Tiny looked up at him. "I'm sorry, Senator, but as I said, it's only a guess. Right now that's the best I can do. When we make the contact we'll probably know a lot more and maybe we'll be able to come up with something better." She looked at Anne Bostwick. The girl had gone even paler, as if she was about to lose the last vestige of her self-control. "Sir, I think someone should get Mrs. Bostwick a glass of water."

Colville swung around to look at his daughter. "I'm sorry, my dear. I don't think we need to keep you any longer. General, is there someone who can take my daughter over to the Thayer? Perhaps if she lies down for a while she'll feel more like taking the trip back to Washington."

An aide was sent for and Colville helped Anne Bostwick to her feet and took her to the door. She looked back at Tiny.

"Thank you, Colonel. You're very considerate. I know you'll do everything you can to bring my husband home."

When she'd left the room Tiny asked, "Can I take it, gentlemen, that we are authorized to proceed as we think best?"

There was a sudden silence in the room. Tiny was a lieutenant colonel and a woman. She was asking for a hell of a lot. If they gave her free rein, they might find themselves in over their heads if she screwed up. It wasn't the kind of thing you do without a lot of thought.

I guess it wasn't anything out of the way for the Chief of Staff. An army officer knows he has to accept responsibility for what his people do. He tries to get the best he can find and then he puts his own career on the line. If they come up smelling like a rose he gets his share of the credit. If they goof he takes his share of the blame.

For politicians like Kenzie and Colville it was a different matter. At the first hint of any scandal that might affect his boss, there would be a fast request for Kenzie's resignation and he'd lose his big office, his private plane and the rest of his goodies, to become another statistic in the unemployment figures.

For Colville it could be just as bad. He'd spent a lifetime working his way up the seniority ladder to the upper levels where they handed out the big committee chairmanships and the rest of the really effective power. To risk all that, to gamble on the good judgment of a lieutenant colonel and a captain, was asking a lot in a matter so close to his own family.

In his position he was used to being deferred to by the topmost levels of the military. Generals and admirals lit his cigars and mixed his drinks. The merest hint would get him a military jet and crew, ready to fly him anywhere in the world, or an aircraft carrier for a pleasant warm-weather cruise when the snow got too deep in Washington. Now he was being asked to put everything in the hands of two people he'd never laid eyes on until just a few minutes before.

I don't suppose you can get to a position like Colville's without taking some risks. I'll say this for him: He had guts.

"Colonel Eriksen, you were brought here because you were the person recommended by her superiors as best qualified to direct this operation. You and Captain Keefe have a track record. We acknowledge that—right, Kenzie?"

Kenzie said in a low voice, "That is the opinion of their superiors."

"Then I'd be the worst kind of damn fool if I didn't get out of your way and let you get on with what you've been trained to do." His tone softened a bit. "Still, I'm sure you can see my position. I'm a father with a daughter who wants her husband back again with her and their children. I've got to balance that against my duty as a public servant and, I hope, a good citizen."

That was straight enough. We had clearance to do as we thought best. At the same time it wouldn't hurt to think, every now and then, about consequences.

When Colville spoke again it was in his normal assured tone. "What do we do next, Colonel?"

"We do as we're told. If we're going to play ball with this man, then we go back to New York and place the ad he wants in the Sunday *Times*. We just insert the ad and follow instructions. Today is Thursday and that gives us more than two days to get set up for the contact. When we know a little more we can make an intelligent assessment and come up with a recommendation."

Kenzie stood up. "That makes sense but I want to give you a few guidelines. There is to be no hint of Army involvement in this business. By all the rules, we are supposed to leave this sort of thing to the civilian authorities. If it comes out that we've bypassed them, there's going to be one hell of a stink. You're to make use of any support the three services can furnish but you will not expand the number of people who know the real purpose of the operation without express orders from me or these gentlemen. Senator Colville agrees that it is in the national interest that we handle things this way until we have good reason to involve anyone else. You are authorized to communicate directly with the Chief of Staff without going through channels or, if he is not available, with the Chairman of the Joint Chiefs." He gave Tiny a sharp look. "You already know something about how to do that, I'm sure."

Tiny nodded and he went on: "Now what will you need right away?"

"First I'll need a précis of everything we have on Captain Bostwick. Physical data, personal characteristics, pictures taken as

14

recently as possible, reports—anything that may be of the slightest use."

"No problem there. I can get that done right from my own office."

"Next, a copy of the after-action report on the operation during which he was captured and the interrogations of the surviving members of the company." She paused for a moment and then said, "It may be that we'll need funds."

The senator looked up. "I'll take care of that. I'll transfer what you need as soon as I get back to Washington in the morning." He took a card from his wallet and scrawled a number on it. "That's my unlisted phone. If I'm not there, whoever answers will know how to reach me." He looked at Tiny narrowly. "Don't scrimp, Colonel. I'm not the richest man in America but I have enough and I'm willing to give every last dime to get that boy back."

She nodded. "Thank you, sir. I hope that won't be necessary."

Kenzie broke in. "What else do you need?"

"There were two of them, sir."

"What do you mean?"

"Two men from that patrol are missing. Captain Bostwick, and"—she paused—"the other man. Sergeant Bailey, the radio operator."

There was a sudden silence. They'd been so busy worrying about the missing officer, they'd forgotten all about the enlisted man who'd been captured with him. Colville was the first to get back his cool.

"The same thing applies to him. You're to make every effort to bring him back along with my son-in-law. Anything else?"

Tiny thought for a moment. "One thing. We'll need a code name for the job."

"Any suggestions?"

"I have one you may like. How about 'Operation Home Run'?"

Kenzie nodded. "So ordered. Now if there's nothing further I can contribute, then I'll get back to Washington."

He took just enough time to shake hands and then he was gone. A few minutes later I heard his helicopter take off and by that time we had wound up with the Chief of Staff. Evidently he had other business at The Point and excused himself, leaving the two of us with the senator. For some reason Colville seemed to be in no hurry to go. He stood at the window and watched as the general and his aide walked across The Plain toward the club and then he turned to me.

"You haven't said a word, Captain. Don't you have any thoughts?"

I had a lot of thoughts but none of them seemed proper to discuss with him. Until we knew a lot more, all I could do was make conversation.

"Senator, I'm way down at the working level. Down where you sometimes get your hands dirty. Frankly, the less you know about what I do, the better for everyone."

He smiled. "Well, you're a candid young man." Then his face sobered. "Just try to remember that what you do can affect a lot of people. Most of them will never know it but it might change their lives more than you'd think. Right now I'll just wish you the best of luck. You already know you've got all the backing we can give you." He nodded to us both and left the room. Tiny and I followed him to the entrance hall on the way to our car, but as we were about to go out the front door, a white-coated servant handed Tiny a small envelope. She tore it open and read the few lines on a sheet of notepaper and then passed it to me.

Dear Colonel:
    If it is at all possible, would you and Captain Keefe stop at the Thayer for a moment. I'll be in my room.

                                                            Anne Bostwick

She had led us to a spot where we could look out over the Hudson. There was a light spring breeze which stirred her blond hair and she held her collar closed against the chill. Anne Bostwick was not a beauty by conventional standards but she knew how to make the best of her good points, mainly her fine hair and her good eyes. Despite the slight edge to the wind and the fact that she must have been very tired, she breathed in the clear air hungrily, seeming to draw strength from it. We had called her

16

room from the lobby and she had come down to meet us and to lead the way to the spot where we now stood.

"You know, I have a lot of happy memories of The Point. The football weekends, the big proms, the parades and all the things a young girl likes. I was at school in Washington and coveys of us would come up for dates. The boys we'd meet are scattered all over the world now. Most of them are married. Some of them dead in Vietnam. A lot have left the service but none of them will ever forget the years here. I know I won't.

"I didn't begin to date my husband until a few months before graduation. He hadn't dated anyone his first three years. Then, just as though he'd reached a deadline he'd set for himself, out of a clear sky he wrote and asked if I'd like to go to the next prom with him. At first I couldn't imagine why he'd picked me. There were lots of really beautiful girls and almost all of them were better partners than I. You know—brighter chatter, good dancers, all the things that most boys like. Duke was First Captain and he could have had his pick of any of the regular prom-trotters but he chose me. I was on top of the world.

"After graduation there was the usual rush to the chapels and the whole thing with the arch of swords. Duke hadn't proposed or really said anything but it was just understood that he wanted to marry me but not until he'd made the list for captain. In fact, now that I think of it, he never did really propose. One day he just let it be known that the marriage had been scheduled and he'd let me know when it was time to have my trousseau ready. He wrote regularly once a week and half of every leave he'd spend with my family, doing the things he planned when and where he wanted. Even his gifts to me were selected to fit his plans. One birthday he gave me a copy of *The Officer's Wife* and every so often he'd give me a kind of quiz, just to keep track of what I'd learned.

"My husband isn't an easy man to know. I suppose all the Bostwicks have been like that. People respect them, they may even admire them, but nobody really likes them. Do you know how he got that nickname? It began as 'The Iron Duke.' Some cadets hung it on him when my husband said that the man he most admired was Wellington. It stuck but Duke never seemed

17

to resent it. He took it as a compliment, not realizing that it meant something different to the others.

"He always called his father 'sir,' ever since he was a little boy. He even suggested once that our girls call him that instead of 'Daddy.' " She broke off and looked to the north, toward the cemetery. "The old general never came to see me even once after Duke was captured. My mother-in-law did until she died last year but when I asked her why he hadn't come she always evaded the question. Finally one day she let it out. The general had never forgiven her for having just one child. She had borne a boy, though, and now I was the only one who could assure that there would be more Bostwicks. It seems ridiculous if you didn't know him but he wouldn't have anything to do with me until I provided him with a grandson." She shook her head sadly.

"Maybe I shouldn't say it but I'm not sorry I haven't given Duke a son. Not that I want to hurt or disappoint him; it's just that I can't bear the thought of my boy being forced into living the kind of life his father and grandfather planned for him. Just suppose he doesn't want to give his life to the service. Maybe he'll want to build bridges or be a farmer or a forest ranger. He'll have to choose between breaking the family tradition or living out his life the way they have. Either way, once he's made the choice, he'll have to live with the thought that perhaps he should have chosen the other way."

I had no idea why she was telling us all this. I did realize that she was saying things that had been on her mind for a long time, which she had never chosen to speak of to someone else. She took a step toward Tiny.

"When you find my husband, don't let what I've told you here make you think any the less of him. He's not easy to understand and often he doesn't act as another man might, but don't let that put you off. No matter what I've said, I want him back."

She turned away and half ran toward the hotel and we walked to where we'd left the car. We didn't have much to say during the ride back but just as we started across the bridge I asked, "Who's going to make the contact?"

Tiny swung around in her seat and looked right at me. "Don't be silly, Mike. You are, of course."

18

⊰ 3 ⊱

I'd never been in New York before and I had some idea that once the ad had been placed in the Sunday *Times* I'd be able to get around a little and see the sights with Tiny. I wasn't even going to get to do that.

The first thing I had to get through was a stack of material that arrived next morning with a courier and a guard to keep him company. They must have had every clerk in the Pentagon up all night pulling stuff for us to review. When the Army does something, it never seems to know when to quit. You ask for a man to help you lift a box and they send you a full battalion, a hundred-ton crane and rations for a week. That kind of thing.

The pouch had the personnel file on every man in the company, his whole life story from the day he'd enlisted or been drafted, and most of it made damn dull reading. I skimmed through the files of the survivors, then turned to those of the dead and missing. Bostwick's story I knew a little of, so I went on to check the radioman's bundle.

Bailey was twenty-four when he was captured, a farm boy from the Florida Panhandle. He was a Regular, five years' service and a good record. The only negative thing in the file came from his wife's bad habit of spending his pay faster than he could make it. There was some correspondence about it but he'd finally got her straightened out. No other bad marks. A pretty good soldier.

Most of the others were about the same but the company had a poor reputation. Some of the senior NCOs had seen Vietnam as a kind of Klondike, a get-rich-quick opportunity that might never come again. A slack CO had let them take over and by the time the battalion commander had caught on, the thing was out of hand. The Inspector General and the MPs had moved in and the investigation began turning up a king-size stink. There were pages and pages of it.

The old first sergeant had been the kingpin but all the senior NCOs were mixed up in it one way or another. The acting first, the one who was killed later in the action, was due to go next and probably shouldn't have been taken on the patrol. There was plenty of evidence that he'd been the one behind the fragging of the executive officer, the one who had begun asking questions. As soon as he started getting answers, he died suddenly of the multiple wounds you get when you share your cot with a live fragmentation hand grenade. That's what finally brought the Inspector General and a CID team. It was all in the file.

Next came the after-action report.

The patrol was supposed to be nothing more than a long recon. There were no reserves available to help out and if they ran into any kind of resistance, Bostwick's orders were to mark the spot and pull back. Later somebody would come and clean up the area but until then, the patrol was supposed to gather intelligence and stay out of trouble.

The real purpose of the exercise was to pick up what was left of the company and give it a good shaking. The battalion commander must have figured that a hard-nosed West Pointer like Bostwick was just the man for the job. He'd clean out the rotten spots and then rebuild on the good wood that was left.

He formally assumed command and headed straight for G-2. They gave him a nice quiet area, one where there had been no report of hostiles for some time, but rugged enough to let the men know they hadn't just been out for a stroll. Bostwick drew rations and ammunition for a week. What the men couldn't pack on their backs would be airlifted in but essentially they were on their own for seven days. When he got back he'd know who his problems were. Those who weren't set for court-martial would be disposed of in other ways and he'd draw the replacements he needed to get back to full strength. That would include a new first sergeant. The acting one Bostwick would keep right under his eye until they returned to base.

They moved out as only two platoons. A reliable lieutenant had the first and a steady sergeant first class, who hadn't been involved in the mess, was leading the second. There were no other officers and company headquarters was just Bostwick, the acting first, Bailey, the radio-telephone operator, and a couple of riflemen, barely a squad.

Physically the men were in shape. They had been airlifted into the sector they were to cover and when the choppers left the drop zone, Bostwick moved them right out. He'd had to take into account his shortage of bodies and his march plan was based on what he had to work with.

Instead of the usual diamond formation, which kept flank communication between the platoons and the command post, he set them up in echelon, one forward on his left flank and the other to the rear on his right. That way he hoped to keep visual contact and still cover a front of a couple of hundred meters, each element in position to move to support the other in case of trouble. That's the way they were moving when they got hit.

The terrain, as I've said, was pretty hairy, and it had been slow going for quite a while. It was one of those stretches where you hit a tangle of gulches and gullies, the jungle spilling out over rocky outcroppings and sheer drops into deep-cut stream beds, with patches of swampy ground for a change of pace. It's no wonder they hadn't been able to keep close contact and it hadn't taken long for them to get spread farther and farther apart both left to right and front to rear. The first platoon had the easiest going and they'd moved pretty far ahead while the second kept dropping back. They'd run into a tangle of fallen trees that had been taken down by a landslide.

Bostwick still had radio contact and, like any well-trained company commander, I guess he was just about to give the order to regroup when it happened.

The CP, right in the middle, got hit first. They'd marched straight into a small but well-set ambush that the first platoon should have sprung before Bostwick and his handful reached it.

The way it was they got the full force of it. The first platoon heard the firing and tried to wheel and come back to support him but as far as they'd strayed, that took time. The second was still in the fallen trees and by the time they got through, it was all over. They were taking moderate fire all the time and never did get to the place where the CP had caught it. Both platoons, following their orders, withdrew and finally made it back to the drop zone. The lieutenant and a few others had been zapped and the steady SFC assumed command, taking his casualties with him.

As quickly as they could get there the choppers came in to extract the survivors. There was no thought of trying to get back to the ambush site until enough of a force could be scraped together from other operations in progress. That would take a couple of days at least. Meanwhile the SFC was written up for a Silver Star and everybody who'd been involved began to think of reasons why it wasn't his fault.

Operations said that based on what they'd had from Intelligence, there had been no reason to keep Bostwick from taking his short-handed outfit into the area for the purpose of shaking it up without getting anyone killed.

Intelligence said that while they had been the ones to make the selection, everything they had on the area showed no signs of Vietcong or North Vietnamese activity anywhere near it for months.

Air Operations came up with all kinds of pictures that were supposed to prove they had detected no movement or sign of hostile occupation and anyway, they had put Bostwick right where they'd been told.

It turned out to be just the beginning of their troubles.

Suddenly the air was full of messages, demands, orders, with everything marked "For Immediate Action," or the equivalent. The Pentagon called Hawaii, Hawaii called MAC-V in Saigon. From there the demands for action and information grew even more urgent. U.S. Army–Vietnam, Second Field Force, division, brigade and battalion were all on the mat. They all had the same question to answer. What had happened to Bostwick?

Burton Bostwick III, Captain, U.S. Army, fifth-generation graduate of the Military Academy. The first Bostwick had commanded a brigade at Bull Run, his son had won a Medal of Honor as the youngest battalion commander in Cuba. The next had led a machine-gun outfit in the AEF in France. The one we'd just buried had been on MacArthur's staff in the Pacific, served in Korea and was waiting for his fourth star. While he waited he was burning up the channels for word of his only son.

For more than a hundred years there had always been a Bostwick in the Army Register, Volume I, Active-Duty personnel. The latest was the standard model.

From his first day at West Point he'd been a marked man. Never had a cadet arrived so well prepared, emotionally, physically and mentally, for the Academy. While his classmates had yet to learn the difference between their left and right feet, Duke Bostwick had already been steeped in *The Officer's Guide, The Soldier's Handbook,* and *Infantry Drill Regulations,* along with everything else that a compleat officer really needs to know.

The old-timers around the Academy recognized the marks of the breed right off. The Bostwicks had all been smart, they were better-than-average athletes, they were tops in their classes academically, they were rich, well connected and insufferable. They earned top grades in their courses, they wore varsity letters on their sweaters and a long row of stripes on their sleeves and they made few friends.

At graduation they never failed to make the top 10 percent, automatically earning the right to assignment in the Corps of Engineers, a posting they always declined in favor of a combat branch, where the increased visibility would help earn them promotion as fast as the law and Army Regulations would allow.

Even more carefully than they chose their assignments the Bostwicks selected their mates, researching the available prospects with special attention to such factors as health, social, political and economic status and a proven ability to produce sons. No Hapsburg princeling was ever mated with more caution.

As noted, Duke had married Anne Colville, only daughter (after three sons) of a senior member of the Senate Armed Forces Committee and the multimillionaire founder of the Colville Syndicate.

Lieutenant General Bostwick wanted his son back. Senator

Colville wanted his son-in-law back. It was assumed that Anne Bostwick wanted her husband home. The pressure was constant and intense. G-2 got the brunt of it.

Information was slow in coming in. Even while the units in the field got ready to mount an operation in force to enter the area, the spookmasters were bearing down on their nets. Every available agent was urged to his maximum effort in finding out what had happened to the missing captain. Cash bonuses were offered and a lot of people took extra risks they should have avoided.

It didn't take too long to establish that whoever Bostwick had tangled with had not belonged to any regularly organized Vietcong or NVA unit. G-2 was able to prove that they had been right in their original assessment. There were no known hostiles in the region where Bostwick had led his patrol. They knew exactly who had not laid the ambush. They just didn't know who had.

A beefed-up team of debriefers had been brought in to interrogate, closely and at length, the men who had survived. From the data they assembled the Intelligence officers had been able to pinpoint the spot where the attack had come. A volunteer team had been airlifted as close as they could get and the whole area had been fine-tooth-combed for clues as to exactly what had occurred.

The place where the CP had been hit was located and it was there they found the bodies. Each was matched against the names of the known missing. It wasn't easy. They'd been lying out there, unburied, long enough to attract the local animals and most were identified by their dog tags and personal belongings. They were scraped up and shipped back to the States. The remains of the acting first sergeant were found close by Bostwick's radio, closing his file and saving the taxpayers the cost of court-martialing and punishing him. Of Bostwick and Bailey, his operator, there was no trace. "Missing in Action—Presumed Captured."

The news was flashed halfway around the world to the Pentagon, to Senator Colville and, presumably, to his daughter. In time someone probably got around to telling Mrs. Bailey, who was at Fort Jackson waiting for her husband to come home.

Putting a name on what had happened to Bostwick didn't take the heat off.

24

If anything, the flak started to rise higher. A lot of people stopped doing what they were paid to do to put in full time on the search for Duke Bostwick. While the Army was using its resources, the State Department was taking pressure to open every available clandestine channel to the VC and Hanoi through third-world nations and even the antiwar elements at home in the States. A group of show-business personalities who weren't so radical that they couldn't recognize the value of good publicity from the Colville Syndicate were urged to ask their friends across the DMZ for any word that might be available about the man. They returned from their visit with word that their inquiries had been met with what they considered to be honest denials. The belief that Bostwick was not in the hands of the NVA was bolstered by the fact that there had been no attempt to use the young officer in their propaganda campaign, a move they certainly would have made with such a prominent captive.

The South Vietnamese were kept busy as well. They had a fine appreciation of just how important a man the senator was when it came to filling their needs for weapons and money assistance, and word was filtered to the Vietcong that any information about Bostwick would earn the bearer enough reward to keep him in comfort for life. Actual delivery of Bostwick, alive and well, would get the man or men responsible even more.

Nothing worked. Gradually the pressure eased and the men in the field were permitted to go back to doing what they'd been sent to do. There was a flurry of interest in the press when Anne Bostwick and Mrs. Bailey were invited to the White House to receive the decorations their husbands had been awarded. Bostwick was given his promotion to major and there had been posthumous awards for the others. A few days later there had been a commotion at a national cemetery out on Long Island. Press and TV had been alerted and were on hand when the widow of the acting first sergeant dumped all his medals and other decorations on the grave his remains had occupied since their return from Vietnam. Her six kids stood around grinning while their mother addressed her late husband in words so direct and explicit that most of her diatribe was lost to the censor's bleeps.

For the next year little more was heard of Bostwick and Bailey except for a one-inch piece in the papers when Bailey's wife tried to get her husband declared dead. The lady was anxious to re-marry but the judge rejected her application out of hand with a scathing lecture on loyalty to her prisoner husband, who was being held captive so that she, her children and the rest of the nation should be free.

Back in Washington, Senator Colville was sworn in for his fifth term and General Bostwick got his fourth star and what would probably be his last active-duty assignment, at a post in Europe.

The peace talks dragged on and finally ended. The NVA opened their POW camps and the men began to come home. Getting those in the hands of the Vietcong took a while longer but at last they were released, flown to the Philippines and then home to be lionized, briefly, and then forgotten. It was their tough luck to have been in a war that nobody wanted to think about anymore. There were no victory parades, no monuments, no memorial plaques. The benefits for the men who had been taken from their homes and told to make the world safe for people they didn't even like very much were given slowly and without grace.

Of Bostwick and Bailey there was no trace. Their names appeared on none of the lists furnished by the other side and they were still carried on the rolls of the Army as "Missing—Presumed Captured." Bailey's wife lived on with her children in quarters at Fort Jackson, working her way through the pay check that arrived every month. Anne Bostwick and her daughters lived quietly with her father.

◄ 4 ►

The phone finally rang. We'd had breakfast sent up and, a little later, more coffee was delivered and drunk and there was still no sign of anyone paying any attention to the ad in the paper. I'd about given up hope of getting a quick response when the sound of the bell sent me out of the easy chair I was slumped in. I waded across the floor and the thirty or so pounds of newsprint you get when you buy the Sunday *Times* and I reached the phone on the third ring.

"Is this the party that advertised the Edsel?"

"Yes."

"Well, look, friend. You don't say nothing about it. There was four models in that line. Which one have you got?"

Something was wrong. He hadn't said anything that included the recognition word so I figured I'd better use it first. "Don't you want to ask about the radio?"

"Sure, but what model is the car?"

By the rules his answer should have included the word "photo." I waited and so did he and finally it hit me that this wasn't my guy at all. This dude on the phone really wanted to buy an Edsel. He was willing to pay good money for it, too, and it took a couple of minutes to convince him that he was too late and finally get him off the line. There were a couple more like that but I got them headed off by saying the car was already taken. Finally I connected.

"Does your Edsel have a good radio?" I nodded to Tiny

27

through the open door to her room and saw her switch on the recorder.

I answered, "Yes, it has a radio and you may want to come up here and see the car in a photo."

"No, I don't think that would be best. The operator who answered said that your number is that of the St. Regis Hotel. That is near Central Park, is it not?"

From the few words he'd spoken I was trying to identify his accent and to visualize the man from the voice.

"Yes."

"Then will you be good enough to leave there in precisely ten minutes and walk north on Fifth Avenue? Enter the park at Fifty-ninth Street and walk north to the zoo. Enter it through the south entrance, where you will find a vendor of balloons. You will buy a balloon and hold it for a minute. Then pick out a child and give the balloon to it and walk north to the large building and out to Fifth Avenue. At the bus stop allow two buses to pass and board the third." I heard a click and realized that he'd rung off.

I replaced the phone and checked my watch. Through the open door I could hear the sound of the tape recorder being rewound. I went in and stood listening as Tiny played it back. His instructions were clear enough but he seemed to be making an awful lot of fuss about our meeting.

"What do you suppose all that's about? Why the business with the balloon?"

"I told you this guy was no fool," said Tiny. "He must have called earlier and found out where we're staying and then worked out this gimmick. This way he's going to get a good look at you before he lets you see who he is. If he thinks there's something not quite kosher he'll be able to pull back and try again later."

"Then what's that about the bus? The third bus, at that."

"Time, Mike. Three buses will give him time to make sure you're alone. He's willing to meet one man but no more."

The way she explained it the deal sounded logical enough. While she got busy on the phone I took my raincoat and went down to the lobby. Five minutes later I started up the avenue.

Even on Sunday there was plenty of traffic, lots of window shoppers and family groups going north toward the park or south

28

toward Radio City. When I got to Fifty-seventh I crossed Fifth in front of Tiffany's and then went uptown past Bergdorf's and the big fountain near the old Plaza Hotel. I waited for the light at Fifty-ninth, getting a good look at a cute girl waiting in an old hansom for a fare. She was wearing blue jeans and a bright dashiki shirt that didn't quite go with the battered old coachman's hat on her head. Maybe an actress filling in between parts, and the look she gave me said that she might be available for more than just once around the park. Maybe something like dinner for a start.

Inside the park there was a paved path lined with benches, leading to the zoo entrance a few blocks up. The early spring sunshine felt good and lots of people were seated on the benches and even on the grass with a piece of newspaper to keep their tails out of the damp. Any one of the men could have been the guy I was to meet and I was beginning to get that old prickly feeling at the nape of my neck as I entered the zoo grounds.

The balloon seller had found a sunny spot and he looked like he was doing a pretty good business. I waited while he took care of a couple of kids, then I picked out one of his stock and paid him. It was a big yellow one and I felt more than a little stupid standing there holding it. A couple of people gave me funny looks, and when a minute was up I looked around for a kid to give it to.

The first one I saw was a little girl about four in a pink coat and a frilly kind of bonnet. I held the balloon out to her and she stuck out her little hand but before she could latch on to the string she was suddenly yanked away by a large woman in a fur coat. I was treated to a five-thousand-candlepower glare and then I heard her say something to the man with her about calling a cop. That was all I'd need.

I walked away a few paces and looked for another candidate. This one turned out to be a boy about five, his black face gleaming as brightly as his crisp white shirt. He took the string from me and looked up into my face with a pair of big eyes that shone like headlights. He didn't say anything to me but instead he yelled to a whole bunch of kids grouped around an ice cream stand.

"Hey, lookee. He gimme a b'loon. That man there."

Before I could retreat a step I was engulfed by the whole swarm, all screaming at me and demanding their "b'loons." If I was going to keep my date I had to get out of there and without a Pied Piper trail of yelling kids. I stepped back to get room and reached into my pocket for a couple of bucks, and when I'd picked out the biggest kid, a girl about twelve, I said, "Here, buy as many as you can with this."

The girl immediately took my place as the center of the whirlpool of gyrating kids and I made my getaway, red in the face and the target of a lot of curious looks. It was only a few yards to the exit at the old arsenal building and I went straight up the steps to the bus stop. I stood there as I'd been instructed and let two buses go by before flagging down the third. I was the only one boarding and I began to think that my man had changed his mind about making the contact. I got on anyway and ran right into another problem.

"How much?"

"Thirty-fi' cents. Exact fare only."

"Well, all I've got are three quarters and some singles."

"Can't ya read, bud? Sign right on the door. Exact fare. We don't make no change. Everything goes in the lock box and that way I don't get held up."

"Look, I don't have the exact change."

"Sorry, bud. I gotta let ya off."

He was starting to swing the door lever when I heard a new voice.

"Perhaps I can help. If the gentleman needs ten cents to make the right amount perhaps he will accept it as a loan from me."

I saw a hand extended with a dime nestled in a pink palm. I started to hand my quarter to the driver but that still wasn't the right drill.

"In the box. You gotta put it in the box."

I took the dime and dropped it into the chute with my quarter and turned to thank the man but he had already started down the aisle to the rear of the bus. There was a long seat there that stretched across the full width of the vehicle and I followed him to it. I had only the last few steps to get a quick look at him before he turned and looked out the window. I still wasn't sure that he was the man I was to meet but any doubts I had were dispelled when I thanked him for the dime. He didn't reply immediately but waited until a roar from the engine almost drowned out his words.

"It is my fault. I should have mentioned on the telephone that the exact fare is required on New York buses. It did not occur to me that you might not be familiar with the customs of this city."

He ended his comment just as the sounds of the engine settled down and I guessed that he would not say any more until the bus stopped and started up again. I could hear him without any trouble but all the recorder in my pocket was getting was sound effects. He sat quietly until the bus stopped at Fifty-seventh and then, when the driver raced the motor, he said, "We will be getting off in a few minutes. You will come with me, please."

With his face turned to the window there wasn't much of it I could see without leaning forward and staring right at him but I could tell that he was a short man and heavy for his height. His black suit, complete with vest, was well worn and had never come from any of the stores we were passing along Fifth Avenue. His chubby thighs strained against the hard-looking material, coarse, thick-woven stuff that salesmen always say "wears like iron." If the suit had ever been pressed it had been a long time before and the overall impression I got of the outfit was that it was certainly not American. I'd seen that kind of suit on characters in French films, usually the village lawyer. The one shoe I could see was a black oxford with a slightly bulbous toe, somewhat scuffed and in need of a shine.

It was the broad hand resting on his thigh that drew my attention; the stubby fingers like little sausages had more than a hint of grime under the ragged nails. The skin was almost gray, with a yellowish overcast as though he'd once had malaria. Even the fumes coming from the bus engine couldn't drown out the stale, unwashed smell of the man, which wasn't disguised in the least by his cheap cologne.

He said no more and didn't move until he suddenly stood up and tugged at the signal cord. I followed him to the door and down to the street when the bus stopped. A few blocks ahead I

31

could see Forty-second Street as he headed west along the side street lined with office buildings and shuttered shops. For a man his size he moved quickly, glancing about him with little darting looks. The street was one way in the direction opposite the one we were taking. If anyone was trying to tail us he wouldn't be doing it in a car. If it was someone on foot he'd have to lay back pretty far on that almost deserted street.

When we crossed the Avenue of the Americas he didn't slacken his pace and I'd about decided he was heading for Times Square when, without warning, he turned into a run-down-looking establishment with a flaking sign over the door, RIALTO TURKISH BATHS.

Five minutes later I was sitting beside him on an unpainted bench in a tile-lined room with clouds of steam rising around us. All I was wearing was a towel around my waist and an elastic cord with a key on my wrist. The key was for the locker where I'd left my clothes and with them the pocket recorder, still turning away.

Finally he was ready to talk.

⊰5⊱

"First I must tell you that I am not a principal in this matter. I am, in fact, an agent, acting for others. To be perfectly candid, I have never met my principal. He deals with me only through an intermediary. If their dealings are in any way criminal or even unethical you may be sure that I am not involved in any such thing."

He was a careful son of a bitch and I could see that no matter what, he would be sure that Number One was taken care of.

"Okay. You're only an errand boy bringing a message. Now, what is it you've got to tell me?"

He didn't really appreciate being called that. He made a little gesture with his hands palms up and open, as though trying to show how clean they were.

"My principals believe that you may be in the market for something which they have in their possession. They have directed me to advise you of the price they have set and to arrange terms. Are you authorized to receive them?"

"Suppose you just say what you've been told and we'll take it from there."

His left shoulder lifted slightly. "As you wish. First I am directed to tell you that they have no interest in money changing hands."

That was a new twist. Ransom generally means money. Cash of some kind.

"They propose, instead, something in the nature of an exchange—their property for yours."

33

"And what have we got that they want in trade?"

"They will exchange the property they have for ammunition."

"What kind of ammunition?"

He paused for a moment as though making certain that he would get it all correctly.

"They require one million rounds of fresh rifle ammunition equally divided between the types used in the M-1 Garand rifle, the M-1 carbine and the new M-16 automatic rifle."

This guy had to be out of his mind A million rounds of ammunition for one slightly used but still serviceable U.S. Army captain. They might as well be asking for a secondhand A-bomb useful in starting a small brush-fire war.

"Do you know what you're asking?"

"Certainly. I have just told you."

"But do you really know what it means? For example, do you know that ammo for military use is packed a thousand rounds to the case. Each one is plenty heavy and you're talking about a thousand cases."

"I did not know that." From the way he said it there was no doubt that the matter was of small importance to him.

"I'm not sure what that adds up to but with the weight of the packing material, that much ammunition is going to weigh out at damn near fifty tons."

He didn't deign to comment, merely waving his hand slightly to show that he was personally dismissing that part of the problem.

"You've got to know that fifty tons of ammunition isn't something you can hand over on a street corner. How could you ever set up a delivery?"

"That will be arranged. You will be given instructions."

"Tell me one thing. Why not just take the money? I'm ready to negotiate right this minute if you want to talk about cash."

The way he answered left no doubt that he had clear orders not to deal that way.

"No. The amount is one million rounds. That part is not negotiable."

"Look, friend, you're taking me pretty far beyond my instructions. I don't know if I can even discuss such a deal."

34

He gave me a mean little sidelong glance. "Is it possible that you, too, are only an errand boy?"

I guess I had that coming. "Okay. You're right. If you won't talk in terms of cash then I'll have to go back for fresh instructions." A sneery smile from him rattled me a little. "Nobody ever dreamed that your people would come up with a crazy idea like this. If you want to settle the matter right here and now I can offer two hundred and fifty thousand dollars or its equivalent in any currency you choose for the safe return of the two men."

This time it was his turn to be surprised. "Two men?"

"If they're both alive. Spend the money any way you like."

That had been a trial shot and I'd learned something. This guy didn't know much. He may even have been telling the truth when he said he'd never seen his principal. In any case, it was a waste of time dickering with him. He could carry the cash offer back and we'd see what happened. He fooled me, though.

"This I can assure you: money in any currency will not be accepted. The terms are as I have given them to you on that point."

"Okay. Now suppose you listen to our terms."

"You have terms?"

"Why not? Why should you have all the fun? Now get this and make sure your boss gets it. So far the only thing you've shown us is a box with two rings. You're going to have to do a lot better than that. You're going to have to bring us solid proof that the owner of those rings and the other man are really alive and well. Nothing hokey. Real proof that will stand up."

"What sort of proofs do you require?"

"That's your problem. Just make sure they're good, that's all."

"And once we have established that both men are alive and well . . . ?"

"Then we'll begin to talk about the next step."

"You will deliver the ammunition?"

"We'll talk about it. We're not going to rush into anything."

He shook his head. "I urge you not to create delays. I have been told to tell you directly that if my principal even suspects that you are not negotiating in good faith, he will begin to send you what it is you want in his own way." He wiggled the fat little finger that

35

lay on his hairy thigh. "He will send it a little at a time."

That was pretty specific.

"If he's in such a hurry, tell him he can speed things up by setting some other price we can pay. Where does he think we can lay our hands on anything like a million rifle cartridges? Hell, the M-1 has been obsolete in the American Army for years since we converted to the NATO weapon. The old M-1 carbine hasn't been used in the services since Korea and the M-16 is used only in the kind of war we just finished with in Southeast Asia."

"Then I take it you do not know where to obtain such ammunition?"

"Not just like that. Do you?"

"My principal thought that might be the case. It is suggested that all three types are available in large amounts in just one place." He paused, I guess to build up a little cheap suspense.

"You'll find them all in Vietnam."

So that was it. There was nothing stupid about this bunch. I hadn't been on my toes when he'd listed the three weapons. There was just one country we'd given all three to in large quantities. There were lots of other nations who'd got our obsolete World War II and Korea equipment. Half the free world and the third world, too, were toting the weapons once used by GIs. Just one of them had lots of the nasty little M-16. That was Vietnam.

Even though the Americans were no longer fighting in the area, they were still sending in a flood of matériel as "replacements," allowed under the peace treaty. Every time Nguyen pulled a trigger another cartridge started on its way from America. The ammo dumps of the Saigon government were kept full.

The question was whether a million rounds could be sneaked out without touching off a stink that could reach people who didn't like to be embarrassed. A thousand cases of cartridges wasn't something you could just slip into your hip pocket either. It would be a hell of a job to move that stuff legally, let alone trying to sneak it out in exchange for the prisoners. I had no way of knowing whether the people I worked for would even consider the idea in the first place. It wasn't up to me to agree to assemble that big a chunk of matériel and then haul it off for the purpose of ransoming Bostwick and Sergeant Bailey. The only thing I could do right now was to try to get some useful information out of this character in the time I had.

"Let's just say for the purpose of discussion, mind you, that the ammunition could be gotten together. Now, how would you take delivery?"

"You will be given detailed instructions at the proper time."

I shook my head. "That's not good enough. You're going to have to give me some kind of an idea so that my people can decide if it's even possible. Hell, we could get ourselves all set and then your side might come up with something that just can't be done."

That stopped him for a minute. I watched him sweat until he said, "I can say that you will make the delivery within three hundred miles of Saigon."

"That covers a lot of territory, wet and dry. Can't you tell me if they are going to want land or water delivery?"

"I am not empowered to tell you that as yet."

"Well, for Christ's sake, when will you be?"

"First we must be sure that you actually have the matériel in your possession. When you have demonstrated that, you will be given instructions for delivery."

"Okay. I'll go back to my people and tell them what the demand is. They'll make the final decision about accepting the deal but I'm going to recommend that we do nothing until you show up with solid proof that you can deliver what we want. Right now the whole thing may be nothing but a swindle, so the next move is yours."

He gave me another of his one-sided shrugs. "That is most reasonable and I, in turn, shall recommend to my principal that he accept your condition."

"Then all that's left is to set the time and place for our next meeting. Just name them and we can both get on with this."

"I think it is perhaps a little premature for that. Tell me, you are familiar with the Continental Palace Hotel in Saigon?"

I nodded. It was like asking a Parisian if he's familiar with the Louvre.

"This is a lovely time of year to visit Vietnam. The rains will not begin for some time and the climate right now is quite delightful. If you can arrange a visit you will be contacted there."

37

"Okay. That's no problem. Do you want to set up another recognition and response for the meeting there?"

He stood up and gave me a funny kind of half bow. "That will not be needed. My name is Dupont, notary, at your service."

"And don't you want to know mine?"

He bowed again. "But that is not necessary. You are better known in Saigon than you realize, Monsieur Keefe. I recall that you were, for a time, associated with a certain Monsieur Toguri, a passing acquaintance of mine. Now if you will be so good as to give me ten minutes in which to make my departure, I will say *au revoir* and look forward to seeing you in Saigon."

He turned and waddled toward the shower room, his gross, hairy body covered with sweat.

There was no point in staying in New York any longer and when I got back to the St. Regis I told Tiny about the meeting while I packed. She taped what I had to say, putting in an occasional question. It didn't take long to cover it all and when I finished she packed quickly, then called the desk for a bellboy and a cab. We paid our bills and rode out to La Guardia to catch the air shuttle. She kept pretty quiet all the way and during the few minutes we had to wait for the next plane she placed a couple of calls from a booth in the waiting room, finishing just in time for us to board. The plane was well filled with people going back to D.C. after the weekend and we had no chance to talk.

The man who waited for us at the top of the steps in the terminal led us to a car in the parking lot, handed over some keys and made himself scarce. I drove, following Tiny's grunted directions, going through Alexandria toward the parkway to Mount Vernon. She came out of her brown study just long enough to show me where to turn off for the safe house we'd be using.

It turned out to be in a big apartment complex along the river. Parking in the underground garage, I got out the bags and we rode to an upper floor. There was a door key on the bunch I'd been given and I opened up on a decently furnished place, two bedrooms, living room and a small kitchen with most of the basics for a short stay, things like vodka, vermouth and generally what grownups need for civilized living.

While Tiny unpacked and changed, I mixed us some drinks and took mine over to a window facing the Maryland shore on the other side of the river. Sipping, I tried to count the major rivers I'd crossed in the last few days, starting with the Yukon, still locked in ice. By the time I'd worked my way to the Potomac Tiny joined me.

Out of the clear she suddenly asked, "Who do you think they are?"

I shrugged. "I don't even have a glimmer. You got any ideas?"

"A couple. One is based on the fact that they don't want cash."

"I suppose they have no way to use it."

"So whoever they are, they can't do their own shopping or get someone to do it. That rules out the VC or some outfit like the Cao Dai."

"Okay. Now who does it leave?"

She didn't have a fast answer for that one. She took a few paces around the living room and then came over to join me at the window.

"They want delivery within three hundred miles of Saigon but he wouldn't say if it was by land or by water. Damn. If he had we'd have something to go on."

"Tiny, this character may be a repulsive little creep but he's nobody's fool. He doesn't know much and he doesn't want to know more, that's for sure."

"Okay, fine. But what's he getting out of this? No matter what, he's not going to take his payoff in ammunition. He's got to be getting his in cash or something he can turn into money without much trouble."

I was about to answer when the phone rang. Tiny reached it in a couple of her long strides. Whoever was calling did all the talking, Tiny just grunting now and then to let him know she was listening. When she hung up she was smiling grimly.

"Well, at least we know who your fat friend is."

"I told you. He said he's a Saigon notary named Dupont."

"Dupont, hell. That's just the French equivalent of Smith or Jones or Doe."

"Okay. What's the word?"

"The New York detachment stayed right with you to the

Turkish bath. When he left he went right to the air terminal. I wondered why he'd set the contact for New York instead of Washington. Now we know. He was already booked and checked in on the SAS polar flight for Tokyo. From there he has an open connection to Hong Kong on Pan Am and another for Saigon on Korea Airways." She checked her watch. "Right now he's probably having dinner somewhere over the Canadian North Woods."

"Speaking of dinner, are we ever going to eat?"

"You're damn right. Just as soon as I make one call."

She dialed quickly and the line must have been answered on the first ring.

"Signal to Saigon. Agency code and priority. Message follows: Subject Fargot, Jules Etienne, en route Tokyo SAS to Saigon via Hong Kong. Vietnamese passport." She gave the passport number and as good a description of the man as I'd been able to supply and orders to initiate a close but covert surveillance from the moment he landed at Tan Son Nhut. "Prepare and forward dossier of subject and initiate background check. Report all known associates and any pertinent data using all available resources. This is a maximum effort. Report every twelve hours reference Operation Home Run. Message ends. Now read that back."

She listened for the time it took then hung up and turned to me.

"Now let's eat."

My watch said four-thirty when I awoke to find her sitting up in bed beside me. She had her long legs pulled up under her chin and even though her eyes were wide open I could see that her thoughts were miles away. I reached over and punched her solid thigh.

"Why the hell don't you go to sleep?"

"Not yet. I can't anyway. I tried but there's too much to think about."

"You're sure it's not just something you ate?"

She laughed and slid down beside me and I edged over so she could share my pillow.

40

"No, it's not that even if we did kind of overdo it. That was one hell of a good meal, wasn't it?"

There was no argument about that. We had driven into Alexandria to eat at a seafood place on the river. I saw right away that Tiny was well known there. The hostess led us to a table in a far corner of the low-ceilinged room, just beyond a tiny bar tucked under an angle of the building. We ordered drinks and were studying the menu when the proprietor came over. He and Tiny went into a huddle.

"Try the broiled lobster," he said. "These are locals I get from the bay and not the poor things that have been dying on ice all the way down from Nova Scotia or Maine. While they're on the fire you'll have just about time for a dozen Chincoteagues and a cup of chowder."

We took his advice and for the next hour we feasted. I'd always thought I knew something about fine seafood but that night I found out that what came out of the Chesapeake beats anything you can get out of the Pacific. Our lobsters were brutes that weighed in at about two pounds each, tender and succulent, a far cry from their clawless cousins I'd eaten before. Except for some coaching from Tiny on getting out the more elusive tidbits, there was damn little conversation. She always was a two-fisted eater and if, as a result, she couldn't sleep, at least she'd had her fun.

She lay beside me now, breathing deeply, until I turned to her and slid my hand under the hem of her nightgown and up the back of her leg to her bottom. I rolled my hand over its smoothness and then slapped her lightly. With one lithe movement she sat up and flipped the gown over her head and tossed it aside, making her breasts swing heavily. Then she slid down beside me and stretched her length to mine. I could feel her toes scraping lightly against my ankles and then she reached up and grabbed me by the ear, pulling my face to hers.

It was a while later when she suddenly said, "Do you think they'll be crazy enough to do it?"

"Do what?"

41

"Give a million rounds to those people?"

"As of right now, I neither know nor care. Anyway, we'll know in the morning."

She shut up then and fell asleep.

◄6►

Actually we didn't find out until late that evening. Tiny and I had come to Senator Colville's apartment, in civilian clothes and trying to appear harmless. He'd let us in himself, leading the way to a book-lined room that looked out on the balcony circling the whole building on every floor. Through the glass doors I could see a picture-postcard view toward the shaft of the Washington Monument and, a little farther off, the Capitol.

There was only one other visitor, who arrived right after we did. He was in civilian clothes, too, but I didn't have to be told that this was the big boss, the man who runs our outfit. Never mind his name and rank but when he came into the room Tiny and I stood up until he waved us to seats and took his own. It was clear that he and Colville knew each other and no introductions were made or needed. Evidently the number of those who knew the objective of Operation Home Run had been increased by one.

"What did you get from Saigon, Tiny?"

"Sir, their first response came in about an hour ago. I didn't want to be late for this meeting so I just took it off the decoding machine, gave it a quick look and brought it along."

She held her hand out to me and I passed over the envelope she'd had me carry. She broke the seal and brought out a length of paper, perforated down the sides and showing the red bands that marked it as classified.

"I won't waste your time reading it word for word. What it adds up to is that Fargot is known to our people and we've had a local dossier on him for years. He's a little too slippery for any of the organized groups to trust but he's useful to them when they want to communicate or set up an informal escrow. He's a kind of stake-holder, not involved directly in very many transactions, but earning a small commission from one or both sides for services rendered. Sometimes he'll get a finder's fee for introducing people who want to do business and every so often it'll be a minor piece of the venture they set up. He owns some small parcels of real estate in Cholon and it's pretty well established he isn't fussy about what he does. His dossier has entries on several protests filed with the National Police by the Saigon provost marshal about him and about establishments he was connected with during the American presence, but no formal action was ever taken.

"Our local office is still checking out the people he is currently doing business with and it will take a few days to run them all down. Naturally we haven't yet told them exactly what we're looking for so we're going to get a lot of useless data until we can narrow the investigation without using communications channels.

"Fargot, as we already knew, is a Vietnamese national, son of a French father and a Chinese mother, both dead. He has several grown children by his first wife, who died some years ago, and two younger ones by his second, a former bar girl.

"He is known to have dealings with French nationals in Saigon and elsewhere but he is not accepted socially by them. He belongs to none of their clubs and is not received in their homes. It is possible he may be a channel for them to the VC.

"He drinks sparingly and uses opium but is not addicted heavily.

"He was fifty-seven years old on his last birthday and in good health.

"Attended lycée in Saigon and spent the war years, supposedly at school, in Paris. He was suspected of being the Gestapo's informant among the Indochinese residents but was never charged, having left just before the liberation."

She looked at her watch. "Right now he should be getting pretty close to home and the surveillance will begin as soon as he clears the authorities at Tan Son Nhut."

She replaced the report in its envelope and waited for questions. The first came from Colville. "What's the next step, Colonel?"

"That's up to you, Senator. Do we trade the ammunition for your son-in-law?"

I could see he wasn't ready yet to give a firm answer to that.

"Before we get to that, tell me something. Who do you think these people are and what do you think they might do with the million rounds?"

"Sir, about all I can tell you now is who we think they're not. That would be the VC, the Khmer Rouge in Cambodia, the Cao Dai or any other group with some pretension to legality or international standing. It's not their style anyway.

"Possibly they are something like the Nationalist Chinese troops left behind when their government evacuated to Taiwan. They might be an ethnic tribal group, descendants of mercenaries brought into Annam by the Chinese and left to settle. It's even possible they're simply bandits, organized enough to have carved out a piece of real estate that they can occupy while the Saigon government and the VC are busy with other matters.

"They are armed with American weapons, captured or stolen but nothing heavy. They have no external source of supply sufficient to fill their needs for ammunition and no way to buy it. They need it to hold what they have and for use if they decide to expand the territory they now control. Money has little use for them."

"And how will we be affected if we give them what they demand?"

Before she could answer that our boss broke in.

"We talked about that at our meeting this afternoon. The consensus is that such an action would pose no threat to the United States or its direct interests. How the South Vietnamese might react is another matter, to say nothing of what we might hear from the VC or the North Vietnamese were they to find out."

Colville nodded and for a moment he didn't reply. When he did, it was in a low tone. "General, I need your assurance that what I'm going to tell you will not leave this room. I cannot, of course, order you to withhold this information when you make your report to the Chief of Staff, but I can ask it of you and these officers. Do I have your word on that?"

"As far as it's consistent with my responsibilities, yes, and I think I can speak for all three of us."

"That's good enough for me. Now you all know the position I occupy in the Senate. My subcommittee is currently considering the new military aid bill, most of which deals with the type and amount of aid we will furnish the South Vietnamese in the next fiscal year. Several of their senior officers are in Washington to meet with us in executive session. This morning I met with their Chief of Mission and ambassador. Naturally I was guarded in what I told them but they're pretty good at reading between the lines. If we decide to go ahead they will impose no obstacles and will cooperate fully. They can recognize the risks but I assured them the affair will be handled with discretion and, of course, complete secrecy."

I wondered just how many details he'd given them, and how. Colville, in his position, was certainly more than able to do a little straightforward arm twisting with some reminders of just how unfriendly he could be if they didn't agree to go along. Still, I didn't think it was his style to take that route. He hadn't lasted all those years in politics without learning to handle all kinds of people, including Asians. Probably he'd just stated his problem and left it up to their mother wit to figure out what they ought to do. In the end they'd recognized the implications and decided it was best for them to string along.

The general asked, "Did they have any specific ideas about what they could do to supply the ransom?"

Colville nodded. "Yes, and I think it will work. They will decide shortly to reduce their inventory at certain depots and the surplus will be offered for cash sale. The buyer will deposit the full amount with the embassy here in Washington and will be required to accept delivery in Saigon. At some time in the future the funds on deposit here will be allocated to a specific purchase or purchases which will be exported, under license, to their government. It may be unusual but it's perfectly legal and ethical in every way."

"They didn't make any other conditions?"

46

Colville smiled. "Naturally certain things are understood. They are more than a little concerned about that much matériel and exactly where it's going to wind up. They will name a liaison individual who will work with us and report to them. I had to agree to that. The only other major condition is that they will not deal in any way with an official arm of the U.S. government but only with private individuals or concerns. You know, they read the papers, too."

"And how do you propose to handle that, Senator?"

"Hell, you're the experts. Suppose you tell me."

Tiny spoke up. "I think we can work that out if Senator Colville is willing to go along with the idea."

The general swung around to look at her and then nodded for her to go ahead. I saw her take a breath and then she got to work digging my grave.

"Senator, you still own the Colville Syndicate, don't you?"

"No, not precisely. You might say that I have a measure of control. The actual ownership is vested in my children and grandchildren and the Colville Foundation. In a practical sense I still control a major interest."

"Newspaper, radio and TV stations, all that?"

"Fourteen daily papers, four AM radio stations, four TV outlets, the wire and picture services and some minor holdings."

"Bureaus in all major U.S. cities and foreign capitals?"

He nodded and I finally realized what she had in mind. "How about Saigon?"

"Not any longer. Not since the U.S. withdrawal, in fact. We rely on the other services for coverage there. That was not my decision. I exercise no control over the day-to-day operations of the syndicate and ever since I first ran for elective office I've made it a rule to have nothing to do with editorial policy as well."

"But the people who make those decisions would be likely to take the hint if you were to offer some suggestions?"

He allowed us a little smile. "They generally do."

"Then I think it might be just the right time for the syndicate to consider reopening the Saigon bureau. There's even a man available you might recommend for the job."

"Go on."

47

"Captain Keefe is about to leave the Army. He's a trained reporter and cameraman and he's already spent a lot of time in Southeast Asia and has contacts there."

That was the first I'd heard about my getting out of the service so I tried not to look surprised. Later I'd have some notes for Tiny about her habit of volunteering my services.

"He should be able to put together a first-rate staff with men he can hire in the States and some he can pick up in Saigon. We can have the U.S. citizens here in Washington by tomorrow for their accreditations and passports. Your Washington bureau can handle that, can't they?"

"I don't think there will be any difficulty."

"Then there should be plenty of time for Keefe to get his people together, take care of the paper work, acquire the equipment he'll need and still get to Saigon in time to coordinate with the Vietnamese and be ready for the next contact with Fargot."

And that, children, is how I came to be sitting in an airplane on my way back to guess where.

⊰ 7 ⊱

It turned out to be a wild few days. With only a limited amount of time to get set up, it was clear I wasn't going to be able to pull together any kind of elaborate organization. I'd take with me only the absolute minimum I'd need to get the job done. Additional men I'd hire locally in Saigon. The one man I positively had to have was a top cameraman who knew the terrain. It didn't take a lot of thinking to decide who that was going to be. I wanted Pat Brice.

Pat came into the Army during World War II. That's on the record. Nobody knows how old Pat really is but he's a legend in his own time among military cameramen. He's been in and out of trouble for years, dodging courts-martial mainly because he's known most of his superiors ever since they were shavetails. For twenty years or more he'd staged a nonstop battle with the bottle before he met up with the cutest little Thai girl you'll ever see. She's smart, too, and when Pat brought her back to Hawaii he settled right down to raise the kids she produced every year. After his long slide down the ladder, his promotions were coming along regularly now and Pat's work was beginning to attract a lot of notice. A couple of the TV news outfits had made offers but Pat was happy where he was.

For a start there was only one other man I had to have. He's been with me, on and off, as long as I've been in uniform and it's no secret that I wouldn't still be walking around and drawing pay if it hadn't been for the quick work of Sergeant John Potter. His military job title is Still Photographer and he's good at his work

49

but he had a lot of other qualifications for the kind of job we had.

To begin with, Potter is one of the most physically powerful men I've ever known. If he'd gone to college instead of lying his way into the Army, John could have had a slot in the defensive line of any pro team in the nation. He's always in top shape, doesn't drink or smoke and his only vices are ice cream and toothpicks. The first he eats as available but the second he uses every waking hour of the day, feeding a steady supply into the corner of his mouth. He's strong, smart, hard-working, but for my money his greatest asset is his talent with weapons. He's top man with a wide range of hardware from handguns to mortars but his favorite is the riot gun. As a matter of fact, one of my fondest memories is of John Potter, his shining black face divided by a happy grin, toothpick clamped firmly, while he performed on his ten-gauge shotgun like Heifetz with a fiddle. He had that kind of smile for me when I met him and Pat Brice at Dulles Airport.

On the way into town I briefed them on as much as they'd need to know about the operation. No more and no less. One thing they had to understand was why we were all going to have discharge papers before we could get started. That had been the one stipulation before the agency would get involved in Home Run. The papers would be drawn and put in a safe place. If we stubbed our toes and Home Run got blown, then the Army could claim we weren't on their payroll. If we came through okay, the documents would be torn up and we'd go on just as if nothing had happened. Meanwhile we were employees in good standing of the Colville Syndicate and getting top money, at that.

There was no delay about getting civilian passports issued and as soon as they were ready we whipped over to the Washington bureau of the syndicate. While we were taking care of being put on its payroll, drawing expense money and getting shots, our passports were already at the Vietnamese embassy for visas. The next day we took the air shuttle to New York to get our equipment.

With plenty of Colville's money in my pocket, I didn't stint a bit. I bought a new 16-mm Arriflex camera with all the accessories, a spare Nagra recorder and a load of sound gear, including a wireless mike and anything else I'd always wanted but hadn't been able to afford. I didn't waste any dough but I didn't pinch any pennies either. Maybe our setup with the Colville Syndicate was nothing but a cover, a phony, but I had some ideas of my own about that.

We'd be feeding what still coverage we could get to the Colville wirephoto service, so Potter got a tasty selection of still boxes for the kind of work we'd have. Since there wouldn't be any handy neighborhood camera store and we'd be on our own for any repairs, I got plenty of spare parts, extra lenses and meters, a tool kit and everything I could find to go in it. For the first time I could buy anything I saw and thought I'd need. What happened to it when I'd finished was someone else's worry.

We were back in Washington in time for a late dinner. Our visas were ready and, unfortunately, so were our tickets. This time we'd be heading eastbound to Europe instead of the usual route over the Pacific. It was a direct flight to Bangkok, one last night in a city at peace, and into Saigon in the morning.

That night I had my first real fuss with Tiny. It all started when she suddenly announced that she was coming with us. What she expected to accomplish underfoot in Saigon she couldn't say but I wasn't willing to buy any part of the idea. I won't bother with all the long list of reasons she had. All I knew was that I didn't want her clucking around while I tried to get my job done. Finally I agreed to let her set up shop in Bangkok at the agency office there. That way she'd be close enough to consult with, but if push came to shove, we could always claim that she'd had no part in the deal. The rest of the evening, once we'd made the compromise, was a lot better and the next morning she drove us out to Dulles to catch our flight back to the Paris of the Orient. She'd be heading to Hawaii and then on to Bangkok on her own. With luck we would clean up the whole mess in a couple of weeks. Bostwick would be home with his Anne and Bailey could try to get things going with his wife. I began to think about putting in for some leave.

I'd reached the point where I had to decide what I was going to do with my life. The first time I'd gone into the Army it was because I had to. I'd served my two years and then taken my discharge in Saigon and tried to make a go of it with my camera.

51

I hadn't done too well and I'd wound up back in uniform to save my neck. Without anything better in sight I'd just stayed on, most of the time on photo missions with time out every now and then to cover a special assignment for Tiny's outfit just as I was doing now. This time was a little different.

This time I had a cover that was a legitimate job with a reputable outfit. It was the kind of setup I'd tried to get on my own without much luck. Now it was being served up on a platter. Even though it wasn't the name of the game, still I'd be turning out the kind of work I really can do. If it was good enough maybe the Colville Syndicate people would be sufficiently impressed to keep me on after the job was done. And should I manage to spring young Bostwick and get him home in one piece, the senator's gratitude might cause him to pass the word to take care of me. It was one hell of an incentive but it wasn't really the way to approach a delicate assignment. I was going to have to make sure that I didn't get so eager I'd be tempted to do something stupid. It was going to be tough.

The first leg of our flight was to London, then we'd go on to Frankfurt and Istanbul. The morning went by quickly enough, as we dozed and read, and then lunch took up some time. It wasn't long before we flew into the approaching night and the plane began to let down for the London landing. A few minutes after the first lights appeared below us we were in the pattern and then the wheels gave that painful crunch and we were on the ground. Somehow travel isn't as bad in first class, where the syndicate had us booked, as it is back in tourist, where Uncle Sam travels the troops.

We had to deplane there and switch to a 707 but that didn't bother me a bit. I'd never been in England and even though we wouldn't see much besides the transit lounge, at least I'd be able to say I was there. There should be time to get a couple of drinks and something to read, and there would have been if I hadn't been handed a note as I deplaned, with a Washington number to call.

There was some kind of delay as my call was patched somewhere else but finally I heard Tiny's voice.

"I've had word about that shipment we were keeping an eye out for. You know the one I mean?"

That could only mean Fargot but there was no need to mention names.

"Yes. Did it arrive okay?"

"Well, there's a little problem. We seem to have lost sight of it."

"How the hell did they manage to do that?"

"Well, you can't really blame the people at the other end. They were right on hand waiting for it where we'd told them it would be off-loaded but there was no sign of it. When it didn't come off the flight they just assumed it had been delayed and would be coming along later. When they got around to checking they found it had come in okay on the right plane but it had never been off-loaded. Instead it was kept on when the flight took off."

"Do they know what happened to it next?"

"They're still checking but the next stop was Phnom Penh."

That was one hell of a note. We'd all been expecting that Fargot might lead us to someone we might be able to identify as his "principal." It might have dispelled a little of the mystery and given us a lead to whom we were dealing with. Now we were still fumbling around trying to get organized.

"I'll tell you what. I'll call this number at every stop and you can relay whatever you get. Then we can compare notes in Bangkok."

"Okay. I'll be there first. I'll get something fast to Utapao and look for you at the Diana when you check in."

She was going to have a rough flight in a B-52 or a spook ship but at least they didn't take long to get you where you wanted to go. I hung up and came out of the booth, to see Brice and Potter hovering outside the door. We made it to the gate on a dead run and that's as much as I saw of England.

By the time we landed at Don Muang in Bangkok I didn't know much more. I'd spent every stop wrestling with operators with strange accents who only wanted to know who was paying for my calls. I had words with several censors and similar busybodies. I learned what kind of coin was needed to get a dial tone in half a dozen assorted countries. Most of all I had indigestion.

Traveling eastward against the clock meant that every time my stomach got all set for ham and eggs, it got chicken Kiev or curry or grilled water buffalo tenderloin or whatever joke the airline caterers felt like playing on the cash customers. By the time we were letting down for Thailand I had a bigger load of gas than the aircraft and all I wanted was to be let alone for a shave and a good long shower followed by a twelve-hour stay in the sack.

In most other countries I'd have checked the camera and sound equipment and the heavy baggage right at the airport and taken just what we'd need for the night, but I'd spent enough time in Thailand to know better so we hired a couple of cabs and loaded everything in for the half-hour trip to the hotel. There was no Colville Syndicate office in Bangkok so we were strictly on our own, just like any civilian crew without the military to fall back on. Normally I'd have called a number in town and someone would have appeared to pitch in and get us moving but if anyone got the idea that we weren't just another news-film crew, the Vietnamese would yank back and the three of us could return to filming maneuvers and retirement ceremonies.

The trip into the city was probably no worse than it had ever been. Perched on top of a pile of gear with something full of sharp corners on my lap, though, I felt it was taking forever, and when we finally pulled up in front of the hotel I was right on the ragged edge. The usual swarm of juvenile bellboys began hauling our baggage into the lobby as I got the taxis paid off. No sooner had I signed my name on the register than I was given a note in return. Tiny was around the corner on Sukhumvit, waiting for me in the Chinese restaurant.

She was at a table up on the second floor, by the window that looked out on the traffic streaming by, English style, to the left. One look told me that her mood wasn't a bit better than mine. I sat down and ordered some food I didn't want just so the waiter would leave and give us a chance to talk.

"Have they found him?"

She nodded. "Finally. He got off at Phnom Penh, all right, but by the time our geniuses discovered that, the trail was just about

54

cold. He spent the night at a third-rate hotel. There's no way of knowing who he contacted. He left the next morning for Saigon and went straight home to his wife."

"Any ideas about what he was doing in Cambodia?"

"How the hell do I know? Maybe he wanted to decorate his grandfather's grave."

"He doesn't spend like a man on an expense account unless he's working on a guide to flop joints."

"Well, that figures. His principal hasn't asked for money and we still don't know how Fargot is going to get his piece."

"It looks to me like he's paying his own way in hopes that he'll get paid off when his boss collects. If he's half French and half Chinese, that doesn't add up to someone who's likely to throw money around."

Tiny didn't reply until the waiter had served me and gone back down to the first floor.

"I'm beginning to think this crowd doesn't have much of an organization outside their own bailiwick. For Fargot to pass on what happened in New York, he had to have a face-to-face meeting with either his principal or a messenger. If it was the man at the top, he's got his orders and he'll be around in a day or so to give you the word. If it was just a messenger, he's going to have to wait for instructions. That's why he wants you standing by in Saigon, so you'll be available as soon as Fargot knows what to tell you."

"That's what I'm going for."

"Yes, Mike, but just be sure that your cover isn't blown. Remember, once you land in Saigon you're in his territory. He's going to be as careful as a cat with a strange tom in his alley, and I can't say I blame him. I don't know if they still have those posts and sandbags set up across from the Central Market, but if the White Mice find out what Fargot's doing, he's a cinch to be decorating one of them."

I finished my food and paid our check with the American Express card the syndicate had issued me. Tiny left first for the place where she was staying. I watched from the window as she hailed a cab and went off. Then I walked up the narrow *soi* and finally got to bed. The next pillow I'd hit would be in Saigon.

◄ 8 ►

Covering the war from Saigon turned out to be a whole new ball game. There was no more JUSPAO, the Joint U.S. Public Affairs Office, which had served the press with all the goodies Uncle Sam could provide. He had run the press the same way he'd tried to run the war. Massive doses of aircraft, ground transport, mail service, PX rations and cheerful handouts every day. If a correspondent showed interest in a pig-breeding project at a village in the Delta, or in some remote orphanage, there would be a helicopter, an escort officer, an interpreter and suitable drinks and accommodations along the way. There was access to commanders at every level who could be set up for interview purposes, even for those whose dispatches were clearly antiwar or even out-and-out anti-Army. The JUSPAO building was conveniently located in the heart of the city just a block away from the Caravelle and the Continental Palace, the two hotels where most of the press bureaus were installed. For those who wished to cover the war from the comfort and safety of downtown Saigon it was only necessary to walk the two hundred yards to the daily briefing, the "Five-O'Clock Follies." Here, in air-conditioned comfort, the indolent newsman could get the latest official optimism served up complete with mimeoed handouts which, with a little rearranging, could be filed as a story most editors would accept. It was a nice comfortable war, the kind Hemingway would have enjoyed, located in easy commuting range of the fighting just a few miles away. It was customary for the newsman to sleep well in a modern, air-conditioned room, arise to enjoy a first-rate American break-

56

fast, nicely served by uniformed waitresses, at bargain rates, and then, at your leisure, go to work. You could be transported, by road and air, right from the hotel door up to where people were dying, get a nice story and still be back for an early lunch and an afternoon of golf. In an economy inflated to the point where a university professor was hard put to keep his family in rice, a little discreet dealing in currency could bring the price of lobster thermidor down to the cost of a Big Mac at home. With the taxpayers paying the freight, you bought Beefeater gin and Johnnie Walker Scotch for the price of wino muscatel back home. The PX had been a bargain hunter's paradise, with Japanese cameras, cultured pearls, fine dinnerware, electronic gadgets and even cars, all at duty-free prices. It was a hell of a nice war if you happened to be in the right slot.

Things had changed.

JUSPAO was gone. The fleets of helicopters and jeeps and free GI buses were no more. The few Americans officially in Vietnam were told to keep a low profile and the drop from hundreds of thousands to merely hundreds of well-paid servicemen had wiped out a sizable portion of the local economy. Without the armed MPs on patrol downtown, an American had to learn that when a National Policeman shouted, *"Dung lai,"* it was a good idea to stop what one was doing until somebody came up to explain. The press corps, formerly coddled and pampered by the American info officers, now had to rely on the Vietnamese for their transport and news sources. The ARVN failed to grasp the importance of keeping the American public informed with its morning coffee or after dinner each evening. Transport was hard to arrange, possibly because with big pieces of its territory in hostile hands, the government wasn't all that keen about the foreign press seeing things for themselves. Generally speaking, when it came to newsmen they didn't give much of a damn.

At least one thing hadn't changed. The Continental Palace was just about as it had been in the days of Somerset Maugham and Graham Greene as well as ten thousand other writers and newsmen who had enjoyed the open-sided café on the ground floor. As always, the wicker chairs and tables were set up every afternoon, to be tended by a platoon of uniformed waiters. Custom

57

may have dropped off a bit but it was still the place to go to see who was in town and perhaps pick up the latest rumors.

It was about half filled when the three cabs we'd needed to haul ourselves and the equipment pulled in. With the Americans gone the traffic had moved a lot more easily and we made good time coming in from Tan Son Nhut. It had been only a short flight from Bangkok once I'd seen our baggage loaded and the hatch locked tight. There was the usual routine hassle when we'd landed but the judicious distribution of five-hundred-piaster notes had lubricated things nicely.

The hotel had been expecting us and we moved right in and started getting organized. There were two adjoining bedrooms with a connecting door, one for my own use and the other for our office. The furniture was cleared out of that one and the hotel sent up some extra tables and chairs to use until I could get out and order some desks and files. Its bathroom would have a lock installed on the door and the windows covered with black cloth for use as a darkroom for loading and unloading film; spare equipment would be stored there, too.

The office was a corner room, looking down on one side at the old Grand Opera House, where the French once got their culture and the Vietnamese House of Representatives now did its deliberating. On the other side was Tu Do Street, seeming a lot more sedate now without its string of deadfall bars and cocktail lounges.

My own room was fine, large enough to spread out a bit and a hell of a lot better than the last place I'd had in Saigon.

We'd already decided that Pat and John would get a place of their own as close as possible. That way we'd have an extra spot to meet and at the same time have more freedom of movement. If I could get them a phone we'd be able to communicate if I needed them in a hurry. I brought the two of them up to date and then turned them loose to go apartment hunting.

While we were waiting for Fargot to make contact we had to look like we were really working, to keep our cover legitimate-looking. We'd already decided that we'd leave spot coverage to the services and put our effort into feature stories and documentaries. Pat had come up with a few ideas and as soon as we could

58

get organized we'd begin. One problem I hadn't foreseen was with Potter.

"When can I draw my weapon, Captain?"

"Look, John, there's not going to be any weapon unless I give a direct order. We're supposed to be the harmless civilian press protected by all the force and majesty of the Geneva Convention. I'll admit that most of the newsmen here who have tried to make that point with the VC have wound up pretty dead but that's the way we're going to have to play it, too.

"Next, that 'Captain' is going to have to go. We're not in the Army and I'd just as soon not remind anyone that we ever were. I know it's going to be tough, but you're going to have to get used to calling me Mike. Okay?"

He shook his head dolefully. "If you say so, Captain. I'll call you Mike, sir, but it's going to take a little time."

"Okay, John, just keep trying, and look out for the 'sir,' too."

John has never been a big talker and with the handicap I'd given him he'd probably wind up barely opening his mouth.

When I'd unpacked I got busy on my chores. First I went over to the bank and deposited the letter of credit I'd got at the Washington bureau. I had asked for enough to more than cover the first month's operations. By that time I'd have a better idea of what kind of budget I'd need if we had to stay any longer. I'd have to pay the rent, hire cars, pay the local people I'd be hiring and give Pat and John their living allowances, plus my own.

With cash in my pocket, I went shopping. I bought an office typewriter and a small adding machine, a couple of desks, a file cabinet and some other stuff originally supplied by U.S. taxpayers for the use of the troops. Why these things hadn't made the boat when their users left wasn't explained but I couldn't complain about the prices. While I was at it I got a small Japanese refrigerator, a hot plate, a teakettle and a coffeepot, all essential to an efficient operation.

I'd once had some printing done and I remembered the little shop on one of the narrow side streets off Nguyen Hue. I ordered a batch of stationery printed and the other supplies we'd need. To show his gratitude the printer sweetened the deal with a couple of hundred business cards. On one side I was Mike Keefe, bureau manager, Colville Syndicate, with the address and hotel phone number. On the other side, in Vietnamese, it was a little different. Mike Keefe translated out as "Mai Ky Pha," as close as the printer could come to the original and still make something that a Vietnamese could pronounce. The whole order was promised for the next day and I headed back to the lower end of Tu Do Street to pick up an old contact.

Way back when I'd been the local cameraman and correspondent for the now defunct IBC, the bureau manager, as he liked to call himself, had been a character named Isamu Toguri. Now if you stated categorically that Toguri was crooked, you'd be giving him the best of it. If there were two ways to do anything in the way of making a buck, Toguri would pick the shady one ninety-nine times out of a hundred by preference. I never did find out about more than a few of Toguri's deals but those I knew about were all felonious.

The most visible of his enterprises was the Jockey Club, a bar he owned on Tu Do Street. That is, it was called the Jockey Club on its sign. Its all-GI clientele uniformly referred to it as the Jockstrap, for its total and utter grunginess. The air was unbreathable, the drinks unpotable, the food inedible and the ladies who entertained there largely venereal. Madame Toguri, a Vietnamese, ran the joint and while the pickings were good it must have been a gold mine. I had made it one of my hangouts, restricting my drinking to black market canned beer at a hundred piasters a throw. (I always opened my own cans, though, after I found out about Madame's bad habit of refilling empties with Ba Muy Ba, the local brewery's poison.) I didn't have a lot of hope that I'd find it still in business and I was right. The spot was now occupied by something new.

The neon sign over the door and the gilded notice on the small show window now displayed a string of Japanese characters and beneath them in English, GINZA RESTAURANT, PROP. I. TOGURI. The window itself was half blocked with a shoji screen, in front of which stood a vase containing a single plastic chrysanthemum. The door was now a matching shoji on which a local artist had drawn his version of some kind of stilt-legged bird with a long sharp bill.

I pushed open the door and got my real surprise. Everything was exactly the same—the padded bar, the tiny tables and the eye-straining illumination. The only difference I saw was that while Madame T. still occupied her regular spot behind the bar, her kimono was slightly stained. She was engaged in her favorite sport, computing some victim's bill on her abacus before padding it and ringing it up on her ancient French cash register. There were about a dozen customers in the place, a few Vietnamese but the rest sons of Nippon. None seemed to be eating and I learned later that those who chose to live dangerously, former Kamikaze pilots, for example, were directed to the floor above, where a couple of Japanese-style dining rooms had been installed. Madame finished her calculations with her customary flourish and carefully wrote out the bad news on a check. It was when she passed it to the nymph who was serving that she spotted me.

For the first time in our long acquaintance I saw Madame surprised. Her jaw dropped and I'm sure that if there had been a bit more light I would have seen her grow a shade or two paler. I stood still while she held this interesting pose and then I saw her hand dive for the bell that I knew would alert Toguri up in their private quarters that he was needed and right now. I walked back, took my regular seat and asked for a beer. She still hadn't found her tongue but probably more from force of habit than anything else she reached into the chest behind the bar and brought out a San Miguel and a church key. By the time I had the can opened and the contents poured into a slightly finger-marked glass, Toguri had appeared.

"Mike, what you do here?"

"What do you think? I'm drinking a cold San Miguel."

"But in Saigon? You must be crazy man."

"No more, Toguri. I'm smelling like a rose now. Got a new job, too. Best I ever had and with a great outfit."

"Not like IBC?"

He'd touched a sore nerve. I'd parted from IBC on less than the best of terms. To put it bluntly, they'd stranded me in Saigon.

61

Just pulled the rug out from under and left me to fend for myself.

"Hell, no. This is a real outfit. The Colville Syndicate. Newspapers, radio and TV. I'm bureau manager with a staff and everything. I've taken a place in the Continental Palace and we'll be operating in a couple of days."

"Anything I can do for you, Mike?"

He had no shame at all. After the way he'd dumped me when I really needed his help he really had a lot of gall, but then Toguri never had been bashful when he saw a chance to make a buck.

"No, I can't think of a thing."

I'd already decided that there might well be a chance to get some mileage out of his contacts but it seemed like a good idea to wait and let him become a little hungry first. That way he'd be less likely to try to pull a fast one.

"There's just one thing you can do for me as a favor."

"You just say what, Mike. We are friends long time now and if I can't do favor for old friend my name is not Toguri."

"Do you remember the guy we used to call The Tiger?"

"Sure. Vietnamese fella. Nice guy. Number one sound man."

"Well, I'd like to get in touch with him. Maybe I might even have some kind of work he can do. Last time I heard, though, he was back in the army."

"No more. Got zapped in leg. Sometimes he get work for couple weeks on film job but nothing steady. You want him—I get him."

He smiled as though he'd just awarded me first prize in the lottery. Later I'd find out from The Tiger just how much Toguri had squeezed him for the tip to look me up.

"Okay. You tell him to see me at the hotel."

"No sweat. What else you need? Maybe nice girl for secretary?"

Toguri is probably one of the few people in the world who can make a simple word like secretary sound dirty. Chances were that anybody he'd dig up would be someone too old to work the bars anymore and was looking for a meal ticket. Still, if it hadn't been for the Toguris I never would have known Co and maybe she'd be alive today. I'd met her in their place, right upstairs in the top-floor apartment where they lived.

"Not yet, Toguri. Let me get settled first and then maybe I'll think about it. Right now I want to talk to your wife. Alone."

He looked up in surprise. I'd never had any real dealings with Madame but he probably figured that it might be something he could make a buck from. He had his wife set another San Miguel on the bar and then took off, probably to start looking for The Tiger.

I could see that Madame was puzzled, too, but she didn't say anything as I poured the second beer.

"Tell me about Co," I said.

"What to tell? She die."

"I know. What happened then?"

"We bury her. That's all."

"Toguri?"

She gave me as scornful a look as I've ever seen. "Not Toguri. My family pay everything." Co had been her cousin.

"Where?"

"In Gia Dinh."

That was the suburb of the city where Co had lived before we met.

"Did you make prayers for her in the pagoda?"

She nodded. "Small prayers. Toguri watch to see I don't spend too much."

I reached into my pocket for my bankroll. Slowly I counted out ten five-hundred-P notes and pushed them across the bar to her.

"You go to pagoda now, Madame. Tell the priest to make big prayer for Co. Okay?"

She nodded and tucked the bills into some recess in her kimono. When she spoke again it was almost gentle. "You come back, Mike, but watch Toguri. He still number one son of a bitch."

I smiled and finished my beer. When I tried to pay for my drinks she waved my money away. "Toguri too much rich already."

As usual I ate too much. That's what happened every time I went to the Piccadilly. When we'd come out of the hotel for dinner I'd had no intention of going there at all.

The last time I'd eaten there had been with Co. It was our last meal together and we were both on cloud nine. I was about to make the biggest piece of money I'd ever seen and we'd be pulling out of Vietnam for a new start in another country. Two weeks later Co was dead and I was on the run for my life.

I stood at the hotel entrance with Pat and John while we tried to decide where to eat. Everything around us looked the same as always, barring the absence of American uniforms. A covey of Tu Do Street quail hopefully awaited the patronage of any of the male clientele of the terrace café. The Opera House still needed a coat of paint. The double-amputee beggar lay in his regular place at the corner of the wall around the Brink BOQ, holding out his filthy fatigue cap to every passer-by with a grin and a mock salute. The homeward-bound traffic was choking Tu Do Street from curb to curb, with a bad jam right where it crossed Le Loi, the broad boulevard, once tree-lined, that led down to the circle at the Central Market. There were dozens of places to get a good dinner and Pat and John left the choice up to me. Sooner or later we'd have to go to the Piccadilly and I decided to get it over with.

We rounded the corner and walked up Tu Do, looking into the shopwindows and getting the feel of the city back. At the next corner, Le Thanh Ton, the small park with the bandstand was bright with flags and banners proclaiming some sort of propaganda. As part of the government's attempts at building up national consciousness, somebody had decided that band concerts were just the thing. I don't know if it got the approval of anyone but the members of the local chapter of the pickpockets' guild but the concerts did draw a crowd. As we passed, workmen were setting up folding chairs and a few people were already gathered.

At the next corner, Gia Long, there was still a tangle of barbed concertina wire and a few sentries controlling access to the army headquarters across from the restaurant. The usual ten-year-old in a page uniform held the door open and in we went.

The big welcome I got did a lot to help but I still sat with my back to the table where I'd eaten with Co. Gradually my mood changed and it wasn't long before I was having as good a time as the others.

We ate too much, as I said, and then settled it with brandy

before we started back to the hotel. The band concert had begun and the sidewalks were filled with shoppers taking advantage of the cool of the evening. Pat pointed up to a corner third-floor window across from the park. They'd found a furnished flat there, complete with maid, on a month-to-month lease. The location was perfect, only a minute or two away if I needed them in a hurry. The place had a phone, too.

We were all pretty beat but it was too early for bed so when I offered to buy a drink they joined me on the terrace. We got a table right by the railing and I settled down while my dinner elbowed around in my stomach trying to find a good, comfortable arrangement. We ordered and then spent a couple of minutes trying to convince the sprites around us that while each of them was a vision of beauty and grace, we still wanted to sleep alone. They finally gave us up as a bad job and left us in peace. I was having trouble keeping my eyes open when Pat leaned over.

"Just across the street, Mike, by the corner. The guy fixing his bike."

I glanced over as casually as I could. From what I could see he was just another citizen in a white shirt and dark slacks doing something to the front wheel of his bike. "What about him?"

"He's been playing with that thing ever since we sat down but I'm damned if I can see anything wrong with it."

If the guy's real interest was in us there was one way to find out.

"I think I'll get a paper to read before I turn in. Be back in a minute."

I left them there and walked to the corner until I saw a chance to cross. I went along Le Loi past the lumpy pair of larger-than-life bronze soldiers. As I walked by the man with the sick bike, it was suddenly cured of whatever ailed it and he stood there trying to look like someone deciding where to go. I crossed at the park in front of the city hall, found a bookstore and bought a Saigon *Post* and a copy of *Time* that I'd missed. I was back at the café in less than five minutes.

"Where is he now?"

"He's crossing the street and heading for the steps over there."

I lifted my glass to drink and looked over the rim. This time he'd picked the drive chain to fuss with. If we stayed in the café much longer he was going to run out of ailments. Just how many relapses can a bike suffer? It was going to be fun to watch the poor guy.

Finally, though, he got a break. Just as he was getting ready to try changing the tires, his relief arrived. This one looked pretty much like the first except that he was on foot and carried a folded newspaper. When the bike-fixer wheeled the patient away, this guy found a place on the steps across the way, where the light was a little better, and settled down to read.

Pat said, "What do you think that's all about?"

"I'm damned if I know and I can't say I care. If somebody wants to know what we're doing, they can send all the snoops they like just as long as they don't make a crowd and begin to get in the way."

I sipped the last of my brandy. "Right now I'm ready for bed."

I paid the check and waved them good night. As I rode up in the rachitic French elevator I knew that Saigon hadn't changed a bit.

◂ 9 ▸

I was just finishing breakfast when he came in. He peered around the dimly lit dining room, his eyes still adjusting after the glare of the street. I hoisted myself out of my chair and he finally spotted me and limped over, his hand out.

"Sit down, Tiger. It's good to see you."

"Good to see you, Mike. You don't change one damn bit."

"Neither have you. Maybe a little fatter, that's all."

He shifted his bad leg and gestured toward it. "Damn leg still number ten. They make me some kind crazy brace but I don't wear him. Damn brace hurts worse than damn leg. Crutch no damn good either. Most time I sit on my tail, eat rice. Nobody give work to number ten Tiger. Get fat like pig."

"You looking for work, Tiger?"

"You damn betcha." He looked at me hopefully. "You got job for beat-up sound man?"

"If you want it the job is yours. I'm with a top outfit now. No tin-pot affair like IBC. Wait till you see your equipment. Nothing but the best."

He was so tickled he couldn't find any English words. His mouth opened in a big smile, flashing the large white teeth that had got him his name.

"When we start to work? Maybe today?"

"Take it easy. Have a cup of coffee, then we'll get the others and get over to the ministry for our cards. You're okay with them, aren't you?"

"No sweat. I keep nose clean."

"Maybe I'd better tell you we've got something coming up that might be rough."

He brushed that off and, while he drank his coffee, told me what had happened. He'd been with the ARVN film unit over on Hong Thap Tu, trying to live on army pay by moonlighting whenever he got the chance. He was working with an American TV documentary crew when he got zapped. It wasn't even enemy action.

The Americans had been pretty green and first thing you know, they had managed to set up for a shot right in the middle of an old minefield. The Tiger said he'd tried to tell them but they'd brushed him off. Of course the one who stepped on a mine was Tiger. Luckily the charge must have deteriorated over the years but it still packed enough kick to cripple him pretty badly.

After their stupid mistake the TV people had treated him well. They had him flown over to Bangkok for the best medical care they could get him and then they worked it out with their insurance company to pay him a small pension. For more than a year he hadn't done much. During the war the networks had trained a lot of local men who still had two good legs. The ARVN didn't want him back and the civilian jobs were going to those with lots better connections. No wonder he was hot to trot.

He finished his coffee and then I took him up to the room to sign the forms I'd need to put him on the payroll with the syndicate. When I showed him his recording equipment he damn near glowed and he was still beaming when Pat and John came up to the office. I finally pulled him loose and we went over to get our press cards.

We were expected. For once the red tape was down to a minimum and we zipped right through the procedure without the normal delays. I was just about to leave when I got word that one of the brass wanted to see me. I was shown to an office on an upper floor and kept waiting just long enough to establish the importance of the man I was to see.

Now the Vietnamese have a real subtle way of showing how they rate you, and you know it by what they serve to drink. Lowest rung is Coke or orange drink. That means they're glad to see you but you don't stand too high. Next comes local beer, La Rue or

Ba Muy Ba served over ice, and American beer or San Miguel is up another notch. It's good but not as good as the next rung. That one is tea, served in tiny cups, and the better the tea the better your standing. Top drawer is whiskey but that's up at the ambassadorial level and you don't get there very often.

Colonel Tan served tea.

"We are glad to have you back in Saigon, Mr. Keefe." Since I had known of Tan as one of those "official spokesmen," that was pretty good.

I sipped my tea. Even an amateur drinker could tell that it was pretty good stuff.

"It is very kind of you to say so, Colonel. I am glad to be back. Of course there was a time when I was not the most popular foreign cameraman in Vietnam."

He favored me with a short laugh. "That was a long time ago, Mr. Keefe, and I assure you that it has been completely forgotten. In point of fact, my government feels in your debt for several matters which I don't need to speak of now."

My not needing to speak of it either was a good part of why they felt they were indebted. A lot of people would be in a bad way if I chose to run off at the mouth.

"Now I think that perhaps we can try to repay a small part of that debt. I must say that I know none of the details of precisely why you are here and I hope you will not feel that it is necessary for you to tell me." He gave me a kind of sly glance. "We in Vietnam have learned much from your military and also your civilian leaders."

It wasn't so much a snide remark as it was just taking advantage of the chance to needle an American a bit. If I'd thought there was any point in making an issue of his crack I could have come up with a few things, but it wasn't worth it. He went on.

"My superiors have told me that you will need some assistance in your project. One of our officers has been detailed for the purpose and I'm sure you will be able to make good use of his talent and experience. Would you care to meet him now?"

I said I would and while he dialed and then had a short conversation I congratulated myself. With an official contact man I'd be able to really do a good job for the syndicate while I waited for Fargot to show up. It wasn't every member of the press who rated this kind of red-carpet treatment. I'd know more when I saw the kind of man they'd given me. I didn't have long to wait.

There was a double rap at the door and in he came. He saluted Tan and there was a short exchange in Vietnamese before he turned to me.

"Mr. Keefe, this is Captain Hieu."

Hieu saluted but I didn't return it. Instead I got up and held out my hand. He took it and from the firmness of his grip I got my first impression of the man. His hand was smaller than mine, dry to the touch and with a hint of strength. When I sat he took his seat beside me, turning to Tan for what more the colonel might have to say.

"Captain Hieu has been detailed to this ministry for as long as his services are required. I am sure you will work well together and score a real home run."

There was a funny little gleam in his eye. Maybe he didn't know what it was all about but at least he knew the name of the game.

"Captain Hieu will not report to me. He will, instead, make his reports directly to Tan Son Nhut."

That meant that my man would be supplied with a channel right into the ARVN Joint Chiefs. It also meant that I would be watched by some important people.

Tan stood up behind his desk. "Much success, Mr. Keefe. I hope you will be able to tell your people in the United States that we are taking good care of you."

I didn't need a diagram to understand that one. Senator Colville's name drew a lot more water in Saigon than those of others who thought they were big men in Washington. I took a moment to thank Colonel Tan and then Hieu and I left the office. We gathered up the others on our way downstairs and then crossed Le Loi to a stand where we could get our new cards sealed in plastic. It was time for lunch.

Now I could have taken Hieu back to the hotel for a big meal on my credit card or even to one of the fancy European-style places. I would have picked up the check and right away he'd be indebted. That meant I'd go down a peg in his estimation.

Maybe it sounds odd but Asians tend to rate you by the way you rate them. It's an exercise in subtlety. You buy a man a meal for a few hundred lousy piasters and he feels that you're not much if you put that appraisal on what he's worth. Not in money but in how you see him in relation to yourself. If I was going to work with Hieu I had to show him that I valued the association. What I had to do was demonstrate as best I could that I accepted him as an equal in every way. That ruled out any cheap gestures with credit cards and expense accounts.

Instead we all went into an open-front restaurant I'd gone to before on Nguyen Hue, the Street of Flowers. It was a decent place, clean and well kept. We all had the same thing—a bowl of the standard Chinese soup, broth with a few noodles and bits of meat, and a heaping bowl of rice with pork, chicken and pieces of shrimp and other seafood. I doused mine with nuoc mam and passed the shaker bottle to Hieu, then dug in with my chopsticks. Each man paid his own check and the whole meal didn't take fifteen minutes. When we finished we were all well fed and nobody owed anybody. We were all equal.

During lunch I sat across from Hieu and, without being too obvious, got my first good look at him. I put him at right around thirty, slim and wiry with the slightly stooped shoulders of a man who's studied a lot. He was dressed in a crisp fatigue uniform that had been tailored to him and was not the regular issue. His English was almost perfect, only the slightest hint of accent noticeable. He'd had two years at a college near Atlanta and Potter was won over when Hieu said he was a Henry Aaron fan. After he'd been commissioned he'd attended both information and photo schools in the States and he'd had some of Pat Brice's friends as instructors. With The Tiger he was just a little restrained—not unfriendly, but a trifle tentative about a former sergeant.

After lunch we went back to the hotel, stopping just long enough to pick up the stationery I'd ordered. Hieu watched the others begin to unpack and check out our equipment while I did some odds and ends of paper work. When I finished Hieu and I went into the bedroom to talk, closing the connecting door so that the others wouldn't disturb us. First of all I had to find out just how much he knew about Home Run.

Right away I discovered that he knew everything there was to be told about the ARVN part of the operation, what we were getting and how much from their stock. If he knew what we were getting in return it was because he'd figured it out for himself, not because he'd been told. As long as it didn't affect his ability to pitch in and help, there was no point in raising the issue.

"Anyway," I told him, "there's nothing we can do about Home Run until we get some kind of word from our contact. Until then we act like any other news team."

"What do you have in mind, Mr. Keefe?"

"Well, I want to talk to you about that. I've got a couple of ideas for special documentaries that I think will work. See how this one sounds to you."

He settled into his wicker chair and lit a cigarette, taking care not to blow the smoke right into my face.

"Essentially it's based on the simple fact that the war here has had a pretty bad press in America. That's something we have to accept without going into all the reasons, pro and con. Still, two or three million Americans were here. Some of them had a completely miserable time and think of it as a year lost out of their lives. Some didn't like it but were content to have had a look at a strange part of the world. The biggest percentage had a ball, brought home a lot of memories—and I've even heard some say they wanted to come back and show Vietnam to the wife and kids. The one thing all of them have in common is an interest in this country.

"What I'm thinking about doing is a kind of 'then and now' story. A program about the places the Americans remember best, both good and bad. That means everything from the R and R center down in Vung Tau clear to the battlefields along the DMZ. We'll hunt up Vietnamese who worked with and for the Americans. Find out right from their own mouths how their lives were changed when the GIs came and again when they pulled out. We'll find out what was good and what was bad. How does that sound to you?"

He didn't give me a fast answer. Instead he thought for several minutes and finally said, "From what I myself know of your countrymen it sounds good. I'm sure the ministry will like it and I'm sure they will cooperate. We still want to keep those friends we have in America and, if possible, make more." He smiled. "Not everything in Vietnam is war or politics. There are many good things that no one thinks to speak of and others that were once not good but are now much improved. Yes, Mr. Keefe, I think your project is a good one and I think it should be done."

I got note pads and for the next hour we worked up a list of the things that should be seen in the documentary and the kind of people we'd want to talk with. He had a lot of good ideas and they went in along with my own. By the time The Tiger returned we had a big selection to work from.

Tiger had been rustling up some transport for us. He'd found a driver with a brand-new Renault and another man with a well-kept panel truck. Both spoke some English and were able to travel if they had to. It took only a minute to talk to both men and agree on their daily fee and some other details.

While I talked to them I noticed Hieu and The Tiger speaking quietly in Vietnamese. When I sent the drivers off Hieu asked, "Mr. Keefe, did you know you're being followed?"

"Yes. We spotted two of them last night outside the hotel. Why?"

"Now there is a new beggar across the street. A blind man with a small child."

He pointed down into the street. I looked out and saw the man he spoke of, squatting in front of a small jewelry store, his eyes masked by a pair of those mirrorlike sunglasses. There was a small rice bowl on the pavement in front of him and a little boy about two or three played listlessly at his side. Beggars know they make more if they've got a kid along. If you don't have one they can always be rented.

With those glasses there was no way to tell if the beggar was one of the men we'd seen the night before or a new entry.

Hieu said, "If he disturbs you I can have him removed."

That would really stir things up. Whether the tail had been put on by Fargot and his bunch or by some third party, that was okay with me. If I did nothing to bother them they might get just a trifle careless and then, when I really needed to slip the tail, it would be that much easier.

I didn't say anything about the chance that the surveillance might be official but Hieu must have known the possibility was in my mind.

"It is not the way it would be done," he said. "In any case, strict orders have been given that you are not to be hindered. Now, Mr. Keefe, is there some other way in which I may be of assistance?"

Since he asked, there were a couple of things.

"I'll be needing a first-rate secretary—English-speaking, of course, and I'm ready to pay for the best I can get."

There had to be plenty of good secretaries available after the withdrawal but I had a reason for asking Hieu instead of doing it myself. It was normal for the people who are interested in what the press does to have a source of information in every bureau office. I didn't have anything to hide except Home Run and it might not hurt a bit if I made it easy for them to be convinced of it.

"I will make inquiries, Mr. Keefe, and perhaps we can find someone suitable whom you would like to engage. Is there anything else?"

"As a matter of fact, I was going to ask your help in getting a telephone of my own here in the room. A private number if that's possible."

"Yes, I think that can be arranged. It would be best if you could use your telephone without the call having to go through the hotel switchboard."

Captain Hieu was nobody's damn fool. He looked at his watch. "Now if there is nothing else I will return to Tan Son Nhut. Tomorrow morning, if you will not need me, I will go to my office. There I can see about your telephone and do what I can to find you a suitable secretary. Also I will report, unofficially, on your proposed film project. If the reaction I get is favorable, then a formal request can be drawn up and submitted for approval as quickly as possible. I know how anxious you must be to get to work."

He got up and put his cap on. "Perhaps we can meet after

lunch and I will be able to bring you word on what has been done."

He bobbed his head at me and then left, his heels clicking on the tiled floor of the corridor.

I looked around to see The Tiger, with a big grin. "I think now you must be number one big wheel, Mike."

"What makes you say that?"

"This Captain Hieu. His father is big general. Many stars on collar. Big man, General Truong. Someday, maybe, this captain is big general, too. When this captain say he can do, you better believe he can do. In Vietnam some people have to ask. Other people only have to tell. This Captain Hieu is number one teller and when he tell, people do." His grin grew even wider. "Very good, Mike. Very good."

He turned out to be right. First thing next morning two men showed up from PTT, the local Ma Bell. By good luck or good planning they wired the phone right out to a pole in the street instead of using the hotel's system. That would make it damn hard to put a tap on the circuit unless you had access at the exchange, something that only the government could do. While the men were still at work the desk called. The caller was the first applicant for the secretarial job. Her name, she told me, was Miss Binh.

She was armed with a wad of impressive references from a news syndicate, a big construction outfit which had departed and at least one firm that I knew for sure had been a front for Uncle Sam's spooks. They all spoke well of her shorthand and typing as well as her familiarity with filing and bookkeeping. She was both neat and punctual, knew her way through the mazes of the local bureaucracy and a number of other useful matters. She was fluent in English, French and Cantonese, with experience in translating from and into Vietnamese. If Miss Binh was half as good as her references claimed, she was a real jewel, and I hired her on the spot. Her first duty was to phone Hieu and tell him no more applicants would be needed.

I didn't have any doubt that Miss Binh was also a full-time employee of the kind of outfit Tiny and I work for but she sure

75

wasn't your stock model Mata Hari. She just about made five feet in her sandals, a pudgy woman, past thirty, probably at least half East Indian, judging by her warm cocoa color. Her face was composed of a series of soft curves that descended through a cascade of double chins to the collar of her ao dai. If she ever felt the need to smile I was never present for the occasion; what little expression her face showed was limited to a slight flaring of her wide nostrils and a minute rise of her thick, unplucked eyebrows. Most Vietnamese girls enjoy a small flirtation consisting principally of giggles and some gentle needling, but not this daughter of the Orient. Miss Binh was strictly the utility model, not supplied with any of the decorative extras and unsuitable for racing or recreation; she was a damn good secretary, though.

When she'd given Hieu the good news she passed the phone to me. He'd bounced my idea around among his bosses and the word was to make it a formal proposal as quickly as possible. The sooner I could get it out there, the sooner I could get to work.

I assembled my notes and Miss Binh and I got to work, stopping only for the new furniture and my other purchases to be hauled in and set up. I did my best to keep the proposal short and loose enough to be flexible about what we'd do without making it too vague for them to approve. It took about an hour and then Miss Binh got busy typing up a first draft to show Hieu when he came in.

The Saigon bureau of the Colville Syndicate was beginning to look like a going concern, the phones ringing and people coming and going. I had lunch at my desk and Miss Binh nibbled at something she'd brought wrapped in a half sheet of newspaper. When the others came in about one it was time to get them to work checking out the gear.

The Tiger had his drivers waiting downstairs and Pat and John brought down the big camera and the sound equipment. This was the closest thing they were going to get in the way of a dress rehearsal before we started filming material for the documentary. They'd expose some film to make sure everything was operating properly and record some sound as well. Whatever there was to do, they could handle it without me. Pat would want to try out various loading setups in the panel truck to get the best arrangement of items that he might want to get at in a hurry. Once he'd decided, then it would be up to everyone to make sure that his gear would always be right where he could find it.

When Hieu arrived Miss Binh had the rough draft of the proposal ready and she brought it to him neatly clipped into a folder. I looked to see if any sign of recognition passed between them but either they had really never met or they were both honor graduates of a good acting school. It didn't matter.

He had a couple of thoughts about the draft and then he and Miss Binh had a short discussion in Vietnamese about translation. When she got to work I took Hieu into my room for a cold drink and a quiet chat. He was the one who opened the topic of Home Run.

"I'm not sure you know that my father is also in our army, Mr. Keefe."

"Yes, I'd heard something about it."

"My father has just returned from your country. He was serving as Chief of Mission to advise your leaders on what our country hopes to receive in the way of military aid next year. He spoke of one man in particular with whom he had dealings."

That had to be Colville and it meant that Hieu's daddy was the one who had given the commitment. Why Hieu couldn't just say so without all this hinting was something I'd just have to learn to accept.

"My father has told me how pleased he was when he found that he might be of some special help to one who had been such a good friend to our cause. He has told me to spare no effort in making your project a success."

I read that loud and clear. General Truong was going along with Home Run but he had his son right where he could keep an eye on my progress and keep the old man both informed and protected. It was a cinch that he'd briefed his son on the whole story as it had come to him from Colville. If I was going to get the most from Hieu I'd be wise to tell him everything I knew. If Assistant Secretary of Defense Emerson Kenzie didn't like it, he could have a crack at coming to Saigon and running the operation himself.

It didn't take long. I gave him the hard evidence as we knew it and added the guesswork as well, the whole ball of wax. When I finished he knew about the rings, the call to the St. Regis, the contact on the bus and the talk in the Turkish bath. I told him as much as I could remember from Fargot's dossier and how the man had been lost between Saigon and Phnom Penh.

He took a minute to get it all orderly in his mind. "So it is possible that he may contact you anytime now."

"No, I think it's still too soon. He only had enough time in Phnom Penh to pass my terms. He left before they could have assembled what they intend to show. That means the proofs are not yet in Saigon. Now they'll either have him come back for them or send the stuff, whatever it is, to him by messenger. That will take time."

"Do you want me to have a watch set on him?"

I shook my head. "There's no point in taking a chance on frightening him off before we see what they've got. The way I see it, he's as anxious to get the job over with as we are. All he wants out of this is the payoff they've promised. From what we know of him, he's not normally what you'd call an action type. To me he looked like a man who's in a lot deeper than he likes to be and it scares him."

"So we wait."

I nodded. "We wait and I act like the Colville Syndicate's Saigon bureau manager."

"And Home Run must be deferred until they bring you the proof you demanded."

"That's it. Solid proof. That's their ticket to ride. It's as simple as that."

Hieu got up slowly and walked over to the window, looking down on the traffic I could hear passing below. Then he turned to me.

"Forgive me but I think that perhaps there is something we can be doing."

"What's that?"

"Even with the small amount of information we have there may be a few things we can build on. For example, the man Fargot told you that they would take delivery within three hundred miles of Saigon. Is that correct?"

"Yes, he did tell me that much but what good is it? That's a hell of a lot of territory. Some of it isn't even in Vietnam."

"That's right. That would seem to give them a great deal of choice but if you look at it on the map you'll see that a lot of it we can eliminate right away. A lot is salt water, some of it is almost totally impassable."

"That still leaves a lot."

"Yes, but consider this. Most of what remains is held firmly either by our government or by the invader. Even at a minimum, if we judge the size of this group by the amount of the ransom, it means a sizable force with enough room to operate and not come into contact with either side. We have to look for those unoccupied spaces between them that are suitable."

"And when you've found them?"

"Very likely the information will be of small use. Still, as you know, in our work it is sometimes possible to erect a large structure of educated guesswork on a foundation of very few hard facts."

If he had the manpower to put into that kind of exercise it was okay with me. He hadn't had to remind me that long after I'd collected the two men and gone home, he'd still have the problem of all that ammo out on the loose.

A few minutes later Miss Binh came in with the finished versions of the shooting plan in English and Vietnamese. We checked them over and Hieu took the copies that would go to Tan Son Nhut for presentation in the morning. He took a rain check on my drink offer and left just as the crew came in from their day's work. They spent only enough time to put things away and then were gone. I signed the mail and told Miss Binh she could close up for the night. The day before, the first back in Saigon, I'd been full of vitamins and minerals and without any sign of the classic jet-lag symptoms. I suppose I'd been kidding myself that after all the traveling I'd done I'd built up an immunity. All of a sudden I was brought back to earth, convinced that it's not nice to kid Mother Nature. Anything I had to do was going to have to wait until morning.

A shower and a change of clothes made me feel a bit better but I couldn't face the idea of picking out a restaurant and getting there and the whole effort. Instead I decided I'd have something light to eat right there in the hotel and get it over with. I took the elevator downstairs and chose a window table in the dining room, looking out toward the hotel entrance. The sun had set but that whole neighborhood is pretty well lit, brightly enough to see the passers-by reasonably well. I was just finishing my dessert when I saw a taxi arrive at the hotel door. The rear door swung open and the passenger got out and fumbled for his wallet to pay the driver. It wasn't until he'd got his change and turned to the entrance that I got a good look at his face.

It was Fargot.

⊰ 10 ⊱

I tossed some bills on the table, enough to cover the cost of the meal and tip, and without taking time to wait for my change, I went straight to the reception desk. Before he could get the attention of the clerk I was at his side.

"Are you looking for me, Monsieur . . ."

"Dupont," he put in quickly. "Yes, I was about to ask to be connected with your room, Mr. Keefe."

"You have something for me, then?"

"A few small things of interest. Perhaps we might speak privately. . . ."

I nodded and gestured to the elevator, stepping back to let him go first. He walked heavily across the tiled floor and I could see that he was bone tired. The grille clanged shut behind us and as the car rose I looked him over.

In spite of the heat he was wearing both jacket and tie, this suit a slightly lighter-weight version of the one he'd worn in New York. It was black, with a kind of mottled greenish overcast to the shiny fabric. He was still using the same cheap cologne, which failed to hide the fact that his last bath was probably the one we had shared at our previous meeting.

When the grille opened he let me go first down the corridor, waiting at my side as I unlocked the door to the office. I switched on the lights and he looked around the room, noting the furniture and stacks of equipment with interest but offering no comment. I took my seat behind the desk and he lowered himself into the chair that faced me. Without a word he reached into an inner pocket and brought out another of the hotel envelopes he favored. It was passed over to me and then he waited quietly as I inspected the contents.

The first things I drew out were Bostwick's and Bailey's Army ID cards. I had no doubt about their being genuine but by themselves they didn't prove a thing. They were going to have to do better than that.

Next was a snapshot, a 2¼ by 2¼ print. I lifted it to my nose and sniffed. The odor of the chemicals was still there, indicating that the print, at least, was new. It showed two men sitting at the base of a jungle tree, both big guys, one black and one white. The sunlight had been patchy but it was easy enough to read the name tags on their tattered fatigue jackets. For what it was worth, one was BAILEY, the other BOSTWICK, with a captain's double bars visible on the collar. The exposure wasn't very good and the focus might have been better but it was possible to see that Bostwick looked pale and drawn, his face gaunt under his shaggy hair like that of a man who's had a long bout of fever. Sitting behind the men were two Asians, their faces in shadow but their weapons clearly visible.

I put the snapshot aside and brought out the last item. It was part of a page torn from the Sunday *New York Times*, the classified ads. It had been issued the day I'd met Fargot and circled in black crayon was the ad for the '57 Edsel. Scrawled across the top of the page was one line.

"For God's sake give them what they want and get us out of here."

It was signed, "B. Bostwick, Captain, Infantry."

There was plenty of space left but he hadn't bothered to add any message for his family or to let Bailey add something for himself.

I went through the items again before I put them down and looked at Fargot. He had slumped a little in the chair but his eyes were giving me their full attention.

"You realize, Monsieur Dupont, that these things will have to be examined and authenticated by our experts and the men's families, both the photograph and the handwriting. I have never

82

met either man and until I can be assured that these items are genuine I cannot proceed."

That brought him upright in the chair. He was frightened and he showed it.

"But I understood from what you said that you had full authority, Mr. Keefe. You gave me to understand that you were the man in charge."

"That's right, but if you will think back you must admit that I was very explicit. You were required to furnish solid proof not only that the men were alive but also that you are in a position to deliver them. When we are fully convinced that you have met the conditions we will be ready to move to the next step."

I almost started feeling sorry for the man. His skin had gone even grayer and a thin film of perspiration gleamed on his upper lip.

"Please, Mr. Keefe, I implore you, do not delay. You must realize that my principals are not such men as you and I. They are people of little learning and do not have the sophistication that is necessary in dealings such as these. If they begin to suspect that they may be betrayed, they are capable of much violence. If they feel you may not be dealing in good faith, there is no way to predict what reckless action they might undertake."

"But you told me in New York that you had never met your principals, only an intermediary. Does this mean that you have met them since I saw you last?"

He brushed that aside. "No. I have not met them nor do I wish to do so. Still, what I have learned from their intermediary has convinced me that they are not people with whom I should want to have a disagreement." He shivered slightly as though hit by a sudden chill. Even the thought seemed to have a strong effect on his metabolism.

"How long will it take, Mr. Keefe, to complete your examination?"

"That's hard to say. Possibly a week, give or take a day or so."

"As long as that?"

"Look, my friend, I'm ten thousand miles from my own country. It will take a couple of days for this stuff to get there. It will be examined and I'll get the verdict back when they're finished. It takes time."

"And then how much longer before you can be ready to deliver?"

"A few days. After that it's just a matter of the time it takes to get to the place where I meet your principals."

"How will I know that you are ready to move?"

"I've got my own telephone now, a private line. Suppose you call every day at about five in the afternoon. Ask if I'm ready for the tailor to measure me for a suit. When everything is cleared I'll make a date for a fitting and we'll meet again."

He fished out a grubby pencil stub and a scrap of paper and wrote down the number. He wasn't happy about it but he didn't have any option except to go along with me.

There really wasn't anything more for us to settle but, scared as he was, there was a chance that if I could keep him talking he might just let something slip. We knew so little that anything might be useful. As he put the bit of paper in his pocket and gathered himself to get up I stopped him.

"Of course there might be some way we might find to speed things up."

"Anything, Mr. Keefe, anything to finish this business."

"Well, we're going to have a big job just lining up transport for a shipment of that size. Then we'll need men, I suppose, fuel for the trip out and back, food and water, all that. Until I know what kind of place I'm heading for I can't make any plans.

"For example, are we going by boat or truck or plane, or even oxcart, for that matter? How much time will I need to get to the rendezvous and back? Can I make it in one day or will it be longer? I know your instructions are to tell me nothing until I show you the ammunition ready to travel. Okay. I can see how you and your bunch want to keep the meeting place to yourselves as long as possible. That's what I'd do in your place if our positions were switched.

"Still, you want to speed things up and I think you can do it safely if you'll just give me something I can use for planning. What I really need to know is just a few simple facts. What kind of transport will I need and how long is the trip from Saigon? Give me something to go on and I'll have everything ready as soon as word comes from the States."

He was tempted. There was no doubt about it and from his face I could see the struggle he was having. On the one hand he was dying to get the whole affair finished and over with and off his back. He wanted to collect his payoff and come away with his precious hide reasonably intact. From his dossier I knew that he was playing with a crowd a lot rougher than his usual borderline clientele, and he didn't like it a bit.

But still, he had to weigh all that against the chance of some kind of doublecross on my part. If anything went wrong because he'd had a loose lip he would have to face a bunch of very unhappy customers and it was a thought he didn't care for very much. That was what probably clinched it.

"No, I think not, Mr. Keefe. I have told you too much as it is and you have doubtless made good use of even that. As I told you in New York, delivery will be taken within three hundred miles of Saigon. Details of transportation, travel time, meeting places and things of that nature will be given to you when our dealings have reached the proper stage and not before."

Just to make sure he wouldn't let anything loose, he got up and departed without another word. I heard his heels clicking down the corridor and, in a minute, the sound of the elevator door.

By that time I'd dialed the number Tiny had given me and in less than ten minutes the courier had picked up the envelope and was on his way to Tan Son Nhut and the first plane to Thailand. Tiny would take just long enough to check the stuff and photocopy it before shooting it along to the States. Until I got the word, Operation Home Run was strictly on "Hold."

The next day turned out to be a real killer and I got back to the hotel flogged to my socks. Miss Binh had a few messages and there was mail to take care of but I put it aside while I destroyed a cold beer and indulged in a long shower. I'd taken on a full load of the old familiar laterite dust, the red, clinging stuff that's as much a part of life in Vietnam as the heat and the rain. Most of the day had been spent riding the roads with Hieu, selecting the locations we'd film and gathering background material. With the big mass of possibilities, it was going to be a problem picking which things we'd decide would offer the most.

I'd just come up from breakfast when Hieu called. All indications were that the project would be approved and backed, a new record for official action in Vietnam, and we could go ahead, pending final action. Our driver ran me out to the Joint Chiefs in Tan Son Nhut and Hieu was waiting to take me in to see his bosses. I had to drink some more tea with some more brass before we could hit the road and get to work. Hieu had drawn a jeep and as we bumped along I briefed him on what had happened the night before.

"Do you think his proofs are genuine?"

"That's something I'm not going to even bother having an opinion on. The ID cards belong to the men we're looking for but they could have been taken from their dead bodies a long time ago. The photo the same way. The print was fresh but who knows when the negative was actually shot? The newspaper has to be current but it's going to take an expert to make an evaluation of the handwriting. I just hope that he'll have enough to work with. Even if it is genuine, though, it only proves that the man who wrote it was alive last week."

"And Fargot would tell you no more about the delivery?"

"If he knows anything he's keeping it to himself. He's scared but not so scared that he's going to give something away for nothing."

"Perhaps if I were to have him picked up we could convince him that it might be best for him to tell us what he knows."

"I don't think it's worth the risk. He's ready to talk right now if we can show him we're ready to move. He'll sing like a bird without any persuading at all. If we lean on him on the off chance that we just might get something useful, we run a big risk of scaring his principals off. You know what he said in New York. They'll send our men back a piece at a time."

"So we wait?"

"We wait and while we're at it we improve our cover by working."

As we'd talked Hieu had been maneuvering his jeep through the traffic around the air base. We were on our way to look over

86

some of the fire bases the Americans had built ringing the city. One by one they'd been turned over to the ARVN to occupy and the new tenants had made changes to suit their own life style.

Mostly the new look was simply a result of the fact that these troops hadn't been brought halfway round the world to stay a year and then head for home. The ARVN was home and in service for the duration. They moved in with the whole family and the pigs and chickens, too. The barbed wire and revetments were gay with drying laundry, while the poultry and even an occasional goat browsed on the grass that sprouted from the ruptured sandbags. There were kids playing under the muzzles of the tower machine guns and between the tracks of revetted tanks. Gone were the battalions of mama and papa sans who had made the beds, washed the clothes, shined the boots, served the food and washed the pots and mess trays of the Americans. The deadfall bars and improvised car wash establishments which sprang up wherever there was a chance to pick up a stray piaster were gone, their place taken by ramshackle teahouses and eating places, most just a few tables and stools roofed with thatch against the sun and rain.

This close to the city we were on government-controlled ground and every structure bigger than a privy displayed a red-striped yellow flag. How much was due to an increase in patriotism and how much to the efforts of the National Police was anybody's guess.

Every so often I'd see something that stirred my memory, places I'd seen before but were already changed almost beyond recognition. A few years more and you'd have to look hard for relics of the American presence. The largesse that had sifted out of the military supply system to filter down into the local economy was being replaced now by imports from Japan, Taiwan and other Asian nations. Once more the French were in evidence, their renewed activity indicating that the sins of their fathers were now remembered only by the older generation who had fought to expel them. The few remaining Americans tried hard to be unobtrusive.

Toward the end of the morning we stopped at the big Cong Hoa Hospital, one of the places the Americans had poured money and personnel into in an attempt to raise the pitifully low level of care the population had got. It was still a far cry from the Mayo

Clinic but it was a hell of a lot better than what I'd seen a few years before. I put it down on our list and when we got back to the jeep Hieu asked if I was ready to break for lunch. It sounded pretty good and I asked him to pick out a place in the neighborhood. Instead of taking any of the places along the street, he drove the short distance to the golf course and parked in the lot beside the big clubhouse. I'd eaten there before, either as a guest or when I'd been a little flush. The food was good and the open dining terrace on the upper floor was a nice place to sit and catch any stray breeze that happened by. As we came to the top of the stairs the maître d' hurried up with his sheaf of menus. Not that I impressed him. It was Hieu, and the man made a whole production of finding us a table and snapping his fingers for his flunkies to spring into action. While he didn't exactly sneer at my pronunciation of the French dishes I ordered, he did convey a strong feeling that he didn't think I was much.

We had almost finished eating when I saw a foursome coming in from the last green. They were all prosperous-looking Vietnamese and after they'd dismissed their girl caddies I heard the clatter of their spiked shoes on the stairs. As they came in sight at the top I saw that one of them was getting a good deal of deference from the others, while the maître d' was bowing and gesturing like a man demented. The object of all this attention looked around the terrace until he saw Hieu. He smiled and came directly to us. Both of us stood for him and he slapped Hieu on the shoulder and said something in Vietnamese that brought a smile to Hieu's face.

"Father, this is my colleague, Mr. Keefe." He turned to me. "My father, General Truong."

We shook hands and the general said, "Sit down, please. May I join you for a moment?"

Before either of us could answer he called something over his shoulder and as he drew his chair up to the table a tall iced drink appeared. He drank deeply and then swung around to look directly at me.

"My son has spoken of you, of course. Tell me, how is your project going?"

He could have been referring to the documentary but somehow I didn't think so.

"Slowly, I'm afraid, but there have been developments that are encouraging."

He'd get the details soon enough through his own channel and it didn't seem like the right time or place to go any further.

"As you know, we are watching with a great deal of interest. Sometimes what might, at first, appear to be a small matter can have an effect on the relations between our countries that might last for many years to come. Let us hope that the outcome of what you are doing will be a happy one."

I was reading him loud and clear. If something went wrong it could light a fuse that might cause an explosion almost anywhere. He was more than a little worried that one might go off right under his tail. The fact that he'd put his son where he could keep a close check on the operation showed it as clearly as anything. He'd have his share of sweating before we were done.

He drank off the rest of the liquor and, waving to us to keep our seats, got briskly to his feet.

"I hope we will meet again, Mr. Keefe. Until then I hope that all will go well with your filming." He strode quickly across the terrace to his own table, where he chatted animatedly with the others in the party and paid us no further attention. Hieu signaled for our bill but when I reached for it he took it himself and, with the waiter's pen, scrawled his name across the bottom. Running into his father had been no accident and what better place to arrange it than at their club?

As we got to the top of the stairs three men in uniform were just starting up. They were Europeans, big, vigorous-looking types, and I heard Hieu mutter, "Hungarians."

We were halfway down when they passed us but they showed no interest in me other than a slight turn of their heads when our eyes reached the same level. Even in the noonday heat I felt a slight shiver in my lumbar region. They represented just one more factor to deal with if Home Run came unstuck. The Control Commission was bound to have a lot to say on the subject.

For the next few hours we cruised, Hieu driving while I made

89

notes on what we'd shoot, when the light would be best, traffic density, who we'd have to contact to get clearance. I'd decided to open the film with an extended montage of the places most familiar to the ex-GIs. The hotels that had been billets for both officers and men. Those that had been used as hospitals and offices, and other installations in the downtown district, in Gia Dinh, and the string of apartment buildings along Plantation Road and in Cholon. There were the off-duty hangouts, the bars along Tu Do Street, Cheap Charlie's, Givral and Brodard. The USO and the JUSPAO building and My Canh, the floating restaurant in the river. I'd end the introduction with a look at Hundred P Alley, the red-light section just outside the main gate of the air base. We were both concentrating but the same thought kept coming up in our minds. Finally we decided to get back to the office and settle it.

It had been eighteen hours or more since Tiny had got Fargot's envelope and it was not too soon to look for some kind of message.

It was waiting for us at the office. Sitting opposite Miss Binh was an uncomfortable-looking American, a tall kid in his early twenties. He was in civilian clothes but his close-cropped head and rigid posture screamed out, "I am a U.S. Marine."

Tiny's reply had come over in the daily pouch and after checking my ID and getting my signature on his receipt, he passed it over. I told him not to wait for an answer and as he left we took the message into my room and closed the door.

Dear Mike:

Your exhibits have been photographed for local study and the originals are on their way back to the main store for analysis. The men in the snapshot tally superficially with the ID photos and other data if you take into consideration what's probably happened to them in the last few years. On first glance the snapshot shows signs that it was not printed from the original negative but is a photocopy of another print and that explains the poor quality. We are setting up the biggest blowup we can make and hope that may show any evidence of doctoring.

The handwritten note matches, superficially, the samples we

have here but with more data in the States we'll wait for their verdict.

Allowing for transmission time expect something definite in seventy-two hours. I think you can assume, for planning purposes only, that the material will prove out.

It was unsigned. I passed it to Hieu and he read it carefully. When he'd finished he looked as glad as I felt that the wait was coming to an end.

⫷ 11 ⫸

We spent the next day pretty much the same way. Hieu drove, I made notes, and gradually the final format I would follow fell into shape. However Home Run came out, we'd end up with a film we could all take some pride in. The point we'd pivot the whole story on was a natural.

One of the installations the Americans had left behind on the sprawling complex at Tan Son Nhut was a cantonment known as Camp Davis. It had been named for the first GI killed in Vietnam back in '61. In the years that followed Camp Davis had been built into a typical area of temporary tropical barracks, mess halls and work areas, with all the recreational facilities a modern army needs. It was equipped with running water and electricity and the whole affair had been enclosed by a barbed-wire-topped chain-link fence. When the Americans left the new tenants had moved in —the official delegation from the Vietcong. Right there at Camp Davis was a capsule history of the past fifteen years.

There didn't seem to be a chance in hell that I'd ever be allowed to go right inside with a camera and crew. Even if the VC agreed I knew I'd definitely be marked lousy by the government press people. I could make it a plus. I'd shoot from the outside and, if I could, from the air and not take a chance on messing up. I had to remember the real purpose of the trip.

On Sunday I called a halt. We all needed some rest and a chance to unwind and I wanted everybody at the top of his form for what was ahead. There had been much more to do than I'd expected. We'd started from scratch and made a hell of a lot of progress but only because everybody had hustled. We were keeping our personnel down to the bare minimum for a lot of reasons and each one of us wore a couple of hats. As a combination bureau manager–producer–writer–correspondent, I had my share.

We never could have done it without Miss Binh. She was doing jobs that the other outfits hire three or four people to cover, from early morning until she took the mail to the post office after telling Fargot that I still wasn't ready to be measured for a new suit. She'd really earned the day off and I hoped that after she'd taken care of her report on me her other boss would feel the same way.

For myself, I slept late and then took time for a long breakfast including all the trimmings. With the whole day ahead I could do whatever I liked and I started out by taking a stroll wherever the spirit moved me. I went up Tu Do to the big red-brick cathedral, which was doing a good business, and on to Phan Tan Gian and the cemetery where the VC used to hide their weapons between raids in the city. A few blocks down was the bicycle shop where the suicide squad that had attacked the U.S. embassy to set off the Tet battle had hidden. Just beyond was the nice new concrete canal bridge they'd contributed a big hole to with a rocket, and a lot of other things that brought up painful memories for anyone who'd gone through the mess.

I turned and went a few blocks west and then headed back toward the center of town. I passed the big villa where the American commander had once lived in a style more like that of a Roman governor than the leader of a liberating army. I remembered how he used to be driven through the crowded streets in his shiny car, sirens screaming and outriders scattering the pedestrians and the vehicles carrying less fortunate mortals. If the idea had been to "win the hearts and minds of the Vietnamese people," they had sure picked one hell of a way to go about it.

Before I knew it I was back at the Central Market. As far as the locals are concerned, this is the real heart of the city, a combination of Broadway, Bond Street, the Rue de la Paix and the Farmers Market in Los Angeles. Anything you need from a needle to an anvil, or a sausage to a whole hog, or a hanky to a full trousseau, you can find under that one roof. The whole high-

93

ceilinged center is crammed with food vendors' stalls, and the long corridors that surround it are given over to yard goods, men's clothing and ladies' unmentionables, hardware, stationery, pots and cutlery and dishes, as well as a lot of top-quality antiques if you know what you're buying. Outside are a raft of fast-food stands with a selection to suit every taste. It's a hell of an interesting place and probably the best show in town. I should have stuck around awhile.

Instead I left the market and sure as hell my feet took me on a route I'd covered a good many times before, right to the one place I didn't want to see again. I didn't stop until I got to the entrance to the narrow alley where I'd lived with Co.

It was just like any of the hundreds of alleys all over the city, a few shops and other small businesses on the ground floors of the narrow apartment buildings that make up most of Saigon's housing. They're four or five stories tall and only about fifteen feet wide, with an open stairwell leading up to the pair of flats on each floor. There's no way of knowing how many Vietnamese can live in one of those places but ours had been just perfect for two. Perfect, that is, if you don't mind peeling plaster, cracked tile floors, an intermittent flow of what passes for water and the rich mixture of aromas and sounds that fill the place like a living presence.

I suppose it won't be long before a lot of other guys who spent some time in Vietnam start doing the same thing. They'll take the wife and kids on an all-expense tour to the Paris of the Orient, trying to search out the excitement and glamour of Saigon as they remember it. They'll have made pests of themselves with the too-often-told tales of their adventures and escapades, self-convinced by their own fictions.

They'll remember the almond-eyed maidens only as they looked in a dimly lit bar through a haze of cheap booze and pot, forgetting the bad skin, the crooked teeth and the skinny legs revealed in the harsh light of the morning after. They'll have to face the hard reality of what their memories have cleaned and perfumed and glamorized. If Kipling's British soldier ever got back to Mandalay, I'll bet he had one hell of a letdown.

I hadn't had enough time to kid myself more than just a little

94

but I'd forgotten just how crummy the little warren we'd called home really was. I stood a couple of minutes looking up at the slatted balcony door where I'd seen Co for the last time and behind which she had died waiting for me to come for her. I tried again to call up the way she'd looked but nothing came. A few people passing by gave me a curious look but no one offered a smile or a greeting. When I saw the food cart enter the alley, the vendor bent almost double as he dragged it across the pavement, I forced myself to turn and walk away. At the hotel bar I bought a bottle of brandy and took it up to the room. I'd had enough of remembering for one day.

The sound of typing from the next room woke me next morning. I took my shower and shaved and by the time I was half dressed the waiter was knocking at the door with my breakfast. I ate quickly and then, taking my coffee with me, I went into the office to see what Miss Binh was up to. Actually Miss Binh wasn't up to anything there because the typing was being done by a young woman I'd never seen before. She looked up from her work as I came in and what I saw was as pretty a sight as you'd want first thing in the morning.

Miss Binh might have been one hell of a good secretary but, as I've said, she wasn't really in the running for the Miss Saigon crown. This girl could have taken it hands down.

"Where's Miss Binh?"

"Miss Binh sick today. She give me key. Tell me to come to work for her."

"And who are you?"

She bobbed her head. "I Miss Chi, cousin of Miss Binh. Number one secretary."

I walked over to her desk and picked up the last letter she'd typed. As far as I could see, it was perfect. When I handed it back she passed me a couple of phone messages she'd taken. The names were recognizable and the short note she'd made of each was clear and concise. Not only was Miss Chi decorative but she was efficient as well.

She was a perky little thing. She was wearing an ao dai, which, in the case of most Vietnamese girls, serves as a means of hiding a number of deficiencies. In her case it gave prominence to a number of attractions and the hint of still others. She held herself nicely, her shoulders, a bit broader than most girls', kept well back and accentuating a nicely placed front elevation. Just a hint of makeup brought out her dark, slanted eyes and maybe she wore a touch of rouge. She was a prime example of the classic Annamese type—flattened nose, full, generous lips and pointed chin —but she gave no sign of the subdued attitude most of them affect. Miss Chi had none of that downcast-eye, low-voice, you-are-my-master approach. She looked you right in the eye with complete self-possession even though her tiny feet couldn't quite reach the floor below her chair. Miss Chi seemed completely satisfactory even though she might easily become a bit of a personal problem. If Miss Chi were to become a permanent part of the operation and I let nature take its course, my social life could easily turn into a business liability.

I returned the calls she'd taken and then got busy on a status report for the syndicate. They would need a timetable for the first documentary so that things would be ready to happen on their end when I began shipping film. I was just about finished when there was a firm rap at the door and in came another Marine, the same stock model as the first. He checked my ID and then handed over a sealed envelope. On the small memo sheet inside I read "Go." Just below was more. "Be careful." It wasn't signed but it didn't need to be.

The Marine took one last long look at Miss Chi, filed what he saw under "Pending" and went on his way. It was time for me to get to work.

At sundown I'd closed the slatted shutters on the open windows on the chance that my visitor might like it better that way. The only light in the room came from the lamp beside my bed, placed to shed most of its illumination on the chair where Fargot would sit. The desk had word to send him right up without calling first. The office was dark. I'd sent Miss Chi home right after she'd passed the word that I'd be ready for a fitting anytime after six.

Pat and John were standing by at their place with The Tiger,

Hieu was downstairs in the bar. All we needed was the word from Fargot and we'd be all set to move.

Six o'clock came and went but for once Fargot was taking his time. I had ice and glasses ready and I mixed myself a light one just to keep busy until he showed. I checked to be certain I had a pad and pencil handy in case I had to take notes and made sure I had a fresh reel of tape in a small recorder so I could get everything down on paper after he left.

The closed shutters subdued the noises coming from the street below and seemed to amplify the small sounds I made, the clink of ice and the soft squeaks of my chair. The crash of the elevator door opening and then closing sounded like a full artillery salvo and then I heard the rapping of heels approaching down the corridor until they reached the bedroom door. I waited for him to knock but nothing came. Instead there was a funny sort of shuffling sound as I crossed the room and swung the door open wide.

It was Fargot, all right. He stood in the doorway, still in the same musty suit he'd worn before, his shirt collar limp with sweat. Pallid as he'd looked before, this time he really appeared sick. He looked at me with a strange, puzzled expression, his pudgy fist halfway outstretched. I stepped back to let him come into the room but he just continued to stand where he was. Just as I was about to speak he seemed to pull himself together and took a couple of steps forward. He still had his fist outstretched and I wondered what he was clutching so hard. He still hadn't said a word. In fact he never did.

Instead he uttered a low, animal-like grunt and then slowly collapsed on the floor. For the first time I saw the spreading red stain that was saturating the back of his jacket from a point just below his left shoulder blade. By the time I could snap myself out of it and bend to search for his pulse he was dead.

⊰ 12 ⊱

It was a hell of a struggle to make myself think clearly. After the way I'd built myself up to the idea that we were finally going to get something done, it took some time to get used to the notion that we were right back where we'd been days before. Right now, though, I needed help and in large lots.

My problem was where to go for it. Calling the cops was out. I threw that idea away right off the bat. The whole of Operation Home Run was so delicately poised that it might collapse completely if any wrong questions were asked. If I could just get what was left of Fargot to hell and gone off my premises there was still a chance, but I couldn't do it alone. There was no way for my three guys to get rid of the body without being noticed. I could call our local agency detachment but that would take time and there wasn't much of it. As for Hieu, I had no way of knowing how he might react to aiding and abetting. There was a good chance that with Fargot dead Hieu would decide that the whole affair was beginning to smell bad, and it was time to pull out. Even if he was willing, how would his father react?

Finally I had to admit that I had no choice. It was go with Hieu as the only practical option. I closed the door on the dear departed and went down the hall. Hearing the elevator rise, I started down the stairs, forcing myself to move deliberately. The corridor showed no trace of blood but everything pointed to the fact that whoever hit him had done it just before he got to my door. I came down the last flight and walked as calmly as I could into the bar, trying to look like a man who wanted nothing more than a quiet drink.

Hieu was sitting alone at a small table and I sat down across from him. A waiter started toward me but I waved him off. Then, as calmly as I could, I told Hieu what had just happened. Apart from a slight widening of his eyes, his face never changed expression. For all anyone could see, I was telling him some bit of gossip about a mutual acquaintance that neither of us liked very well.

He listened to what I had to say, then lifted his glass and finished his drink. He got to his feet and after he put some money on the table, we walked out the front door to the sidewalk.

"Go to the apartment where your men are living. Wait there. It will take about an hour to get everything done. Don't come back to the hotel until then."

"Are you going to call the police?"

He shrugged his shoulders. "What for? They cannot bring the man Fargot back to life for us to question. All they can do is get in the way."

"Do you want to give up the operation?" If he did I had to know right now.

He shook his head. "No, I think not. If the other side still want to deal they will establish a new contact. When that happens I will still be needed."

"And how about your father?"

He smiled. "He will, I believe, do as I suggest."

"Any ideas on who might have gotten Fargot?"

"What does it matter? His friends or his enemies. Either way he is no longer a factor." He reached out and shook my hand as though we were parting after a friendly chat and as I started for the corner, I saw him hail a cab.

It was a long hour. It hadn't taken long to tell the others about what had just happened. The party was beginning to turn rough and they were entitled to know. For Pat and John it was all part of the job and they'd act accordingly. It was a different story for The Tiger. I had to give him the chance to bow out now that casual homicide was in the scenario.

99

It wasn't only that he had a handicap with his bad leg. That wasn't going to hold him back. It was just that no matter how Home Run turned out, we'd be able to pack up and head back for God's Country. He was going to have to go on living in Vietnam. If he got into trouble with the government he'd never again make a nickel at his trade and it could even be a lot worse. It didn't seem to bother him, though.

"Not to worry, Mike. Maybe leg number ten but head still okay. You tell Tiger what you want and you get it. Maybe when the shit get thick you be glad you got me."

For the next fifty-five minutes I sat down, got up and walked the floor. Pat brought me a cold beer and offered to make something to eat but I'd lost my appetite. Somehow I made myself stay in the apartment until the full sixty minutes Hieu had given me were up. Then the four of us went back to the Continental Palace.

I'd half expected to find the reception area swarming with white-uniformed cops but there was no sign that things were not normal. The Chinese clerk at the desk gave me the usual nod and we all went upstairs without anyone paying us more attention than that. I unlocked the bedroom door carefully, prepared to find the remains of Monsieur Fargot still decorating the floor, but there was no sign that he'd even been there. Instead, seated in a chair by the window was Hieu. He'd made himself a drink and was leafing through my copy of *Playboy,* looking for all the world as though he didn't have a care.

"I hope you don't mind my making myself at home."

I couldn't help laughing. Maybe the day would come when I'd see Hieu get excited but this wasn't going to be it. "Everything all right?"

"I'm afraid your friend has met with an accident. He was foolish enough to try to take a shortcut through an alley. Probably some bad man asked him for his watch and wallet and, instead of giving the man what he wanted, he tried to resist. In the struggle . . ." He spread his hands, palms up. "Someone will find him in the morning."

"What's going to happen if the cops find out he's been here?"

"How will they find that out?"

"Maybe he told someone he was coming here. The clerk at the desk will remember."

He shook his head. "Even if he was so foolish as to tell someone he was coming, which I doubt, why would the clerk say that? It would only involve the hotel in what is merely an unfortunate incident. I don't think the management would like that."

He reached into his shirt pocket. "He had this clutched in his hand."

It was a scrap of paper, hardly bigger than a postage stamp. I took it and looked it over. It appeared to be the corner of an envelope where front and back had been glued together.

"You didn't find the rest of it?"

"No, and I think we can assume that whoever got to him took it."

"That means if he was bringing the instructions in writing we still don't know what they want us to do."

Hieu was silent for a moment and when he spoke it was slowly, as he picked his way along his train of thought, putting ideas into words.

"You know, it was too well done to have just been a spur-of-the-moment matter. It took careful planning and split-second timing to do the thing right where it would have the maximum effect on you."

"I don't see what you mean. The man saw his moment and grabbed it."

"No, that is just too unlikely. The man knew exactly when Fargot was to arrive and, probably, what he was bringing. He had only the few seconds when his target was coming down the hall to act. It is almost as if he let Fargot get right up to your door and then made his move."

"Why do you say that? If Fargot saw the man coming at him he had plenty of time to either run or yell. He didn't do either."

"That's it. First, he knew the person who killed him and well enough so that he was not afraid to turn his back as he might to a stranger. Second, the one who stabbed him was a real artist."

"An artist?"

He nodded his head as if there were no doubts in his mind.

"Have you ever tried to stab a man in the back? It's not easy. To do it you have to know a lot more about anatomy than a doctor. You've got to locate the precise spot between the ribs where the knife will slip through and find the heart and do it on the first try. If you miss and the knife strikes bone you've got to stab and stab again until you finally hit the right spot. By that time your victim is likely to raise some objections and even try to get away from you. There will be an outcry and a lot of spilled blood on you and everything else. I took time to examine Fargot's body. Even I could see that the wound was small and perfectly placed; a thin blade did the work and did it to perfection. Fargot's heart was pierced and he bled to death internally. That's why there was so little blood on the floor or on his clothing."

"That still doesn't explain why they let him get right to my door before he was stabbed. Why not do it where there was less risk of being seen?"

"Yes; that occurred to me and I can think of only one explanation. Fargot is no longer necessary to his principal except for psychological purposes."

"What does that mean?"

"I think it was meant as a message to you."

While we waited for a new contact we worked. Bright and early next morning we started shooting. The Tiger had the cars and drivers at the curb when we brought the equipment down for our first real day of work. I had the script outline that Miss Chi had typed and we took off for Tan Son Nhut to meet Hieu. A short hang-up at the air-base gate was fixed with a phone call and we went straight to Camp Davis. I had my first shot planned and while Pat and John set up the camera The Tiger hung the lavaliere mike around my neck and patched the line into the monitor.

Across the road, just inside the camp gate, a couple of sentries were eying us suspiciously. I saw one go for the field phone to pass the word up the line that they had visitors but they made no move to interfere with us. There would probably be some kind of protest filed later but they had no real grounds to object. All they could do now was try to look their best. They were doing a good job of it.

You can figure that the Vietcong were going to man the place with picked men. The few we could see were all husky, well-disciplined-looking types in neat uniforms and the plastic sun helmets that are their trademark now but were once the symbol of the imperialists in hot countries.

The camp itself was immaculate and looked better than when the Americans had been in residence. The sandbags were carefully stacked and unruptured, the ground raked clean and what grass there was had been clipped right up to the fence. Just outside the wire the weeds grew rank and high, the Vietnamese Air Force landlords probably not caring about the mosquitoes that like such places.

Inside the wire I could see some men bent over, tending a lush-looking vegetable garden, and over where the GIs had played volleyball in the evening under floodlights there was a platoon doing calisthenics in the hot morning sun. The young palms and banana trees that our people had planted were well grown now, their green making a nice contrast with the weathered gray of the unpainted barracks.

When both camera and sound were ready I took my place at the roadside and gave the signal to roll. I did the intro I'd prepared, looking directly into the camera to make contact with the audience as I explained what they were going to see, once in a wide-angle shot to get the background and then close for a cutaway. I kept right on talking over the sounds of passing traffic and aircraft, pausing only when they were so loud I couldn't be heard. We printed Take One on both.

Next I brought Hieu into the scene. He'd be doing the interpreting as well as giving his own Vietnamese point of view and I could see that he was going to be fine. There wasn't any need to explain that he was an intelligent and educated guy, the kind of person an American could relate to, but what made him really good was something in his manner. It convinced you that what he said he really believed and that if something was wrong, no matter how bad it made his country look, he'd say so, frankly and openly. We'd agreed on that. The one thing I didn't want to do was make just another propaganda piece for the Saigon government.

103

Once I had him on film we went ahead and did voice-over narration that would be used with the other footage we would get of the camp, both through the wire and from the air. When we'd done that, things moved fast. Without having to worry about sound recording, we got all the footage we'd need by the time we broke for lunch. I was hot and hungry but luckily we didn't have far to go.

Just outside the air base is a big old French-style villa that's been taken over by the Vietnamese Air Force as an officers' club. Like many other things, their definition of a club is a lot different from ours. This one, for example, had a lot of special facilities to offer. There was a dining room that served pretty good American and Chinese food plus a dimly lit bar complete with hostesses and Saigon tea. The lobby had a battery of high-voltage slot machines and upstairs there were other delights available for them as likes them. We'd kill two birds right there.

Since it had been the closest place for a change from ration food and for some amiable feminine companionship, it had been a popular spot for Americans, and after we'd had lunch I planned some shooting right there.

We parked out in front and The Tiger sent one driver off to eat while the other kept an eye on the cars. Hieu went to look for a phone and the rest of us washed up and entered the dining room. It was about half filled and no sooner had we taken our seats than a young Chinese girl was passing out hot towels and a waiter handing us menus. With a long afternoon's work ahead of us, nobody wanted too much lunch and it took only a minute to order. By that time Hieu came in and joined us. He looked a little worried but he didn't explain and I didn't ask. Still, it was clear that something was bothering him.

We didn't waste any time. As soon as we'd eaten we got the camera and started work. It went quickly and as we were finishing I saw that there was still time to move on and knock off another sequence. Hieu had left us again but just as we were loading the equipment to make the move he came out of the club and drew me aside.

"Do you know about Miss Binh?" he asked.

"Sure. She's been out sick but her replacement is fine. No complaints at all about Miss Chi."

"Who is Miss Chi?"

That was funny. I'd assumed that when Miss Binh hadn't been able to come to work her boss had sent in Miss Chi from the bench.

"She's the replacement. Says she's Miss Binh's cousin."

"Miss Binh has no cousin," he said flatly.

Well, that figured. There wasn't any combination of genes that could produce both Miss Binh and Miss Chi. I hadn't really bought the cousin part.

"Wait a minute, Hieu. You recommended Miss Binh. I hired her. To be honest with you, I figured Miss Binh had some special connections but I've got nothing to hide. I hired her not just because she's a good secretary but because you wanted me to. Right?"

"Yes. I didn't think you'd care and having her there has been a help. Now it looks like we have a problem with Miss Binh."

"What kind of problem?"

"Miss Binh is supposed to report by phone every evening. Saturday night she made her call as usual. She said you'd given her Sunday off and that she wanted to use the day to take her mother to Bien Hoa. Last night she didn't make her call and when she still hadn't phoned this morning someone was sent around to check up. Her neighbors said that she had left, as she said she would, Sunday morning and that she wasn't back. As of fifteen minutes ago they still weren't back. They've got a man in Bien Hoa now checking to see if she ever actually got there."

"If she's been away for more than two days I wonder how she got in touch with Miss Chi."

"If she ever did is more like it." He thought for a moment. "Did you let her in when she came yesterday morning?"

I thought back and finally remembered. It had been the sound of her typing that had awakened me.

"No, she let herself in. She said she'd got the key from Miss Binh."

He shook his head. "Miss Binh is too experienced to do anything like that. As soon as she knew she wouldn't be able to go to work she'd have reported in and they would have sent another secretary to replace her. If Miss Chi got a key to your office it wasn't given to her by Miss Binh. Whoever did must have taken it from Miss Binh and sent her over."

"So the next thing to worry about is who sent Miss Chi?"

"That's about it. Maybe that's how he knew about your meeting with Fargot. It must have been Miss Chi that passed the word on."

When it comes it comes in bunches. Now I had a secretary who was the finger for a guy who dropped corpses on clean bedroom floors.

"What do you think I ought to do about her?"

"For right now, nothing. Just make sure she doesn't get a chance to find out anything that could mean trouble for us. Maybe we'll get some extra use out of her."

That wasn't quite what I'd had in mind for extra duties from Miss Chi. Right now it would be hard enough to be with her without giving something away.

◄ 13 ►

It was late when we finally came trooping into the office. Miss Chi was still at her desk and when she saw how pooped we were she got busy with ice and glasses. By the time the gear had been put up for the night she had a cold drink for each of us. I drank off about half of mine before I sat down to tackle the day's scene reports for her to type up. With all the shooting we'd done there was a good deal of paper work to get through and then I dictated a short note for the head office.

We'd ended the day's work at the old MAC-V headquarters. I still thought of it that way—Military Assistance Command, Vietnam—but now it was called the Defense Attaché's Office. We all needed stuff from the PX and, more important, I wanted a secure phone, one on which I could talk in the clear. There was only a short delay and then I heard Tiny on the line. As briefly as I could I filled her in. It all added up to just one thing. Zilch.

"What do you plan to do now, Mike?"

"There's nothing I can do. I've got to wait until someone else makes a move."

"Like what?"

"Well, like setting up a new contact. Even then I'm going to have to be sure that I've really got the right party and not some phony trying to horn in."

"Do you think maybe this new secretary, Miss Chi, has any idea that you know she's a ringer?"

"I think if she has any suspicions she won't be waiting for me when I get back to the office. She'll have cut and run. If she's still aboard I suppose it means that she doesn't know Miss Binh is an agent. She must figure that I've been in Vietnam long enough to know how the locals suddenly take off a day or so and send in a 'cousin.' That way two or three of them can make a living from the job only one of them holds."

Tiny thought about that for a minute. Then she said, "There may be another reason for her to stay."

"What's that?"

"You and Hieu think that maybe she fingered Fargot?"

"It's possible. She knew someone was coming."

"Do you think that maybe the man with the knife might have hit the wrong man? It's a possibility, isn't it?"

"What the hell is this—Make Mike Feel Good Day or something?"

"Never mind the bright remarks. Just be careful."

"Yes, Mother."

She muttered something she wouldn't have said on an open line and I heard her hang up.

When I finished my dictation Miss Chi said she'd just as soon stay a little late and get it all typed up right away. I told her to leave it on her desk when she was ready to go and I'd sign it to be mailed in the morning. John had wrapped the shipment for the syndicate and The Tiger left to take it to Tan Son Nhut on his way home. When the others had gone I went into the bathroom for a shower before dinner.

The first day of shooting any job is always rough. The crew have to get used to each other and the equipment still hasn't settled into its regular places. I was trying to be correspondent, producer and director, planning each shot and thinking ahead to the next move, and I was totally beat. I tossed my dirty clothes on the floor and got into the shower. When I'd soaped and rinsed, the water felt so good I went on standing under the spray while the tension knot I always develop right above my belt buckle began slowly to ease and I felt better about getting on with it. I stepped out and toweled off, then padded into the bedroom. The air had cooled and the tiles were pleasant under my bare feet.

Waiting for me on the dresser was a stack of typed sheets and addressed envelopes ready for signing and mailing when I'd read and checked it all. I took the originals and sat down in my wicker chair to read before I got dressed. They were right up to Miss Chi's standard and there wasn't a thing to change. I put the papers on the table at my side and leaned back in the chair, grateful for the chance to be alone, without having to answer any questions or make any decisions. It was nice and quiet, with no sound coming from the closed door to the office. Miss Chi must have gone for the day. It looked like I was entitled to a short cat nap. I didn't even want to make the effort to get up and go over to the bed. Instead I just leaned back and closed my eyes.

I suppose I dozed right off because I didn't hear the door when it opened and the hands that touched my shoulders were so lightly placed that I never even moved. It wasn't until they began to stroke and knead the muscles at the base of my neck that I discovered I wasn't alone. I must have tried to start forward involuntarily but the hands showed a sudden strength, holding me securely as they went right on massaging. Above and behind my head I could hear a low sort of crooning and then, as she leaned over me and moved her thumbs to the base of my skull, I could see that my visitor was the efficient Miss Chi.

From my neck her hands moved to my scalp, bracing my head against her chest and rocking it gently from side to side so that my ears pressed against her breasts in turn. When she bent forward to stroke my temples and then my face I knew that she was wearing nothing under her ao dai as each breast swung free, stirred by her movements. Slowly her hands descended my face, seeking out each muscle in turn, until she reached my chest. She stretched her arms as far as she could to make a series of long stroking motions, the sharp nails digging ever so slightly into my ribs. Finally, after one long caress, she stepped away and walked slowly, with that lovely swinging gait, to the head of the bed. Reaching one hand down, letting the lamplight shine through her clothing to silhouette her figure, she lifted the remains of my drink and sipped it. She looked directly into my eyes over the top of the glass and then put it down carefully to begin unbuttoning the cuffs of her ao dai.

She was a beautiful thing and she knew it and she made an art

109

of the simple action of taking off the long, flowing gown. As it came away from her body she placed it carefully on the bed and then made a ballet of taking off the rest of her outfit. She unfastened the full-cut satin pants and, with a lithe twist of her slim hips, she let them fall to the floor around her feet. There was nothing more to take off but she just stood there, lapping up my admiration like a cat with a dish of cream. As I started to rise from the chair she turned away from me and swept up her clothes to cross the room to the wardrobe. The lamplight gleamed on her smooth, lightly oiled skin, highlighting every muscle and indentation and reflecting from the glossy black hair that swung free almost to her waist.

Quickly she hung up her things and then padded back to the other side of the bed. With one swift motion she tossed back the coverlet and then knelt beside the pillow, her hands at her sides, and waited for me.

Whatever Miss Chi did she was good at, but to tell in words what she did then would be like describing a Beethoven symphony note by note. As a matter of fact, what she did was more like great music than anything else. It was a superb orchestration of things simple enough by themselves but made magnificent in combination. Only one thing was vaguely disquieting. At no time did she close her eyes, and even at the most climactic moment they gleamed and sparkled at me. They were still open and shining a little later when she broke her silence for the first time since she'd entered the room.

"How long will it take you to get the ammunition ready to move?"

◆ 14 ◆

It figured. If Miss Chi had a message to deliver she had to make a production of it. She couldn't speak her piece and let it go at that, but had to wait until we were looking like Adam and Eve right after they found out that boys and girls are different. It just didn't seem to be the place to discuss serious business.

I didn't answer right away. Instead I got up and looked for some clothes. She watched me silently as I got dressed and put on my watch. I needed time to find out if she came from the right people with her question. There was still a chance that she belonged to some third party we didn't yet know about. It was likely that she'd had her little pointed fingers in the case of the late Fargot and a cinch that she was mixed up in the absence of Miss Binh.

"Okay," I said at last, "what is that supposed to mean?"

She frowned a little and propped her head on her hand. "It is a simple question but I will repeat it. How long will it take you to assemble the ammunition?"

"Look, Miss Chi, you are a very beautiful woman, an efficient secretary and a real winner in the hay but none of that gives you the right to ask funny questions. At least not until you give me some idea of just who you are."

She sat up and let her legs swing over the side of the bed.

"If you want it directly then I will tell you that I come from the people with whom you must deal to get what you came to Vietnam for."

She stood up suddenly and walked lightly into the office. She was back in a moment with a long envelope. Without a word she handed it over and then went back and lay on the bed, her eyes still fixed on me.

The envelope was blank and there was only one thing about it that was of the slightest interest. The lower-right-hand corner had been torn away, showing just a bit of the enclosed sheet. I didn't have to match it with what had been found the night before clutched in Fargot's dead hand.

I didn't open it right away. There was something I wanted to ask first.

"Why didn't you let Fargot deliver it?"

She lifted one shoulder just a bit. "He was no longer useful. A difficult man to do business with. He worried too much about his own interests instead of those of his clients."

"You mean like wanting to be sure he'd be paid?"

"Something like that. I do not know the details."

"What details do you know about Miss Binh?"

She smiled a little. "Miss Binh and her mother are both in excellent health. They are visiting with friends and should return quite soon."

There wasn't any strong reason to believe her. Right there by the door to the corridor had been the proof of that. Before I'd trust what she said I'd want to see Miss Binh alive and well. Right now it was time to see what was in the envelope.

There was nothing but a sheet of onionskin paper with what had to be a tracing from a detail map. There was a network of roads and rivers, a few towns and indications of contour lines. All the really important things were missing. There were no town names, no highway numbers and no coordinates of any kind. There wasn't even a scale and no way to tell how big an area was defined.

"What is this supposed to mean?"

"When the ammunition is loaded and ready to move you will be given the rest of the data, including the exact time and place of delivery."

I tossed it on the bed in front of her. "This thing is useless. It doesn't begin to tell me what I have to know. I don't even know what I'm supposed to load into."

"Is that important?"

"It is if you really want delivery. Do I travel by road or by water? What do I have to provide and load—trucks or barges?"

"Either will be satisfactory. The choice is yours."

"Okay, how long will the trip take each way?"

She gave that a little thought. "By truck it should be no more than three days."

"Both ways? The round trip?"

"Why is that important? It will take as long as it takes."

"Look, lady, it may be of no importance to you but I've got to think in terms of gasoline, oil, drivers and food for them and a few hundred other things. Now assuming I use trucks, how long will it take me to get where I'm going? How long will it be that I have to stay there? Will your side have people to unload or do I have to use my own men? Until I get some answers I can't move even if I want to.

"Maybe you won't believe this but I've been doing my homework. Ammo for the old Garand rifle weighs ninety-eight pounds per thousand-round case. The M-1 carbine is lightweight stuff, just thirty-five pounds a case, and the M-16 loads are more than twice that heavy, seventy-five pounds. A mixed batch evenly divided is going to weigh in at right around seventy thousand pounds. That's thirty-five tons, just to make it simple, or right around a dozen trucks to haul it over good roads. If the going is rough we'll have to cut each load and that means even more trucks, more drivers, more food and more fuel.

"That takes us to the next point. I can get that kind of load on a couple of river barges and use only a few men to work them to your delivery point. Now how long will the trip take by water?"

I didn't really give a damn how long it would be that way. I had no more idea of using barges than I did snowmobiles. With trucks I'd be able to have some manpower and if I got into trouble that might be a big plus. If she picked barges I was going to have to figure my way out of using them. It had to be trucks.

Why did I bother with the problem? For just one reason. I had to know just how Miss Chi would handle it. If she had to wait until she could communicate with her top man, it might tell us a little. First, whether she had good communication, possibly even how she did it, and it might give us an idea about how much water she herself drew.

If she didn't have good communications, then she had to make the day-to-day decisions on her own and this was my way of testing how far she could go without checking first with headquarters.

"If you use trucks you will need many men but barges will not be so quick?"

I just nodded, watching her closely as the gears went around in her head. She was going to make the decision herself but she'd have to be able to defend it. She didn't like the idea much but that was her problem. Finally she made up her mind.

"You will do best to travel by truck. It will take about three days to reach your destination. There will be people to unload the cargo, enough so that it will be done in a few hours. Not all of the roads are of the best, but trucks in good condition will have no trouble if they are not overloaded."

"Okay. We do it by truck." Then, as though I wanted to record her instructions in detail, I added, "I'll get a pad and pencil and write all this down."

I didn't wait for her to answer but just walked quickly into the office to my desk. I opened the drawer, got what I wanted and then switched on the tape recorder, laying the microphone beside a stack of papers. I turned the gain up and went back to the bedroom.

"Now, Miss Chi, I've got a few conditions. First of all, we aren't going to roll a wheel until I see Miss Binh and her mother. No Miss Binh, no go. Okay?"

"If you wish. Miss Binh will be returned when you have loaded the trucks and everything has been checked."

"Okay. Next, there's my insurance." She raised her eyebrows. "I want a hostage."

"What do you need with a hostage, Mr. Keefe?"

"It's simple. If anything happens that's not in the agreement, if I have any reason to suspect I'm going to be had, the hostage is in deep trouble."

"But who could we possibly turn over to you for such a purpose?"

"That's easy. You."

When she finally left it was pretty late but we'd settled the details. D-day was going to be the next Monday. She'd come to work every day in case of any change that we'd have to make. I'd tell her where to meet us to check the cargo and give us the delivery point and instructions for getting there. As soon as I knew Miss Binh was okay we'd pull out. Miss Chi would ride with me in the convoy.

At the delivery point I had to see Bostwick and Bailey in the flesh before I let a single case be unloaded. The distance didn't matter but they had to be in the clear where I could see them. I was firm on that. As soon as everything had come out of the trucks I'd be ready for the handover. It had to be out in the open. They'd bring Bostwick and Bailey to me, I'd give them back Miss Chi and that would be that. They'd have their million rounds, I'd have my men. I didn't care who got Miss Chi. That was his problem.

"You will need men, Mr. Keefe. Where will you get them?"

"I don't know yet but I'll think of a way. That's my concern, not yours."

"Will these be men with arms?"

"I haven't thought about it. Maybe; maybe not."

"It would not be wise for them to be seen at the rendezvous with weapons."

"Why not?"

"It might be misunderstood. Something regrettable might occur."

"I don't know what unless you plan to attack us and hijack the shipment."

She raised her chin. "We are not savages. We will keep our part of the bargain."

I didn't ask her about how they'd kept their deal with Fargot.

"Look at it this way, Miss Chi. If you can use a million rounds, then you must have a pretty big organization. I'll have a couple of dozen men, at most. Do you plan for anything that we might misunderstand?"

"Of course not."

"Well, it's a cinch we're not going to attack you so you've got nothing to worry about from us. We've got to travel a long way past some people who might not feel so peaceable. Maybe we're going to need some protection but that's got nothing to do with you. When we meet your people let them keep the peace and we will, too."

"It is agreed, then. Are you now satisfied with the arrangements?"

"Let's just say that so far I'm content."

"In that case come back to bed."

It took the best part of an hour to get in touch with Hieu, once she'd left. Late as it was, he said he'd come straight to the hotel and in a few minutes he was there. I told him the whole story, just as it had happened, not leaving anything out, and then we got down to cases. The first thing he wanted was a look at the map.

"You say she told you that the rendezvous could be reached either by truck or by barge?"

"That's it. She said that either way would be all right. She didn't seem to care much until I told her that by barge it would take a lot longer. When I said, though, that I'd need a lot more men for a truck convoy she had to think that over. Finally she decided that the barge idea was no good. I guess time is a factor for them."

"Good. That must mean that somewhere on this map is a place that can be reached by road or by water deep enough for a loaded barge to navigate." He studied the tracing closely, holding the flimsy paper to the light. "There aren't too many places on this map that fit that description. We'll give it some study and try to narrow it down."

"What good will that do? Until we know the part of the country that this shows it's not much use to us."

"No, it might be of value. Remember, as I told you, there are just so many areas where an independent group.might be able to

116

operate without interference from either the Vietcong or the government. We have to match this with the places that fit such a description."

"Maybe, but isn't it possible they've picked a spot outside their own real estate? All they need is a spot where they won't be bothered for a few hours."

He shook his head. "No, I'm sure it will be at a point close to their own base. They are going to need a lot of transport to move thirty-five tons to safety." He'd been doing his homework, too. "Also she said they would provide people to unload the trucks. To do that they will have to move them to the meeting place and back. They will want to get finished as quickly as possible, unload, reload and move in the minimum time." He stopped to think for a moment before he went on. "If the problem were mine I would plan to use at least fifty to move a thousand cases. Fewer would take too long while more might begin to get in each other's way. To take even that many from their base means running the risk of attracting attention and possibly even having to fight. They won't risk losing what they've gone to so much trouble to obtain."

He was probably right in the way he'd worked it out but I couldn't see why we were wasting time on speculation. There were too many other things I wanted to get on with first.

"What are your ideas about getting a couple of dozen reliable men?"

He put down the map tracing to give that some thought.

"What are the chances of getting troops?"

He didn't have to think about that. His answer was firm and final. "That is impossible. My superiors will look the other way as much as they can but they would never permit the use of soldiers. There can be no official involvement of any kind. Even my presence with you is dangerous."

That seemed to be that. It looked as if I was going to have to recruit my own army and take my chances with them. Hieu was still thinking, though.

"It is possible that we might find men who have once been soldiers."

That didn't sound like much until he explained.

"I have thought about the matter and perhaps you would like

to hear my idea. My last assignment was to command a company of our Rangers. They are thought by many to be our best troops and to be able to serve with them is an honor. Most of them remain as long as they are fit for active duty but there are those who have left for reasons of age or some wound or illness. I do not think it would be too hard to find twenty or so who are physically fit for work such as this and who would be glad to earn the good wages and bonus you are going to pay them."

That was the first I'd heard about a bonus but if they were good they'd be more than worth it. Having trained men who knew how to drive, handle weapons, obey orders and, best of all, keep their mouths shut could mean a lot. I told Hieu to go ahead and find as many as he could up to twenty-five or thirty.

"I'd like to have enough to put two men in each truck carrying cargo and a couple of good mechanics riding with their tools in a spare. That way if we have a breakdown we can switch the load and keep moving. Now can we get them weapons?"

"Not from any official source," he said, "but if each man chooses to bring one . . ."

That was the thing about Hieu I had to admire. Every time he had to shoot you down he'd come up with something just as good or better.

"Then that leaves the big question. How do I pick up the ammunition?"

"That has been arranged most carefully. It will be taken from the depot and loaded quite openly on a steel barge provided by a contractor. He will tow it to a place I have selected and moor it there. The place is isolated and there will be few people to observe anything unusual. Naturally we will wait for darkness to begin work. I think you will agree that we will not be able to move much more than two hundred cases per hour with the men we expect to have—say five hours from start to finish. Even so, if we begin right after dark on Sunday we will have ample time and also give the men some rest before they have to drive on Monday morning."

It sounded good. There would be nothing out of the way about loading the stuff at the dump. Moving munitions by barge is the normal way of transporting a heavy and potentially dangerous

118

cargo. The bargemen would bring it to the loading point, tie up and go home for the night. Hieu would make sure that they wouldn't noise it around about how their cargo had vanished during the night. They'd just go about their business and not trouble themselves about where it had gone. Best of all, there was no one who could actually say that they'd seen it delivered into my tender care. It wasn't perfect but then, what is?

Hieu stayed on for a while. There were a whole lot of small points that had to be discussed and agreed on and he had a lot of good ideas. One of the things was the problem of feeding that many men the two daily meals they'd need.

"It's just too risky and too time-wasting to try to stop in towns along the way for food. We'd take a chance on being observed and there's no way of knowing for sure that we'd even find such places. No, it's best to be self-sufficient. We'll need rice and tea and canned food for the men to cook themselves. It is the way they are used to doing it. For ourselves we can make what arrangements we like."

That was the first I'd heard about his coming along. I didn't see why.

"I am sure you must realize that there are questions to be answered about who these people are and where they operate from."

"And you expect to find the answers?"

"Mr. Keefe, I have to find the answers. Surely you don't think that our government is going to permit these guerrillas or whatever they are to remain at large with one million rounds of ammunition. With assets like that they will be in a position to resist for a long time, to hold what they have and to seize much more. As you well know, we are doing everything we can to cooperate with Operation Home Run but once it is concluded we have our own interests to consider."

There wasn't any doubt that he was right. If Home Run paid off I'd gather up Bostwick and Bailey and go home, leaving Hieu and company with a very damp baby. The faster they moved to neutralize the men I was dealing with, the easier it would be. The ransom operation would be Hieu's chance to see just who it was he'd have to deal with right where they lived. They'd have to come out in the open long enough to take the ransom and hand over the two men. It might be the last chance to get a good look.

They'd come up to take the bait and Hieu would be there to mark the spot. It was right at that point I began to realize the position I'd worked myself into. It was like a tiger hunt in a way. When you want to catch one you stake out a goat in the jungle and then go climb a nearby tree. You, the hunter, wait for the tiger to smell the goat and work up an appetite for him. When he finally comes for dinner, one of two things is going to happen. If the hunter shoots and hits the tiger it dies. If he shoots and misses, the tiger climbs the tree and the hunter dies.

The only sure loser is the goat.

⊰ 15 ⊱

It was still dark outside when the alarm clock beside my bed went off. I got dressed quickly, went downstairs and over to Pat and John's apartment. While they were busy getting breakfast I gave them a slightly expurgated version of what had happened the night before. Even without the intimate details they were interested and I gave them everything they really needed to know. While we were eating The Tiger arrived, and when I told him about it he brightened up at the thought of finally starting to move. I laid out my plan for the day.

"I'll take care of getting things set up for the trip and you two keep on with Captain Hieu and the filming. You can work without sound so that I can take The Tiger with me."

Pat said, "What do you want us to take on Monday for Home Run?"

"Sorry, Pat. You guys stay here and keep right on working."

Potter blurted out, "Wait a minute, Captain—I mean Mike. This is still a team, isn't it? If you go then we go."

"No way, John. It's not that I don't want you but there's nothing you can do. If the thing goes sour it'll be bad enough for me to be involved. If all three of us get hooked it'll make people ask the wrong questions. I know how you feel and I appreciate it. Maybe I'd even feel a lot safer if I had the two of you backing me up but it isn't worth taking the risk just to make me feel good. The best thing is for you to keep right on filming. That way we'll be done that much sooner and finally get out of here."

The Tiger looked up. "I go. That's right, Mike?"

121

"Do you want to?"

He nodded his head vigorously. "You damn betcha. Pat and Big John stay here so The Tiger comes to watch your ass."

"Okay. Your job will be to take charge of the drivers. Give them their orders, take charge of the rations, make sure the trucks are fueled and serviced."

He laughed out loud. "Okay, Mike. You be like company commander. Do all big thinking. I be like damn first sergeant. Do all damn yelling."

He appeared to like the whole idea and was still chuckling over it when I left and went back to the office.

Miss Chi was at her desk and if there was any change in her attitude after what had happened the previous evening I saw no sign of it. She had been through the bills and made out the checks and there was a batch of government forms that had to be filed with different departments. There was enough to keep me busy until the crew came up to get their equipment for the day's work. When they went down to the cars I went along, and after they'd driven away The Tiger and I caught a cab for Tan Son Nhut. I parked my self-appointed first sergeant in the snack bar and went to get the secure phone.

I got through to Tiny on the first try, and gave her the cleaned-up version of the events of the night before, leaving out the parts she might not appreciate. I left in all the essentials, though, and when I'd finished she had a few thoughts to contribute.

"It looks to me as though the critical moment will be at the actual exchange. Once they get what they want there's no way to be sure they won't change their terms and tell you to go back for another contribution."

"I've had that on my mind, too."

"What can you do to give yourself a little more edge?"

"I don't know. I'll have the hostage but we're playing on their home field."

She said, "Do you think they want her enough to make them play by the rules?"

"I hope so. They went ahead and wasted the first go-between but then I never did think he was any part of their organization. The woman is another proposition. She's right up at their top

122

level, judging by the way she makes important decisions."

"She sounds like quite a piece of work, your Miss Chi."

"You better believe. She doesn't like playing hostage. That was the thing I dug in my heels about. That and the point that I actually have to see the two men before I let a single case come out of a truck."

"Do you think you'll know the right men when you see them?"

"Look, Tiny, I don't think there are too many pairs like that knocking around the countryside. If I see a big white man and a big black man and they look like the ones in that snapshot, I'm going to assume I've got the right ones, give the word and let them off-load the thousand cases. That's when they're supposed to bring our men forward and I give them the lady. It's not foolproof but it's the best I can do."

"I still wish we could give you a little more protection. How about a high-altitude aircraft keeping an eye on you?"

"Lay off, Tiny. Just back off and let me alone. If you start making fancy passes it could wreck the whole thing and me with it. By the way, what about the stuff we got?"

"Well, you know the kind of report you get from lab people. The ID cards are authentic but you knew that yourself. They did some analysis on the photo and they came up with something odd. They claim that it may be a picture of a picture."

"You mean somebody took a picture, made a print and then rephotographed it?"

"Anyway, that's how they explain why it's so grainy and has so much contrast."

"How about the families? What do they say about the snapshot?"

"The black man is Bailey, all right. His wife made a positive identification. I won't go into what else she said but no matter what kind of husband he is, he's hers."

"And Anne Bostwick? What did she say?"

"Well, first she said right off that the picture was of her husband and the senator said so, too. Then she wanted another look. After a while she said she couldn't really tell, what with the weight he'd lost and the long hair and bad light. Her father thinks she's just afraid of getting herself built up for a letdown. He said her doubts are psychological. After living so long with the idea that Bostwick might be dead she's just scared to get excited and then face another disappointment like the one she had when he didn't come home with the other POWs who were exchanged."

"What about the handwriting?"

"Well, the first thing asked was whether Bostwick had ever had malaria. The piece we submitted was a lot shakier than the examples they'd been given. In the end they gave us a mathematical appraisal but they wouldn't say it was a positive match."

"What's your evaluation?"

"I don't know. Everything points to their having the right men. There are some things that can't be explained yet, like why they copied the snapshot."

"What does the blowup show? Maybe they wanted to keep the original."

"We didn't get much. There are signs of what might be retouching but could just be nothing more than finger marks or smudging. There's this much to be sure of: They've got two Americans for sale and we're going to buy them."

"Do you want me to stall and try to get more evidence?"

"No. You've gone this far and even if we had more time or evidence I don't know that it would change anything. I suppose I can't help looking at a thing for some kind of sign that it's really something else. After all, that's the way they train us."

I told her of the rest of the arrangements I'd made and got the usual series of grunts that showed she approved. We talked about getting the men evacuated as quickly and quietly as we could once we had them in hand and then I mentioned that Hieu would be coming with me.

"What the hell is he going to do?"

When I told her what I thought she allowed as how I was right. "Not only that," she said. "If he's as sharp as you say he is you'll be glad you've got him."

"Probably, but either way I can't object after the way they've cooperated. The least we can do is give them the chance to get some intelligence."

"I suppose so. If they're going to move against those people they'd better get busy. With all that ammunition it could be a pretty good scrap."

Thank God that wasn't any part of my problem. I rang off, gathered up The Tiger and caught a cab back to town. The first man I wanted to see was Toguri. I had the length of the cab ride to decide how to handle him. Trying to pin him down was like trying to catch an eel barehanded in a barrel of grease. I didn't dare tell him too much and I'd have to make sure it was worth his while to keep his mouth shut. That meant showing him enough bait to lure him out of the barrel to where I could get a better hold on him.

To catch Toguri, the best bait is money.

"Five hundred thousand P, Mike?"

"You've got it. Half in advance and half when the party is over. A week or less."

"If everything legal why you pay me so much money?"

"I'll say it again. Your part is one-hundred-percent okay. All you've got to do to get the second payment is keep your mouth shut. If I get even a hint that you've forgotten to make like a clam you can whistle for it. Understood?"

"Okay." He looked like a man who believed. "Now tell me what I have to get."

"I need fourteen trucks for a week. Fourteen good—repeat: very good—trucks in perfect running condition. Van bodies with doors that lock. Heavy enough to carry a full load up to five tons. No clunkers, Toguri. If a truck gets sick and dies on my trip it's going to get left by the road. No markings and no more than a couple from any one source. Mix them up, but no diesels. Gas engines only.

"One of the fourteen is to be a smaller panel job, American if you can, not a compact.

"Now this is the thing to remember. The owners deal only with you. You make the bargain and you pay off."

He showed his crooked grin. "If drivers work for you they see you, yes?"

"They see me, no. I don't need drivers. They're not in the deal at all."

He looked at me in dismay. "Nobody rent truck without driver. Is not the way."

"I couldn't care less about the way. This deal is being set my way. All I'm in need of are trucks. Drivers are my problem."

He looked doubtful. "I don't think they do it, Mike. How these men know they get trucks back? How they know what you do with so many trucks? They think if you do bad thing maybe police catch you and take truck away. Maybe you just take trucks and drive away and they don't see you again and truck is gone. You take truck away from man, you break his rice bowl."

"Now you know why you're getting five hundred thousand. You're going to persuade them."

He shook that idea in his head and then, after holding it up and looking at it a couple of different ways, he got back to me.

"How much you pay for each truck, Mike?"

That meant he could do it. From there it was just plain old-fashioned haggling. He started high—I came back low. He came down a little—I came up a bit. At last we got to the point where the owners would still have enough to be content after Toguri had squeezed out his kickback.

"Now here's how we get the trucks delivered. Starting at noon exactly on Sunday I want a truck to arrive every fifteen minutes, the panel job first. Each truck is to have a full tank and crankcase. The driver leaves the keys and papers in the vehicle when he parks it around the corner just inside the alley. He comes in here and gets his money. Then he waits five minutes and leaves. Nobody stands around to see what happens to the trucks. I'll have my own people in the neighborhood just to make sure. One week later we reverse it. They come here for the second payment every fifteen minutes. They wait five and when they come out they'll find their truck where they left it. Again, nobody stands around to sneak any looks.

"That goes for you, too, Toguri. You stay right here and sell the regular drivers some cold drinks when you're not counting a quarter million P in five hundreds. If you feel you've got to do any sightseeing, my advice is to fight the urge."

126

I got up from my stool. "From now on you deal with The Tiger about everything. Remember, I need fourteen trucks. If you can't get the full number, then forget it. No less will do and they all better be number one. Okay?"

I left him deep in thought and walked the couple of blocks to the Imperial Custom Tailors. By luck the proprietor was in and ready to talk business. Mr. Pashti is a man with a mission, his principal aim in life being to provide room in his pockets for any stray pound, peso or piaster that comes within shouting distance. Once you grasp this idea there is no problem in dealing with Mr. Pashti. He is not a man to whom things need be explained twice.

"A thousand-gallon tank truck filled with high-test gasoline for one week and without driver." He reached for a small electronic calculator and gave a short virtuoso performance.

"Now let me see. One-week rental, hm, hm. One thousand gallons gasoline at hm, hm, less bulk discount. Insurance, wear and tear, less credit for driver."

He finished with a flourish and announced the total.

"Mr. Pashti, we are discussing the rental of a truck and not the national debt of the Republic of Vietnam."

He gave me a hurt look and leaped to the fray. Ten minutes later, slightly ruffled but invigorated by the struggle, he shook hands on a drastically reduced figure. We were both aware that the figure was still susceptible to further reduction but the increased profit margin was understood to be payment for utter silence. Again, The Tiger would handle the details from that point on.

We needed a cab for the next move. The driver gave me an odd look when I told him the destination but a sharp bark from The Tiger got him moving. We drove west, right through the city, to Cholon and the establishment of Mr. Tang in a small street behind the market.

I'd done business before with Mr. Tang but mostly as a seller. His shop was an outlet for all vendors and a source for all buyers, dealing, in large part, in the leftovers of the various occupiers of his country back to the Ming dynasty. What he didn't have on hand, which wasn't much, he could get. With plenty of money and a long shopping list, I settled down to enjoy myself.

127

The stack of goods I selected grew quickly: cased C rations, water purification tablets, a sleeping bag and nylon liners with poncho, first-aid kit, machetes and short bayonets, mosquito netting, jungle boots and fatigues. I debated and then rejected a real bargain in tents but was persuaded to invest in some Lerp rations. Those are the add-water-and-wait-five-minutes foods designed for use on Long Range Patrols and the things really work. If you can get hot water for the foods to be eaten warm you can make a damn good meal with little else. When Mr. Tang had finished making his abacus smoke, I paid the bill and arranged for everything to be picked up the following Sunday. One item I took with me.

Mr. Tang had made a really attractive deal on it, a pair of unused artillery observer binoculars, still in the original American factory carton and at a price far below the one paid by the taxpayers. A real buy.

It was almost noon and since spending money always gives me an appetite the logical thing was to stay right in Cholon and avail ourselves of the Tour d'Or, a few blocks away. The Tiger was tickled to death and while we ate too much and the check made him blench to a light ecru, it was coming to us. With a week ahead of C and Lerp rations, I didn't stint. It wasn't until we were in the cab on the way back to the office that I started to wonder whether perhaps we hadn't overdone it.

The others were still out working and I collapsed behind my desk for a few minutes and tried to concentrate on digesting. The Tiger had stumped off on an errand of his own and Miss Chi, looking even tinier than usual, was occupied with some small, mysterious task involving her fingernails, her eyes cast down demurely. Suddenly I remembered that the night before I'd switched on the tape recorder and then forgotten all about it. I slid open the drawer and there it was. The switch was off and the recorded reel had been carefully rewound to the supply side. I didn't have to play it back to know that it had been erased, my discussion with Miss Chi and the subsequent gymkhana to boot. I wondered if Miss Chi had replayed it before she destroyed its value to history. I looked up at her and saw she had been watching, a little smile barely curving her full lips.

"Do not be disturbed, Mr. Keefe. You are not the first man to have his secretary accidentally erase a tape."

Smart. And she read the papers, too.

I'd gone out again before she was due to depart for the day and I half expected her to be waiting for another passage-at-arms but I suppose she needed rest as much as I did. She had left something, though. It was lying on my pillow, a letter that had come in that morning from the syndicate main office. At some time since then the following had been written at the bottom of the sheet in a careful hand I recognized at once.

Dear Mr. Keefe:

I have been told to write and tell you that my mother and I are being treated well and will be released in a few days. My mother asks if you will be so kind as to call Dr. Hieu and ask to postpone her treatment.

Very truly yours,
Miss Binh, secretary

All it signified was that Miss Binh and mother had been okay that morning but it also meant a better chance Miss Chi was keeping the deal. I'd tell the "doctor" when I saw him in the morning.

I don't know how the hell I did it but that night I managed, somehow, to put away another giant meal. Potter had pulled some strings and liberated three really outstanding sirloins and when I showed up at their place after a shower and a nap he was slicing potatoes and tossing salad and firing the charcoal grill. They had a couple of cases of cold beer and Pat and I sat around the kitchen table and talked while John worked. As usual we didn't talk much about the assignment we were on but, instead, about past jobs. Potter still kept in touch with the old bunch we'd worked with on the first tour in Vietnam and Pat Brice corresponded with a good many of the DPOE old-timers. With just the three of us there, John loosened up and chattered along as he worked, still keeping a good grip on his toothpick. He'd turned up a little shop over beyond Hai Ba Trung that carried a brand made in mainland China that he favored.

"Those things they make in the States are just some kind of cheap pine. Taste like turpentine. These Chinese jobs have a real nice flavor."

The steaks must have weighed in at about two pounds apiece and I ate all I could hold without actually foundering and there was still some left. When I said I couldn't hold another ounce John cleared everything away and set out two quarts of ice cream. Pat and I took just enough to be polite but John, with one quart container in front of him, went at it with a soup spoon, each spoonful piled high and the next following right along behind. At that rate it didn't take long for him to hit bottom and Pat shoved over the almost untouched quart in front of us. I don't know how John did it but when the last bit had been scraped up he stood and went to work on the dishes, stacking everything for their maid to take care of in the morning. When he'd finished that and taken a fresh toothpick, we moved into the living room. Pat began a letter to his wife and I found my head beginning to nod. I thanked them and walked back through the quiet street to the hotel.

Most of the preparation I'd had to do was finished. Now it was up to Toguri, Mr. Pashti, Mr. Tang and, of course, The Tiger.

With a firm date set for the kickoff on Home Run, I knew just how much time I had to finish the documentary. If I could get the part I was really needed for done by Saturday, then Pat and John should be able to wrap up the rest, or most of it, while I was away. Hieu had promised to send in another contact man from the bench to cover for him and keep things moving while he traveled with me.

Somehow I managed to do it. I hadn't tried anything tricky, just straightforward camera technique without any *cinéma vérité* or the other gimmicks you use to disguise a weak script. We had more than enough interesting footage to hold an audience's attention without having to dazzle them with footwork.

Miss Chi and I stayed on a strictly business basis. I won't say that a little persuasion on her part might not have changed my mind about some extracurricular but intramural sports, but I didn't press the idea. We kept our distance.

I worked like hell those last few days and it was already getting on for dark when I printed the last shot on Saturday evening.

I was ready to get on with Home Run.

⊰ 16 ⊱

The first look I got at Hieu's Ranger veterans wasn't exactly reassuring. Some of them appeared to be nudging sixty and they were the ones in best shape. Of the younger men there wasn't one who didn't display the evidence of having been involved in something particularly violent. Several had lost a hand or a forearm and been equipped with hooks of one kind or another, a few had lost an eye and just about all would have supplied material for a course in plastic surgery. This was the battered contingent we were going to have to rely on.

It was when I looked at them more carefully that I felt my confidence coming back. They didn't know any more about me than I did of them and none knew a thing about the operation except that it could turn pretty hairy. They were gambling on me and whatever ability I might have to lead them. That array of steady eyes went a long way in reassuring me. That and the faith I had in Hieu. If he thought the men were up to the job I didn't have any reason to doubt it.

They had arrived in twos and threes at the meeting place, a walled-in old motor pool The Tiger had rented. It was just to the northeast of the city on the highway to the new docks at Newport and on to Bien Hoa. They checked in and then squatted in the shade of the galvanized sheet-metal wall that circled the place, smoking and talking quietly, greeting each new arrival as their number grew.

By nine everyone was checked in. The Tiger counted noses and announced that I could begin. When I saw how he was reacting to the men my last doubts evaporated. He was the man in charge but he wasn't using his authority as an excuse to throw his weight around. The Tiger had been in the army long enough to know a good man when he saw him even without a uniform and decorations. He'd had a couple of days in which to meet them all and size them up. By the second day he was starting to refer to them as "my men," and he said it with some real pride.

I'd made a stop the day before at the PX and picked up as many cartons of cigarettes as they'd let me buy. I started a couple going around, most of the men helping themselves to a pack and nodding their thanks as they passed the cartons along. The Tiger and I squatted down with them and those on the edges moved in so they could hear without my having to shout. I knew that all of them understood at least a little English but when I started to talk I had The Tiger make a kind of running translation. I wanted to be sure that everyone had got the word.

I didn't try to play down the fact that the operation was no kind of joy ride—they already knew that from the pay they were getting—but I didn't overdo it either. Now I told them that they'd get the full amount plus a bonus whether we came through okay or not. I didn't want anyone to be worrying about his money and taking chances just to protect it. I finished up by telling them just as much about Home Run as I figured they needed to know.

When I turned the briefing over to The Tiger he gave them the word on picking up the trucks at Toguri's. They could stop at their homes to collect their weapons and personal stuff but everyone was to be back by four-thirty, ready to go. The Tiger had organized the group into squads, using the men's former ranks to establish a chain of command for best efficiency. When he'd finished and answered a few questions we broke up, the men to get downtown on their own while The Tiger and I went back to the office.

I'd been concentrating so hard on getting every last detail out of the way in time to start the operation that now I didn't have a thing to keep my mind occupied. As usual, I started to worry and when noon came and The Tiger left to get the panel truck and send it to Mr. Tang's, I had to fight the urge to go along and see things for myself. Pat and John had given up their Sunday to getting some more coverage and Miss Chi was off so I had the place to myself. She'd be picked up next morning, given a look at the shipment and then she'd hand over Miss Binh before telling us our destination.

I didn't want to leave the phone untended so I called downstairs for a sandwich. When it came I could eat only a little of it. I opened a can of beer and then let it sit and go flat, made a stab at reading *Playboy*, did everything I could think of to pass the time, and I was about ready to crawl out of my skin when first Pat and John and then Hieu got there. Hieu seemed to be as calm and cool as usual but I was sure he was as geared up as I was. John made one more try to get me to take him along until finally Hieu and I said good-bye and went down to wait for The Tiger.

The panel truck he brought looked okay, with plenty of space for the three of us who would ride in it plus some cargo. Hieu and I stowed our personal things and we took off for the meeting place. When the gate was swung open for us I found everything right on schedule and no sign of any of the catastrophes I'd dreamed up. The last truck pulled in right behind us and the driver parked it and waited for us to give it a quick inspection.

Toguri had done a good job. Some of the trucks were anything but new but they were all in good running order and ready to roll. The pickup had gone smoothly and right on schedule. The Tiger had had a few men in the vicinity and they reported that no one appeared to be paying the least bit of attention. He'd sent two of the crew for the tank truck and when it arrived our convoy would be complete.

We were all set to leave at five sharp. The gate opened and the trucks rolled out, following Hieu in the lead vehicle into the evening traffic. It was almost an hour later and getting dark when we turned off a street at the edge of the city into a narrow lane that led through the fields to a canal landing. The lane was too narrow for two trucks to pass but at the edge of the water there was a parking area big enough to hold the vehicles and still leave space to make the turn. When I dismounted I realized I'd been there before.

It had been a busy place then, a regular ammo point where the ARVN had brought the barges loaded from the ammunition ships moored downriver from the city. They'd had a couple of cranes working and a big detachment to handle cargo, but the war had moved to other areas and this place had been abandoned. It still had the same advantages, though: deep water and no inhabitants around to get hurt if the VC sent in a sapper team or got lucky with a rocket. The absence of neighbors served our purposes, too.

The loaded barge was right where it was supposed to be, tied to the shore and hardly moving in the sluggish current in the canal. In the last bit of daylight we got the hatches off and the first truck backed into position. The Tiger had one squad set up bucket-brigade fashion, passing cases out of the hold and across the deck. The second squad, on shore, relayed them to the tailgate, where they were taken and stacked in neat rows. A second truck was standing by to receive its load so there was no break in the work when the first was filled and moved away. I timed the first truckload and while it ran a lot longer than we'd allowed, the pace was sure to pick up as the men got the hang of the work. When the second truck was filled and the doors closed The Tiger called a halt to give the men a short break. Most of them moved away from the barge and lit up but they kept their cigarettes cupped in their hands as old soldiers do at night in the field. Apart from a couple of lanterns in the hold there wasn't a light anywhere and, except for the sound of a starting engine now and then, a person might have passed within a hundred yards and never known anything was happening at the old landing.

That was the pattern we followed. After every second truck was loaded The Tiger gave them a break, a better way than once an hour since the faster they loaded, the sooner they got to rest. Hieu and I tried to make ourselves useful, stepping into the line when somebody had to fall out for a minute. Gradually the barge rose in the water and we had to adjust the operation, passing the cases right from deck level to the truck tailgates. I'd been keeping a rough tally and when the last of the heavy M-1 rifle ammunition came out of the hold I had The Tiger pass the word that the cases would be lighter now. That seemed to be the encouragement the troops needed and the pace began to pick up. When finally the lightweight M-1 carbine loads started coming out it was almost possible to toss the cases, they felt so light. We finished up in a burst of speed, replaced the hatches and came ashore.

Hieu went off into the darkness and in a minute or so I heard the sound of a Honda cycle starting up near the main road. He still had work to do before we could get our convoy past the government checkpoint and out on the open road.

Tired as I was, I was hungry as well and so were the others. Most of them had brought a packet of cooked food from home and I broke out a couple of cases of beer I had in the panel truck. It was still cool enough to taste good with the C ration I opened for myself. The men, pretty well beat, didn't waste any time and as soon as they'd eaten, slung hammocks to the truck undercarriages and climbed in. I found a truck cab that no one was using and climbed up, stretching myself out as best I could. I twisted and turned but the seat cushion wasn't sitting just right and rocked a little each time I moved. Finally I got out of the cab and tried to get the thing set properly in its frame but it wouldn't fit the way it was supposed to. At last I lifted up the whole cushion and felt around in the dark trying to find the trouble. It wasn't hard to locate. Under the seat were two M-16s and several bandoleers of ammo. I laid the cushion on the ground beside the cab and finally dozed off on it, sleeping the last few hours until daylight.

It was about seven in the morning when I got back to the motor pool. The Tiger had ridden the first truck back and then taken the panel job to pick up Miss Chi at the Continental Palace. The rest of the trucks had left the landing at intervals of a couple of minutes and then formed into line at the motor pool, ready to start as soon as we found out where we were going.

On the road the panel truck would lead, with Hieu and our guest and myself. The cargo trucks would follow, then the tanker, and the spare truck, the mechanics and The Tiger inside, would bring up the rear. In built-up areas, Saigon and any towns we'd have to go through, we'd try to stay pretty well closed up but on the open road we'd increase the distances between vehicles and try to look as if we weren't traveling together. If anyone was having trouble he'd signal with horn and lights and the others would pass the word forward to the lead vehicle. Every so often we'd look for a place to take a short break, gassing up and giving the men a chance to stretch. There would be no lunch but that was normal for the Vietnamese, who are smart enough not to eat a midday meal in a climate like theirs.

I didn't have to wait long for Miss Chi. Before I had a chance to worry about her showing up the gate was opened and in drove The Tiger in the panel truck, the lady at his side.

She climbed out and looked around, clearly impressed with what she saw. I was impressed by the way she was gotten up, and even the other men were interested, though girl-watching has never been much of a national sport in their country.

I suppose she was dressed according to her ideas of the right wardrobe for a truck safari across Vietnam, and to tell you the truth, she looked pretty damn cute. She had on a pair of khaki slacks that must have taken a lot of effort to get on, and a matching shirt. Around her neck she had knotted a bit of a scarf, with a matching one on her head. Her shirt sleeves were carefully rolled up above the elbows and the neck was unbuttoned about as far down as the law would allow. What spoiled the overall effect was the pair of black high-heeled pumps she wore. She tried to walk forward across the rutted ground but those heels were never meant for that kind of terrain. Somehow she made it to the tailgate of the first truck in line and I signaled to the driver to unlock the doors and open up for her. Tiny as she was, even in those high heels, she could barely see inside but she went through the motions of peering around and making a rough count of what she saw.

She followed the same procedure with the next couple of trucks, teetering from one to another until she got to the fourth. This time she said something to the driver and after he'd opened the doors he lifted her up and carefully set her inside. He clambered up after her and she picked a case at random and had him open it. She knelt down and pulled out enough of the contents to verify that it was full. I don't know how much she understood about the subject but you don't need a lot of training to tell real cartridges from blank or dummy. When she was lifted down she seemed satisfied that what we had aboard was the McCoy.

137

Damned if she didn't check every last truck, counting the contents and climbing into a couple of others to verify that the full quantity was really up to amount and specification. She even took a look at the spare truck, eying the mechanics' tool kits, the jerry cans of potable water and the fifty kilos of rice in a big straw sack. Finally she came teetering over to where I stood waiting.

"Everything looks quite satisfactory, Mr. Keefe. Now if you will be so good as to come out to the road you will see that I have kept my part of the agreement."

I followed her to the gate and out to the roadside, where she waved to a battered taxi parked on the shoulder. It started up and drove to where we stood.

The man at the wheel kept his face turned away. Seated in the back was a somewhat ruffled Miss Binh and an older woman I took to be her mother.

"Are you all right, Miss Binh?"

You could see that she had been under a strain but her mother seemed to be as sprightly as a canary. "Thank you, Mr. Keefe. We are quite well," Miss Binh said.

"Well, I think you'd better go straight home. When you feel up to it you can resume your work at the office. I'll be away for a few days but Pat Brice will be in charge while I'm gone."

She just nodded, her lips pursed.

"I'm really sorry this had to happen, Miss Binh. I've reported this and I think you'll be thanked in some more tangible fashion."

She didn't have any answer for that so I just passed a few bills to the driver and told her to give the man her address. He drove off and I looked for Miss Chi. She had gone back into the motor pool when Miss Binh had been delivered and when I got inside I saw her on her knees beside the battered suitcase she had brought. She was digging around inside and in a moment I saw what she'd been after: a pair of rubber sandals, the kind half her nation wears. She wrapped up her high-heeled shoes and stowed them away. When she stood up in the sandals she was a couple of inches shorter but obviously a lot happier. All we needed now was Hieu.

When he got there, a few minutes later, he was in civilian

clothes and even though he'd probably got less sleep than any of us, he looked okay.

"Miss Binh has been returned?"

"Yes. I saw them both and they were all right. I sent her home with her mother and told her to take a few days off."

"And Miss Chi has made her inspection?"

"Yes. All we need now is to find out where we're going."

I fished out the tracing she'd given me and took it to her.

"Now if you'll give us the rest of this we'll be ready to leave."

She took the sheet from me and without bothering to look at it she crumpled it in her hand and tossed it to the ground.

"You will not need that, gentlemen."

"Then how do we get where we're going?"

"I will guide you. The map was only to keep you amused."

"Then you planned all along to come with us?"

She smiled up at me. "I had hoped that I would be asked."

"Okay. You've had your fun. Now where do we go?"

The smile vanished from her face. "You will start by going east on Highway 1, not the new, American road but the old, French one. I will warn you in plenty of time before we are to leave it."

I waved to The Tiger to get ready to roll. Hieu took his seat at the wheel of the light panel truck and I took mine, Miss Chi between us. The gate swung open and we moved out to the highway. Wherever we were going, we were on our way.

◆17◆

It wasn't very far to the checkpoint. Hieu pulled over to the side of the road and as the rest of the trucks drew up behind us, he climbed out and crossed to the sandbagged guardhouse. Out of uniform he didn't appear quite so impressive and I hoped he wasn't going to hit a bind. To me he looked like any Vietnamese you might pass on the streets of Saigon. A short-sleeved white shirt, gray slacks and light shoes were all he wore but it was more than just the change of clothing that altered his appearance. Gone were his normal posture and step. Now his shoulders were more stooped and he had taken on the gait of a man who normally wears sandals. No one around the checkpoint seemed to be paying him the slightest bit of attention as he opened the screen door and disappeared inside.

No matter what my impression was, the man in charge must have thought differently about how much authority Hieu had. He reappeared in a moment, a uniformed police sergeant behind him. Quickly Hieu walked back to our truck while the sergeant stepped into the road to halt the oncoming traffic. Our engine started and we pulled out on the pavement, followed by the rest of Hieu and Keefe's Traveling Circus. At last we were really on our way.

I don't know why Miss Chi picked the old, two-lane road when we might have saved a half hour or so by taking the new, American-built highway. Perhaps she just wanted to stay with a route she knew, maybe she expected that the old road would be less well patrolled or possibly she had some other reason, but Hieu didn't bother to argue the point. We just rolled along almost due east, closing up about an hour later to go right through Bien Hoa. As always the traffic was heavy, both civilian and military vehicles from the big air base. A steady stream of aircraft passed overhead, taking off on their regular morning flights, climbing quickly above us to gain altitude before the hostiles outside town might get off a shot at them. It was when we stopped for a traffic light in the center of town that I got a hint of why Miss Chi had picked this particular route.

Right at the corner where we were halted was a small café with a few customers seated at the tables just inside the open front. As Hieu braked for the light I saw one of the seated men rise and look steadily at the three of us in the truck. He looked just a shade longer than someone who was merely curious, long enough to assure himself of our identity. Then he walked rapidly down the street in the direction from which we'd come. Without actually swinging around and staring after him, I couldn't tell where it was he went but I was pretty sure that he'd be passing the word that we were on our way. Miss Chi said nothing and I didn't think it was necessary to tell her I'd seen her man.

As a matter of fact, Miss Chi and I didn't say much of anything. The truck engine wasn't all that loud and we probably could have talked without having to raise our voices but we both preferred to sit and let the sights go by without comment.

About an hour after we got clear of Bien Hoa and passed another checkpoint, Hieu seemed to be looking for something. Finally he pointed over to the right and I could see an old quarry or gravel pit. It looked okay and I nodded in time for him to slow down and pull in. The other trucks followed and one by one the drivers killed their engines and climbed down from their cabs.

Now the climate of Vietnam is a good deal warmer than ours and the indigenes are prone to taking large amounts of liquids. They drink beer, soft drinks and a hell of a lot of tea. All this fluid must, eventually, return to Mother Earth. What I'm trying to say is that your average Vietnamese will take every possible opportunity to urinate copiously. Our crowd was no exception. To a man they walked to the edge of the area and let fly before seeking the shade. I felt the need myself and moved off behind our truck

141

to get out of Miss Chi's sight before shedding a tear. It dawned on me then that the lady had a real problem.

Like lots of other people whom we tend to consider less advanced than ourselves, the Vietnamese consider the simple acts necessary to relieve oneself without any feeling of shame or embarrassment. It's not always the case with the citified and Frenchified, who have had the blessing of contact with Westerners, but it is among those who lead the simpler, less complicated life of the slums and the countryside. There both men and women can be seen responding to nature's summons and the ladies, in particular, have developed little shortcuts that expedite the process. One of these is seen so commonly that only the outlander finds it of the slightest interest.

When the call comes the lady moves off a bit, usually to a roadside ditch, and deftly gathers up one leg of her baggy pajama pants. At that point she stands erect and extends the bare leg at an angle of about thirty-five degrees. The deed is done, expeditiously and without the slightest bit of undue exposure. The pajama leg is dropped and the performer returns to what she was doing.

This just wasn't going to work for Miss Chi.

Those beautifully tailored slacks were made to display her trim legs and her cute little behind. There was no way she could dispose of them quickly and gracefully while she attended to her needs. Not without losing a big chunk of her dignity and holding up the convoy long enough to get everyone annoyed. Miss Chi was just going to suffer.

When the last truck rolled in and halted I waited a minute or two and then we pulled out again. The Tiger would make sure that the rest followed at regular intervals but Hieu held our speed down for ten minutes or so until we estimated that they were all moving again. When he picked up his pace the temperature dropped noticeably as the breeze increased and had we just been out for a drive we couldn't have had it better.

There were people working in the fields on either side, a hamlet every mile or so, schools and, that close to Bien Hoa, Catholic churches and an orphanage I'd once used for a story I'd shot. It had got a lot of its support from the Americans, who had contributed cash and food as well as building materials and books and clothing for the kids and sisters. They also contributed a majority of the orphans, an ethnic mix unlike any other but of small interest to anyone but a research geneticist. Unlike the practical French, who made provision for the fruit of casual unions between their men and the local lasses, the Americans have done little or nothing. Apart from the few dedicated souls who always seem to turn up when they're needed, the rest of us prefer to forget all about our great experiment in imported democracy.

When we got within a few miles of the intersection with Highway 20, Miss Chi broke her silence to warn that we would not make the turn to the north. Hieu slowed down and let the trucks close up so that no one would make the turn and stray from the rest of the herd. I was beginning to regret that I hadn't invested in a pair of walkie-talkies from Mr. Tang's stock so that I could keep in contact with The Tiger back in the caboose. I'd dropped the idea, thinking that we might draw the attention of a bored operator somewhere fishing around for some traffic to amuse himself with. It wouldn't take a genius to realize that our chatter indicated somebody interesting coming down the road. I wasn't worried about the government—Hieu could handle that— but I sure didn't want to stir up Victor Charlie.

Without a map, I had to rely on my memory to anticipate what might lie ahead. Highway 1 was already beginning to climb a bit toward the hills along the coast. The two provinces, Phuoc Tuy and Binh Tuy, that lie along the China Sea have been hostile ground for years, held first by the Vietminh and then the VC. The way we were going, it was only a matter of time before we met up with them. That is unless we took the provincial road, Highway 2, but it would just take us down toward the coast and we could have got there just as easily by taking the good road that went all the way to Vung Tau. The way we kept moving toward the coast, there was a chance that our destination might be someplace where a junk or small ship would be waiting to meet us.

When we got to the intersection and the paved road turned to the east, Miss Chi just pointed one slim finger and we went bumping onto the unpaved road that went straight to the south.

Hieu slowed again even though there was little chance that the convoy might miss the way we'd taken. We were still in the dry season and the road, while bumpy, was passable at reduced speed. The dust boiled up from our wheels to hang suspended in the still air until it was made even denser by each vehicle that followed. I could almost hear The Tiger cursing at the rear, where it must have been almost impossible to see or even breathe. Hieu switched on his lights and I hoped each of the others would do the same in case the man behind might be blinded enough to climb his tailgate.

For the next twenty-five miles we fought the road and the dust and the heat. With the windows down we choked—with them up we boiled like potatoes. Finally Hieu stopped. He went trotting back into the dust and I waited, sweating and spitting, until he came back with The Tiger.

"I think the lady had better wait here while we take a look up ahead."

I could see she didn't like the idea, probably suspecting we might be getting ready to pull some kind of fast shuffle, but she got out of the panel truck and stood beside the road. Hieu pointed to a little grove beside the road.

"There's a place where you can go to rest. We'll be gone at least ten or fifteen minutes if you want to use the time."

Over where he was pointing was a small building, not a farmhouse but what I took to be a family shrine. The red tile roof was pretty battered but the walls were still standing and when Miss Chi saw it she brightened up a little.

"Perhaps I might have my suitcase from the truck."

The Tiger pulled it out for her and as we drove off I saw her lugging it across the ditch. Probably The Tiger had offered to carry it but she was as self-reliant as ever and chose to tote it herself.

We didn't have far to drive. A couple of miles up the line we came to the intersection with Route 15. There was a checkpoint there controlling the traffic to Vung Tau to the south and to Saigon from the road that ran northeast along the shore. Hieu parked under a tree and went into the little office while I found a stand selling soft drinks. I got a coolish bottle of orange soda to try to chase the dust out of my mouth. This time Hieu took a bit longer and I was working on my second bottle when he came out. He got a drink for himself and I waited while he polished off half of it at a single gulp.

"You don't think she's heading us for Vung Tau, do you?"

I shook my head. "What for? If she takes Highway 15 from here all we'll be able to do is go swimming. The road ends when it gets to salt water."

"Then we might have just a little trouble. The VC hold the coast road and if we go that way we meet a tax collector right up the line."

"And what do we do then?"

"We do what the Bible tells us."

"I can't say I get that."

"You know. We 'render unto Caesar that which is Caesar's.' In short, we pay."

That was an idea I was going to have to get used to but I didn't have anything better in the way of a suggestion. Even if we paid up that didn't mean we'd be in the clear with the VC.

"What do we do if they want to see what's in the trucks? They're not going to pass that stuff in a million years."

"We fight."

"Just like that?"

"There will not be more than a few men guarding the collector and we'll have the advantage of surprise. We may take a few casualties but we should be able to get through."

He spoke of it the way you'd talk about getting on the Tokyo subway during a peak rush hour.

"What do you think they'll do when they see me? There's not a hell of a lot of tall redheads in Binh Tuy. They're going to ask questions."

"Do you speak German, Mr. Keefe?"

That was a funny one. "No. Why?"

"A pity. I had hoped to pass you as an East German journalist. There is not much chance of finding a VC who speaks that language but it's best to play it safe." He thought a moment or two. "I think we'd better make you a Finn. You're a missionary who is trying to arrange for Finnish families to adopt Vietnamese orphans. How does that sound?"

"How do I prove it? What if they ask for papers?"

He shrugged. "A pity. Stolen from you this morning by a pickpocket in Bien Hoa. You will replace them when you return to Saigon. Right now you're a Finn who has paid me to take him as far as Ham Tan."

"How do we explain Miss Chi? What do we say about her?"

"She is my fiancée. I am taking her to meet my family in Phan Thiet."

He seemed to have all the answers. I got my attaché case from the back of our truck and passed over enough cash to pay Charlie. He finished his drink and we drove back to where we'd left the convoy. Soon we were going to begin earning our pay.

We hit the roadblock a few miles after we left the pavement beyond Dat Do. The road had been winding along and we descended a short grade from which I could see the glint of a river up ahead, flowing down to the ocean off on our right. We came around a curve and just at the point where the road crossed a well-worn wooden bridge was the tax collector.

A table had been set up at the side of the road in front of a thatched shelter. Seated there was a wiry little guy in khaki shorts, a faded but clean shirt and the inevitable sun helmet. A couple of stacks of papers were in front of him, held down by fist-size rocks and a battered abacus. Lined up waiting their turns were a few men, probably the drivers of the trucks I could see parked on the far side of the bridge. Hieu pulled onto the shoulder and the rest of our trucks drove up and stopped just to the rear. Hieu got out but I kept my seat and tried to look Finnish. Beside me I could feel Miss Chi shrink down in her seat. Any fool could see the lady was scared.

She would have been even worse off if we hadn't made that last stop a long one. When Hieu and I had got back from the government checkpoint The Tiger had pointed over to the little shrine to show she was still there. He called out something and in a few seconds out came a little peasant woman lugging Miss Chi's suitcase. I wondered where she'd come from, not recognizing her until she had almost reached us.

It was Miss Chi, all right, but gone were the tailored slacks and the shirt and scarves. Instead she was wearing black pants, a white rough cotton blouse and the shallow conical straw hat of a farm woman. She looked a lot happier and a good deal more relaxed and she even smiled a little when The Tiger took her suitcase and put it into the truck. A moment later we were on our way again.

When we got to the intersection she pointed away from Vung Tau and to the road up the coast, Route 23. We had a few miles of pavement and then it was once more into the dust and the cheering thought of our meeting with Charlie.

Hieu had got into line and was waiting his turn with the others. The headman snapped a few questions at each payee, looked at his papers and then announced the amount of the assessment. He collected the payment and passed over some of the reading matter on the table. Each driver folded the few sheets carefully and put them in his pocket. After all, you don't get nice soft paper like that every day. They were bound to put the paper to good use. Finally it was Hieu's turn. For the first time the collector seemed to notice the size of our convoy. He pushed his wire-rimmed glasses up to his forehead and squinted down the line that was accumulating, then swung back to peer at the panel truck. I saw his head shift from side to side and then he rapped out something to Hieu. I got the feeling the man wanted a closer look at me and when Hieu turned to wave I got out and joined him, carrying the small canvas bag with my personal stuff.

"I have told this officer who you are and that you speak a little English. He has a few questions and then he will decide if you are to be taxed."

The collector called out something over his shoulder and I saw half a dozen men who had been sitting back in the shade stand and come up behind him. They were a scruffy-looking bunch, dressed in a variety of outfits that showed lots of wear. To my eye they had a kind of wolfish look, lean, hard-muscled little men, with none of the qualities an American officer looks for in good troops. There was nothing slipshod about the way they carried their weapons, though. Each had a loaded AK-47, clean and with the faint gleam of just enough oil, and they showed all the signs of being able to use them quickly and efficiently.

Meanwhile the man at the table was reeling off some kind of diatribe and Hieu was standing there trying to look as though he'd never seen me before that morning and didn't like me much anyway. At last the man stopped and Hieu translated.

The man had barely heard of Finland and he wanted to know how we felt about the War of Liberation and were we a Marxist state or running dogs of the imperialists? I went through the motions of giving some kind of reply and Hieu said, "I'll tell him that Finland is right next to Sweden. He'll like that. The Swedes stand high with the VC."

Whatever it was he told the man seemed to help. The climate got just a shade less chilly and the man gave his verdict to Hieu. I need pay no tax but I must promise that when I got back to Finland I must tell my people of the heroic struggle against the lackeys in Saigon of the American capitalists and a few more of the standard compliments they used to describe the people they were fighting.

I made a short speech promising to do as I was asked and let Hieu take over as the man turned to deal with him. He had his kid gloves off again and he looked as if he didn't believe a word Hieu was telling him. He spread out the sheaf of documents he'd been handed and took his time cleaning his glasses before he ran his eyes over each of them. Finally he gathered them up and tossed them back to Hieu and rapped out an order to his men, pointing to the waiting trucks. He had to be giving orders for a search and I looked down the line to see if The Tiger and his men had caught on.

I suppose they had because there was only one man visible at each truck and the logical assumption was that the other men were crouched down in the cabs with their weapons loaded and ready. I turned back to Hieu to see which way he planned to go when the shooting started. He was staring fixedly at the small bag I carried and suddenly I caught on. I zipped open the top of the bag and grabbed a carton of American cigarettes, then stepped up to the table and placed them in front of the collector and said something about wanting to make them a gift. He didn't need a translation for that. He called to his men, who had only taken the first few steps toward the trucks, and they turned and came back to the table.

Carefully he slit the carton open with a broken thumbnail and extracted a single package before passing the rest along. When each man had a pack the ones remaining were placed on the table and I was rewarded with a full salvo of smiles. The collector tore open his pack, lit a cigarette from a brass lighter and took a long puff before passing it to the nearest man. While the others puffed in turn the headman did a couple of laps around his abacus and announced the total to Hieu. He watched as the money was counted out on the table in front of him, folded it carefully and then passed over a supply of his literature. By this time the cigarette had made the full round of the squad and come back to him. He leaned back, pushing the sun helmet up on his high forehead, and took a deep puff at the tobacco, drawing the smoke right down to the seat of his pants before he waved to us to go. He exhaled and then jabbed his hand toward me. I took it and got the single hard jerk that passes for a handshake and then walked as calmly as I could back to my seat in the truck. Down the line I heard the sounds of the trucks starting and then Hieu edged the panel truck out over the rattling boards of the bridge. I looked back and saw the truck behind wait for us to cross to the far side before entrusting his load to the fragile-looking structure. With three tons of ammunition aboard, he wasn't about to take a chance on having to swim. Hieu braked and then, when the other truck hit the bank, he eased up the hill in low gear and the second load started over. We crawled up the grade, giving everyone a chance to cross and my pulse and respiration an opportunity to get back to normal.

It was about five when we found a place to spend the night. Just before we got to Ham Tan, the provincial capital, Hieu saw a narrow side road leading toward the shore. He halted and waited for the trucks to close up, then turned and headed in, following the ruts that led between the thick growth on either side. We drove along in low gear for about a quarter of a mile and then, just as we were beginning to hear the surf, we came out to an open area of about three or four acres. There were a few granddaddy-size trees here and there but the ground had been grazed over to a short stubble, making as nice a bivouac as you'd want. It looked okay to me and I asked Hieu to let me out while he went back for the others.

It felt good to be able to move around and get my blood traveling along its regular routes. I walked down to the shore and saw the reason for the entrance road. Drawn up on the sand were ten or twelve small fishing boats, the little ones that look so beautiful sailing under their big triangular sails. When you get up close, though, they lose a lot of their allure. Aside from the big eye on either side of the bow, they're innocent of paint and the weathered boards have soaked up the juices of countless fish, gone but not forgotten. Getting downwind of one of the small fleets can have a hell of an effect on your appetite. I gave them a wide berth and walked along the edge of the water to where a small fresh-water creek emptied into the sea. The tide was out and the sand, firm to walk on, was decorated with shells and, of course, the wooden chopsticks that turn up on every beach in the Orient. There was no sign of life anywhere and it seemed likely that the fishermen left their boats here at night to go to their homes in some village nearby.

When I heard the trucks beginning to pull in I turned back. Hieu had led them into a rough circle and when it closed he signaled to cut engines. In the stillness that followed I heard The Tiger calling to his men to gather around and get the word. He knew what he was doing and it took only a minute to get them set up for the night.

They were bivouacked in eight-man squads, each drawing and cooking its own rations and taking one tour of guard duty during the hours of darkness. I could see the cooking fires being lit and in a few minutes the rice was boiling and water was being heated for tea. The tanker was moving from truck to truck, refueling each in turn and passing out oil and water. While all that was happening I got a machete and went over to the edge of the jungle and cut a bundle of saplings. Trimming them, I carried them back to our panel truck. The Tiger and Hieu readied our meal as I lashed the poles with wire into a pair of frames, leaning one on each side

150

of the truck and fastening it into place. I'd done it by eye but when I covered each frame with one of the sheets of heavy plastic I'd got from Mr. Tang they fitted nicely and I'd created a pair of lean-tos that would give us shelter for the night. I tossed my sleeping bag into one and called to Hieu to take the other but he shook his head.

"I'll use the cab. Let the lady have the other."

That was okay with me so I got Miss Chi's suitcase and added a spare poncho liner to keep her off the damp ground. She didn't say anything but ducked right in and I could hear her stirring around and getting herself organized. When The Tiger called that our supper was ready she came out looking a lot better. She had on the same outfit but somehow she'd got rid of some of the dust and combed her hair. I'd fished out some boxes to sit on but she squatted down beside The Tiger and Hieu and dove into the bowl of mixed rice and C ration she'd been handed. While the three of them made their chopsticks fly, I used the plastic spoon that's packed with the rations. There was a small cup of tea for each of us and the hot, strong drink was better than booze to make you feel good.

The whole meal didn't take fifteen minutes to eat and maybe five more to clean up, Miss Chi pitching in, for once, to help. The men were rigging their hammocks and by the time it began to get dark everyone was set for the night. Most of them sat around the dying cook fires, smoking and talking. Every so often I'd hear a laugh. If we had any problems, morale didn't appear to be one of them. As the darkness came across the sky from the east I saw one bunch move out with their weapons to take posts about fifty yards from the circle of trucks. The fires were kicked out and as the last of the color dissolved in the west, everyone had settled down for the night.

We were due for a moon a few hours later but now only the stars lit our little camp. I crawled into my lean-to, opened my sleeping bag and got ready to turn in. On the other side there were some small rustlings as Miss Chi prepared for sleep and I heard the truck springs squeak a bit as Hieu made himself comfortable in the cab. Finally everything was quiet.

I must have dropped off right away. It was a warm night, even there by the shore, and I didn't bother to get into the sleeping bag. Instead I lay on top and used the light nylon poncho liner as a cover. The soft wind from the water was enough to keep the mosquitoes down and the only sounds were from the waves stirring the sand at the water's edge. The stillness was so complete that a few hours later when there were some faint noises from the other side of the truck, I was wide awake. The moon was out now, almost full, and in its light I saw that Miss Chi was astir. At first I thought she might just be moving in her sleep but then, from where I lay, I could see she was sitting up. I looked at the luminous dial of my watch: after one. There was only one logical reason for her to be getting up but I reminded myself that she had a record of defying logic and doing things for special reasons of her own.

Next I heard the rustle of the plastic flap of her shelter and I knew she had come outside. I saw her tiny feet as she moved around to my side of the truck and then, very slowly, the flap of my roof was drawn back. Suddenly I was wide awake and ready to move. She was behind me and I sensed rather than saw her kneel at my head and, without warning, slip one hand across my mouth and fasten a firm grip on my shoulder with the other.

I suppose I must have shot right up to a sitting position. I swung around to face her and, in the moonlight, I could see her smiling. She took her hand from my shoulder and reached down and grasped my hand, pulling gently as she got to her feet. I still couldn't imagine what the hell she wanted at that hour. I stood up and looked down at her. Then I knew.

She was pointing toward the beach, still tugging at my hand, and I let her pull me along. Without her high heels she barely came to my chest but she was a wiry little thing. I followed her out of the circle of trucks and toward the water, looking around and hoping that the men on guard recognized us. There was no point in getting shot by my own people but the only sign of our being seen was the gleam of a cigarette end from beneath one of the trees.

The moonlight was more than bright enough for us to find our way without stumbling and in a minute we were down on the sand a few feet from the edge of the water. She dropped my hand and I saw her lift her arms and free her torso of the cotton blouse and then fumble for a moment at her waist. The billowing pants dropped to the sand and then, without a look back at me, she raced for the water. Miss Chi was a skinny-dipper.

I was so startled that it took a moment for me to pull myself together and get rid of my pants and shorts. By the time I splashed in after her she was a good twenty yards ahead and I ran through the gradually deepening water trying to catch up. She was in almost to her waist when she plunged forward in a shallow dive, her arms flashing in the moonlight. I dove into the warm water and swam after her.

I don't know if I could have caught her or not but abruptly she stopped swimming and turned back to watch me approach. When I got to her side I let my legs drop to the bottom, to stand chest-high. We were almost face to face and then I saw the moonlight flash in her eyes and she suddenly flung her arms around my neck, clamping her mouth to mine, her teeth fastened on my lower lip as her legs wound themselves around me. She twisted and churned her chest against mine as I turned and carried her to the shallower water near the shore. When it was only knee-deep I lowered myself slowly, sitting in the warm surf with her still tight against me. I'm still not sure about exactly what it was she did, but she did it with her usual talent and style.

⊰ 18 ⊱

The second day on the road went a lot better. For one thing, we were working into a routine. About a half hour before first light The Tiger had everyone up. The cook fires were lit and by the time the sun was lifting itself out of the ocean the men were finishing their morning meal. One by one they headed for the fresh-water creek I'd found the evening before and we hurried and finished our breakfast and followed them. Miss Chi went upstream around a little bend to do her thing in privacy and Hieu and I splashed in with the others. The water was a lot cooler than the ocean and I soaped up and washed and brushed my teeth and got out as quickly as I could. The Tiger's men were enjoying the treat and I was sure they'd get a lot of good out of the short time we'd let them have at the creek.

Now I've spent my share of time in Southeast Asia and I've learned a couple of things. One is that there's nothing the Asian loves so much as his daily bath. If you give him the choice of a homesite close to water where he'll probably get flooded out during the monsoons, or another that's high and dry but too far to go for a periodic wash, he'll take the first every time. My place in Bangkok looked out on a small canal running right behind the building. There was a landing with steps that went down into the turbid water and just about any time of day I could look out and see someone bathing. There was one old character who must have been about eighty. Three or four times a day he'd come shuffling down the path and descend the steps, his sarong wrapped around his skinny waist and a bar of soap in his hand. He'd wash his body

154

and then squat in the muddy water for five or ten minutes and just enjoy himself.

Our bunch of battered ex-Rangers were no different. They sloshed around and had fun but as soon as they saw The Tiger climb up the bank, they tagged along behind him. I called to Miss Chi and we packed the last few things and were ready to roll. The fishermen had already appeared and as we drove away I could see them about a hundred yards offshore, raising their sails.

A few minutes later we were rolling into Ham Tan and Miss Chi pointed the way north. I still couldn't figure out what she was doing. We'd made a big, looping detour away from the main highway and now we were heading right back toward it. We could have got to the same place in half the time by just staying on Highway 1. Instead she'd had us go all the way south to take the secondary dirt road along the coast. I didn't think it was just because she liked ocean bathing with variations. There had to be some good reason for not taking the short route through the hills but, if so, she wasn't going to let us in on it. She had no sign of a map or written instructions that I'd seen but she never hesitated once, pointing the way as though she'd traveled the road every day of her life.

Just as mysterious was the way she acted toward me. Evidently she was interested in me personally only after the sun went down. The moment it rose in the morning she resumed her self-possessed coolness. She was polite but standoffish as she rode between Hieu and me in the front seat of the panel truck.

The road north out of Ham Tan was paved. We passed a government outpost without any trouble and a few miles farther on, where the road began to climb, we met another representative of the VC Internal Revenue. He checked the papers and took the donation of cash and cigarettes, and we went on. As the road climbed Hieu had to slow the pace, the trucks behind us having to shift down. A few minutes later he suddenly pulled up and I looked back to see the first few trucks with their headlights burning. We piled out to see what the trouble was. Halfway down the line we found it, a truck with steam billowing from under the hood. The Tiger came stumping up with the mechanics. The driver raised the hood and I saw the chief practitioner climb up to make his diagnosis. He was down in a moment to consult with his colleague and to agree on the nature of the disorder. He passed the word to The Tiger, who relayed it to me.

"Goddamn water hose bust, Mike. All water in radiator gone to hell."

"How long to get it fixed?"

This required another consultation and then I got the prognosis.

"He say he can fix in one, two hour."

I turned to Hieu. "What do you think? Shall we wait for them to do the repair or dump this one and shift the load to the spare?"

"Why don't we put it to the lady? If waiting means we won't get to the rendezvous in time, we'll have to keep going. If we have time I say wait. We may need the spare later."

Miss Chi answered without hesitation. "One or two hours will not matter. It is more important that we deliver the whole amount."

She was still making decisions but I was sure now that there was somebody she was going to have to answer to if she goofed, and she didn't like the idea. I went back to the ruptured truck and passed the word to get going. For a few minutes Hieu and I stood around trying to lend moral assistance by our presence but about all we accomplished was to get in the way. The sun was becoming hot and in a few minutes we were seeking shade at the side of the road where a culvert took it across a small brook.

I saw The Tiger in a huddle with his squad leaders, passing out some kind of directions. When he finished two groups took off up and down stream while two others headed along the road behind and ahead of us. With Miss Chi back where we'd left the panel truck, I had a chance to talk with Hieu.

"How do you think it's going?"

He shrugged. "I'm afraid to say. It seems like we've still got a long way to go before we reach the meeting place."

"It looks to me as though there's no hard and fast timetable she's got to stick to. You notice she's more interested that we deliver the full amount than in staying on schedule."

He reached down and picked up a handful of small stones. One by one he tossed them into the water. "I've been thinking about just who these people might be. One thing I've decided is that they don't have any real organization outside their own area."

"What makes you say that?"

"For one thing, they don't appear to be involved in anything that takes a big outlay of real cash. If they had the kind of infrastructure that the VC maintain it would have to be financed and they'd think in terms of a cash ransom. So far there hasn't been any evidence that they have more than a couple of agents in Saigon."

"How do you figure that?"

He held his hand up and ticked off each point on a finger.

"First there's Fargot. It cost a lot to get him to the States and back but if my guess is right he was working on speculation. He paid his own way against the promise of a later payoff when the deal was concluded. They didn't wait that long, though. When Fargot had done what they needed he was paid off with a knife. His whole trip never cost them a cent.

"Next there's Miss Chi. I think she was sent to Saigon only to make the contact and guide us back to the others. Not much cost in that." He gave me a funny, narrow look. "By the way, did you pay her for the week she worked?"

"Sure. She earned it and there wasn't any reason not to."

"Fine. She probably will even show a small profit on her trip. Last there were the other two, but I get the feeling that they were just hired by the day."

"What other two?"

He smiled. "Well, there may have been three but no more. I mean the ones who kept an eye on you until Miss Chi could get herself right inside your office. There's the bicycle fixer and the paper reader. One or the other was probably the 'blind' beggar and both took care of Miss Binh and her mother while Miss Chi was at work. If there was a third, then he was the man in Bien Hoa."

"You spotted him, too?"

He nodded again. "Now, that leaves an interesting question. Who killed Fargot?"

It was a nasty question and I wished he hadn't asked it. There could be only one answer. Once Miss Chi had set Fargot up to meet me, there was no need to bring anyone else into the Continental Palace. A stranger wandering around or lurking in the hallway risked being found by the hotel staff and forced to explain his presence. Not only that, but Fargot would never have turned his back on someone he didn't know. Our prime candidate was sitting a few yards away down the road. Miss Chi had a perfectly good reason for being in the hotel the night that Fargot had gone to his Franco-Chinese ancestors. She was known to him and he had no reason to worry about her being in the corridor when he came to meet me. I didn't know how much she knew about gross anatomy but so far everything else I'd seen her do showed outstanding competence.

Suddenly I got a funny feeling between my own shoulder blades. When Fargot had been collected from my bedroom floor there had been no sign of a knife, the long, thin blade that had slid so silently to just the right point between the ribs.

From about four in the afternoon on, both Hieu and I looked for a place to spend the night. We were up in higher country, a long stretch of overgrown but still open fields that offered little, if any, cover.

Once the sick truck was back in shape things had gone pretty well. Repairing the damaged hose had run a little over the estimate and by the time the radiator was refilled from the brook I was itching to go.

The men The Tiger had sent off had come back, each carrying something useful. One man had a stalk of ripe bananas, another some pineapples found growing around abandoned farms. There was a nice bundle of bamboo shoots but the best came in last, carried on an improvised litter covered with big green leaves. The Tiger lifted them to reveal a row of bright orange papayas. Most were dead ripe and in a minute each of us had a slice. Even Miss Chi unbent a little, thanking the man who brought her a piece and saying something complimentary when she took the first bite.

The things the foragers had turned up were stowed away to add variety to our meals. A little while later, when the patient was pronounced cured and fit to travel, I couldn't honestly say that the halt had been a total loss. We had all our transport and, to judge by Miss Chi's attitude, we were still right on schedule if there really was one.

There was no hint yet of where she was leading us. So far we'd traveled south, east and north. By following that line of reasoning, and given what we knew of Miss Chi, that meant our final destination had to be to the west. Even so, a lot of possibilities remained. When we got to Phan Thiet, on the coast, she turned us to the north again. We left town, bumping over old railroad tracks that hadn't been used for years, on a partly paved road that needed work but was still serviceable. We'd learned our lesson that morning and at every stop The Tiger had the men check their radiators and hoses. It was midafternoon when we came to the junction with Highway 20, a place we could have reached directly from Saigon in less than a day's travel with a lot less dust and fewer bumps. A left turn there would have got us right back where we'd started in time for a late dinner and a few drinks. A right turn would take us to Dalat and beyond there back to the coast road we'd left a few hours before. She had us turn to the right but, as it turned out, she had no intention of staying on the road very long.

We had been rolling along for close to an hour, glad of the pavement beneath us, when she pointed to a road up ahead coming in on our left. Hieu made the turn and slowed until he was sure that everyone was still with us. Finally we were headed to the west. Not a lot west, more like north-northwest, but still away from the coast and toward the highlands. Most of the way was a gradual, steady climb toward the mountains in the distance. There wasn't a lot of traffic, mostly farmers with oxcarts or pedal-powered cargo bikes. The bridges all showed signs of the fighting, some of them rebuilt or replaced with temporary crossings or fords, and the farther we went along the road, the worse they got. Four o'clock came and then four-thirty and we still hadn't found the right kind of place to spend the night. By five we were beginning to worry.

At last we found a spot. It wasn't perfect but it would do. If we wanted to be set up before dark we couldn't afford to wait for a better.

The road had been going through long stretches of rubber trees

159

broken, here and there, by open rice fields. Some of the fields close to the road were planted but the rubber had been left behind for the woodcutters and the charcoal burners, who were cutting the trees and stacking the cut logs along the road. It was just as we were climbing back to the road from a temporary floating bridge over a canal that Hieu spotted a narrow dirt road that led to the right along the bank.

He braked for a moment and, without taking time to look the place over before bringing in the trucks, led the way toward a stand of trees about a half mile away. When we were well into the grove he turned among the trees, swinging in a wide arc to face the way he'd just come. If we had any reason to make a fast departure no time would be wasted. The other drivers got the message and each drove into the grove and made the turn. It wasn't anything like the place we'd had the night before. Here the trucks were strung out in line without a clear field of fire in case we had visitors.

There was a lot to do before darkness and we got right at it. The tanker went down the line and not until every one had been gassed and serviced did The Tiger pass out rations. I took time to set up the night shelters and then gathered wood for a small cooking fire. I dipped a bucket of water from the canal, adding Halazone tablets just to be safe. The Tiger got things going, making tea and rice and cutting a portion of fruit for each of us. He used the remains of the tea to douse the fire, removing the last bit of light from the darkness under the trees. The sentries were out and when I slid into my sleeping bag the last sounds of the men settling down had stilled.

We must have climbed pretty high because no sooner had the sun set than the temperature dropped like a shot. The padded nylon liner in my bag felt good and I got myself well wrapped and warm enough to sleep. Everything was quiet on Miss Chi's side of the truck until, just about to drop off, I heard a strange little rattling sound. It took me a minute to realize that it was the chattering of her teeth. For all her air of self-sufficiency, Miss Chi just wasn't up to the rigors of outdoor life, but she should have thought of that when she hired out. As always, though, she came up with a straightforward solution.

She simply took the shortest route between where she was and where she wanted to go, rolling like a log under the truck and right to my side. In the darkness I felt her free herself of the cover she had and kneel beside me. There was a rustling as she stripped off her clothes and after a moment of fumbling, she found the long zipper closure of my sleeping bag, pulled it down and wriggled in beside me. Somehow I got an arm free and slid the zipper closed, shutting out the night chill and damp.

I had to feel sorry for her. Her body was like ice and I tried to wrap myself around her and get her warm as quickly as possible. Her body warmed first and then, as she moved her cold hands and feet against me, nature took its course.

Now I'm a fair-sized guy. I'm six one and with all the good living I'd been having I was a lot over my regular fighting weight of 190. There's just so much room in a sleeping bag but Miss Chi was as resourceful as ever. She didn't bother to waste time with mixed hors d'oeuvres, salad and fish, but got right to the main course. Even so it was a gourmet's delight as always and a real pleasure. Ten minutes later she was asleep in my arms and I pulled the switch and joined her.

◆| 19 |◆

The track was narrow, hemmed in on both sides by cliff and rock overhangs, a nice route to take if you enjoyed ambushes and surprise attacks. I didn't like it and neither did Hieu. The track itself was little more than a pair of ruts, a neglected trail that had taken us through a long stretch of rubber plantation and into the flanks of the mountain ahead. The jungle had edged its way right to the road, throwing long, looping strands of vines all the way across in places. A few small saplings had sprouted between the ruts and a couple of times I had to get out and chop them down before we could go on.

Hieu stayed in low gear, not just to get power for the steady climb but also to set the slowest possible pace and let the trucks stay closed up. If there was ever a place where we wanted to keep our troops together this was it. There was no room to maneuver and no way in the world to turn around and get out.

Tired as she looked, Miss Chi had led us without hesitation or mistakes. Even though she had little to do but sit and enjoy the sights, she was clearly showing the strain. Perhaps it was because she wasn't using her makeup but I thought she looked paler and with more than a hint of darkening under her eyes. If there was a temptation to doze off for a quick cat nap, she resisted it. From the moment we'd left the bivouac by the canal she had kept her eyes fixed on the road, watching intently for landmarks or signs.

We hadn't wasted a minute that morning. The Tiger allowed the men only a quick wash-up on the canal bank and a few minutes to eat. By the time the sun broke over the horizon behind

162

us we were already five or six miles up the road.

We had the battered landscape almost to ourselves. The few others we did spot stayed well away, some woodcutters having breakfast with their families beside the rude shelters they'd spent the night under. They didn't wave or show any sign that they'd seen us. Those who had somehow managed to survive in that fought-over piece of country had done so only by giving strangers of all persuasions a wide berth. They saw nothing and they knew nothing. They were merely bystanders in the struggle that had gone on for almost thirty years.

At first the road had been in fair shape, the worst of the damage to it patched with gravel that slowed us only a little. Every so often we'd pass another rubber plantation, long abandoned, the trees rank and untended, the tappers' scars grown over and almost invisible, and the underbrush waist-high in the aisles between rows. After a couple of hours Hieu began to look for a place to stop for a break but Miss Chi picked that point to warn us of the next change of route. It came a mile or two farther along on our left, a gravel road leading west, straight to the mountains.

This road showed few signs of any real traffic beyond an occasional buffalo cart. The fields we passed were pitted with bomb craters and shell holes, the bridges a tangle of scrap iron and weathered planking, forcing us to ford one stream after another. Hieu would stop at the water's edge, wading out to make sure we had clearance for the low-axle panel truck. When the monsoons came in a few months there wouldn't be a chance of taking a cargo truck through.

We finally got some fairly level going when we got to the top of a sort of plateau which sloped gently up to where it met the mass of the mountains. This was montagnard country, the few deserted villages we passed raised on poles, except where time or hostile action had allowed the long community houses to collapse in a jumble of bamboo and thatch. Any level ground had been planted to rubber, one huge plantation that must have made a lot of Frenchmen rich. Overgrown though it was, you could still see the wider spacing where the service roads had led back between the blocks of trees. Over these the raw rubber drawn by the tappers had been hauled out for processing, after which it would

163

be formed into sheets, smoked and then sent on its way to be used in a more complicated society.

Miss Chi was sitting bolt upright in her seat, head up to help her see over the dashboard. We passed one after another of the service roads before she saw what she was looking for. It was a tripod of rough poles, lashed together at the top, from which an empty wine bottle swung slowly in the light breeze. The trail it marked showed no sign of recent use and if it hadn't been for the signpost someone had so thoughtfully provided we might well have missed it completely. Slowly as we were going, Hieu had no trouble making the turn, slowing even more as we heard the drivers shift down to gain traction on the softer ground. I twisted around and got my head out the window, watching the convoy until I saw the tanker turn the corner.

For the first mile or so the going wasn't bad, the ground level and the surface firm as it went between the carefully spaced trees. When we came to the end of the planting, the track began to rise toward the top of a small ridge. Here things began to get rough, the rocky undersurface of the road exposed and, in places, broken by fairly deep ruts cut by the rains. We came over the crest of the ridge and began the descent on the other side. The remains of an ancient roadbed paralleled the track on our left, an occasional rusted rail or rotted tie indicating where once a narrow-gauge plantation railroad had run. Gaps indicated absent culverts or small bridges. The valley continued to narrow and the ditch on our right began to widen into a free-running brook that picked up speed as it was fed from the small streams that drained the higher ground. By the time we were a mile or so along it had grown to the point where the sound of the water could be heard over the noise of the trucks.

The farther we descended, the higher the wall rose on either side. We had been negotiating a series of wide-swinging curves, the old railroad, the track we were on and the stream all following the same course.

We dropped deeper and deeper, the stream falling away from us on our right, its channel farther and farther below the level of the track, which clung to a narrow shelf just wide enough for a truck to pass between the brink and the old roadbed.

The deeper in we got, the less I liked it. It was the sort of place that ten men with rifles could hold against an army. The same ten men, well posted up above, could have stopped us right there without our being able to argue the point at all. If someone decided to hijack us and take all our marbles and baseball cards, we'd be lucky if we got away with something irreplaceable, like our lives.

I glanced down at Miss Chi. She was leaning back in her seat now, her eyes half closed, no longer watching the road. We were coming to the end of the line. There was a louder sound of water just ahead and when we turned one last corner Hieu braked hard. The rutted path we were following, the last stretch of rails, ended abruptly at the brink of a deep gorge. Hieu and I got out for a look around.

First we walked to the edge of the gorge. To our right the stream we'd been following came tumbling down its channel to join a much larger one, almost a young river, that curved down from the higher ground, its water level a good forty or fifty feet below, the bed filled with jagged rocks brought down by the rains. It was pretty clear that at one time the gorge had been spanned by a bridge that carried the tracks across the main stream to their destination. From where we stood we could see the roadbed on the far side ran about a hundred yards off to our left before it disappeared around a bend in the river. There was a lot more room over there, maybe an acre, but on our side there was barely space for more than the first few trucks where the rock wall had been quarried away, probably to provide gravel for the roadbed. It was going to be one hell of a place to get out of if we didn't have much time.

Whatever had taken out the old bridge had made a clean job of it. Not only was there no sign of debris at the bottom of the gorge but even the bulkheads were gone. Across the way the first few rails were missing, by now doubtless reforged into a variety of new objects by some talented and thrifty Vietnamese blacksmith.

In place of the old crossing was a new bridge, if you can call a pair of well-worn hawsers draped across the gorge, with a bamboo walkway dangling between them, a bridge. Hieu walked over and gave one of the ropes a tentative yank, setting the whole rig to dancing and gyrating across its length. I joined him to get a closer look and I could see then that even though the thing didn't get much of a rating for neatness or beauty it seemed to be pretty well kept, the ropework and the catwalk itself tight and in good repair. Still, before I'd trust myself to it I'd want to see someone about my size and weight make a safe landing on the other bank.

The only other thing I got from my inspection was a growing suspicion that over on the far side were the people we'd come to meet.

Hieu and I walked back to the truck to get the word from our guide. She'd got out of the truck and was moving around a bit, paying no attention at all to her surroundings. She looked like someone who has just finished a job for which she had no relish and is enjoying the thought of being shut of it.

"Okay, Miss Chi, what do we do now?"

She looked at me coolly. "You will do nothing, Mr. Keefe."

"Just sit here on our tails?"

"If you prefer it that way."

"Look, lady, it's going to be dark in a couple of hours. What then?"

"Then you will have to spend the night." She turned away as though the matter was no concern of hers.

Maybe it was a slip that she hadn't meant to commit or maybe it didn't mean a thing but she hadn't said that *we* would spend the night. She'd said "you."

I wondered if Hieu had caught it. He looked worried. From what we could see there was no way we could go forward unless we were willing to abandon the trucks and cargo and trust ourselves to the bridge contraption. If we wanted to retreat the way we'd come it was going to take at least a couple of hours to get everything turned around. We couldn't do even that if someone with a rifle wanted to discourage us.

Without any options, all we could do was as the lady had told us. When The Tiger came limping up I told him to have the men dismount and do what he could to get things ready for the night. He didn't like the idea but he was too good a soldier to protest. He yelled at the first driver and I heard the order being passed down the line. The men began to go to the side of the road for the usual reason.

If I'd had any worries about The Tiger being able to take the rough life we were living, all I had to do was look at him. The tougher the going, the tougher he got, drawing on some seemingly bottomless reserve of strength.

He sent some men to hunt for a way down to the river and then had them bring water and gather what dry driftwood they could find for cook fires. There was no way to bring the tanker up but I ordered each truck inspected, the radiator refilled and the oil sump checked. One of the squad leaders came up with a question and I saw The Tiger shake his head.

"He ask about weapons," he explained. "I tell him to keep them under cover but handy. Maybe somebody up there watching and not like to see them."

He was using his head. Miss Chi knew my men were armed but maybe her friends didn't. There was no sense giving away the little bit of edge I had. I had only one hole card and I wasn't sure what it was worth. That was Miss Chi, and I'd have to make damn sure I kept hold of her.

She didn't like it a bit but it wasn't a point I was going to argue. If she wanted to put up a struggle that was her decision; I wasn't going to change my mind about keeping her on a short leash until it was time to trade off. When our meal was ready I unlocked the handcuff that linked her to the length of light tow chain padlocked to the truck frame. The Tiger had gone all out on her farewell dinner—C ration à la Vietnam, rice, the contents of a couple of assorted rations plus bamboo shoots, all laced with nuoc mam, and for dessert, a selection of fruits in season. She squatted a few feet away from me but within easy reach of the pots of food, opening her mouth only to insert her chopsticks, while her eyes burned two holes in my forehead. I don't think it was what she intended but, tired as she was, her anger was better than any makeup, raising her color and giving a lift to her eyebrows and a slight flare to her nostrils.

When we finished eating I led her off behind some bushes and while I didn't stare I still made sure she didn't decide to take off for the tall timber. When she emerged I took her down to the river. Even at low water the current was far too strong to trust but behind a big rock I found a little backwater. She stripped and waded in, her teeth chattering, then suddenly plunged her whole body in briefly and headed back to me, chilled to the bone. I grabbed her towel and dried her, scrubbing her body hard to bring back the circulation before she got into clean clothes. When I'd led her up the trail to the top and back to the truck, I chained her again under her shelter with her suitcase close at hand and when I left her there she was combing and oiling her hair.

I got my things and went down to the river, forcing myself to take a quick dip in the frigid water, and then I shaved. For some reason I wanted to look as good as I could when we met up with the other side. I was just finishing when The Tiger called down to me. I came up the trail on the double to see what the trouble might be.

"Mike, I think maybe good idea to turn trucks around while we got time. I tell tanker driver back up and find place to turn."

"That's a good idea, Tiger. It'll probably make it easier to unload when they get here tomorrow."

"I think so, too, but when driver try to back up, big damn rock fall down from top of damn cliff. Almost hit somebody, too."

I shook my head. "I guess they don't want us to turn around, so you may as well tell everybody to settle down and secure for the night." He was about to turn away when I had a thought. "You remember the old tin can trick for a night bivouac?"

He did and a minute later I saw one of the men edge out a few yards on the rope bridge. He had a couple of empty ration cans, each with some rocks inside. He fastened them to the ropework and as he came back along the catwalk I heard them rattle loudly. If anyone wanted to cross in the dark it would be hard to keep it a secret.

Everything was quiet on Miss Chi's side when I got into my sleeping bag. I was dead tired but sleep didn't come, as my mind traveled ahead to what might happen the next day. To get it off my mind, I thought back to what we'd already done.

We'd been luckier than hell, everything considered. We'd managed to move thirty-five tons of live ammunition right

168

through two contending armies and arrive at our destination without losing a man, a truck or a single round. We'd covered more than three hundred miles even though we'd wound up less than a hundred and fifty from where we'd started. Once we turned over the ammo and collected Bostwick and Bailey, we could be back in one day if we got a good start and hustled. In seventy-two hours they'd be home with their families. I wondered if they'd been told they were going to be freed and what they were thinking about. Bostwick didn't know yet he'd made major and Bailey had a new kid he hadn't seen.

If Pat Brice and Potter had kept shooting around Saigon, I should be able to wind up the job in another week at most. If the wheels at the Colville Syndicate liked what we'd done, I'd be in good shape to hit them for a permanent job. If I was going to leave the Army and try to make it out in the cold world, I'd have to do it soon before I'd built up so much time toward retirement that it wouldn't pay me to quit until I'd started collecting. Tomorrow might make the difference. If I could get the senator's son-in-law back to his wife, I'd be smelling like a rose. It wouldn't be anything I could put in a résumé but the people who counted would know. All those ifs . . .

I lay there for a bit, puffing away at my pipe dream, when suddenly I stiffened. Something was going on over in Miss Chi's compartment. It sounded as if she was doing something with her chain, trying not to make enough noise to awaken me. If I'd been asleep I probably never would have heard it but I was on guard now, alert for whatever she had in mind.

It wasn't long in coming. By some contortionist's trick she had got the chain wound around herself and here she came, rolling over and over under the truck, unwinding it behind her. The last roll brought her face to face with me and in the faint light that came filtering through the plastic I saw her eyes gleam. She tugged at the closure of the bag and I reached up inside and helped her slide it down. She nipped right in, the chain clinking dismally. I probably shouldn't have but I groped for my slacks and finally found the key. I unlocked the cuff that linked her to the chain and snapped it around my own wrist, tossed the chain aside and zipped up the sleeping bag.

If Miss Chi had ever taken up golf she'd have preferred the courses with the toughest obstacles. The cuffs slowed her down a trifle, and maybe even forced some changes in her game plan, but they sure didn't stop her.

Maybe she got a good night's rest but I sure as hell didn't. No matter how I draped myself, she managed to get a sharp elbow into me and I had to settle for a few short naps. Shortly before dawn I gave it up and unlocked the cuff on my wrist. I hooked her to the chain and let her sleep while I climbed out and sat on a nearby rock. Finally, when the sky began to lighten, I went down the trail to the river and washed up. The water hadn't become any warmer but it made me feel a lot better. When I got back up on the bank The Tiger had a fire going and I started looking forward to a hot cup of instant coffee and a nice slice of papaya. Once I got a little food and drink aboard, I'd be ready to deal with whatever the day might bring.

In the growing light I knelt down beside the fire, enjoying the warmth. The pot came to a boil and I held my cup with the brown crystals while The Tiger filled it to the brim. The smell came up to my nose like a kiss and I started to blow on the coffee to hurry its cooling to the point where I dared take the first sip. I was just about to raise it to my lips when I felt a hand on my arm.

It was Hieu and as I lowered the cup I saw he was staring at the top of the cliff behind me. I followed his glance and if I hadn't been so scared, I might have laughed up a storm. Had it not been so frightening, it would have been funny.

What made it serious was that the men ringing the gorge weren't Geronimo's Apaches. They were good old Vietnamese, each one with a rifle, just standing there watching us.

There wasn't a damn thing I could do about it so I raised my cup again and sipped the hot coffee. Things were about to happen and I was sure I'd need it. Home Run was rounding third and heading for the plate.

⊰ 20 ⊱

It didn't take long for the word to get around among our men. By the time the sky was fully lit everybody was clued in but I can't say it had a hell of a lot of effect on anyone's actions. Like soldiers anywhere, ours just went right on doing their thing until somebody gave them orders to do something else. Fires were lit, breakfast was cooked and eaten, hammocks were unslung and stowed away, and there was a steady parade to the bushes, where the VC handouts were put to their best use. I led Miss Chi to the stream for a morning wash-up and then turned her over to The Tiger for some breakfast. I took down the plastic lean-tos and stowed them away in the panel truck, hoping I wouldn't have to spend another night in that damn mousetrap. Miss Chi finished eating and got busy fixing her face and packing her suitcase. When it was ready she placed it on the ground, ready to go with her when she was handed back to her friends. All this time there had been no movement, friendly or hostile, from the watchers who ringed our little camp.

There were about fifty of them up there, more than enough, since they held the high ground, to handle anything we might be crazy enough to try. I found myself moving slowly and deliberately, unwilling to have any sudden action misunderstood.

They didn't seem to mind a bit when I walked to the edge of the gorge and looked down into the fast-moving water. The level was low now but when the sun lifted a big part of the South China Sea and dumped it on the mountains during the rains, it probably was filled almost to the point where I stood. It must have been quite a sight with enough water to carry away every trace of the old bridge. The gap was narrowest right about where I was standing, not above twenty-five or thirty feet across and widening to more than double that a few yards downstream, where the two sources met.

There was still a lingering trace of the nighttime chill in the air but the sun was rising high enough to begin shining down in the narrow canyon. It looked as if we were going to have a nice day for it if we ever got started. I walked back to where Miss Chi was sitting, with The Tiger close by to keep an eye on her. She was still in her cotton blouse and black pants but there was nothing peasant about the perfume she was wearing. It was the real Parisian product. Knowing Miss Chi, she must have had a good reason to pick today to wear it.

I sat down near her and did all the things I usually do to unwind. I made the muscles at my waist relax and slowed my breathing. It was beginning to work and then I heard The Tiger call softly to me. I looked across to the other side of the river and saw the first signs that something was about to happen.

Around the curve off to the left a pair of men appeared. They were dressed in well-worn khaki with regular GI fatigue caps. Above the cap peak each had a bright blue five-pointed star and one man had three blue chevrons sewn to each sleeve. The first man carried a Garand rifle while the sergeant had an M-1 carbine slung over his shoulder. They walked deliberately along the path that paralleled the rusted railroad tracks, straight toward the rope bridge. They were about twenty yards away when four more men appeared and when I saw them I reached for my new binoculars and focused on them.

The man in front was black, almost as big as John Potter but perhaps a little older. He was in a tattered suit of jungle fatigues, as he had been in the snapshot Fargot had brought, and I didn't need the name tape to know it was Bailey. I swung the binoculars and looked at his companion.

It was the other man in the picture, two bars on one side of his collar, crossed rifles on the other and his name on the tape over his right-hand pocket. He looked a little different in the flesh and

I put it down to the patches of gray I could see now at his temples. It made him look about ten years older than the age I'd been given for Bostwick and I got the idea that he hadn't done as well in captivity as his sergeant. Right behind them were a couple more of the troops with the blue stars and they let the two Americans get about halfway across the open area before they were halted. They were waved to one side and I saw them sit heavily in a little patch of shade while their guards found a place a few yards away.

The sergeant who had led this little procession walked right up to their end of the bridge and there he stopped and waited with the second man.

For a moment the only sound was from the water rushing in the channel and then I heard Miss Chi ask, "Are you satisfied, Mr. Keefe? You have seen the two men. Now shall we begin to unload the trucks?"

I didn't have the vaguest idea of how they proposed to get that done but it wasn't my problem. "You can tell them to go ahead, but remember, Miss Chi: you stay put until I have the Americans. Another thing. If you want to speed things up tell them to start with the last truck in line. That way, when it's empty the driver can get it turned around and gassed up and we won't waste any time getting away from here when the exchange is made. Okay?"

She nodded and called out to the sergeant across the way. I saw him salute and then turn and wave to the two guards. One of them called back toward the curve in the track. There was a moment's pause and then came a double column of women.

That's right, women. There were about fifty of them, dressed like any other Vietnamese country women, neither very young nor very old, but just your usual run of mama sans. They came pattering along the path and when they got to the bridge the sergeant signaled to them to cross. There was no hesitation; the only precaution taken was to space out so that there were never more than three or four on the catwalk at the same time. About every tenth woman wore an armband of the same blue material as the stars; they were probably leaders of work gangs.

When the first of them crossed the bridge Miss Chi called

something to her. The woman nodded her head and started down the line of trucks, leading the pack out of sight from where we waited.

At first it looked as if the whole sorority was going to get to work on our side of the bridge but whoever had organized the operation knew what to do. One gang spaced themselves along the length of the bridge itself while the rest didn't cross at all but waited on the far side, squatting in silence until they would be needed. In a couple of minutes I saw how they were going to work the deal.

From the end of the convoy a stream of women began to arrive at the bridge, pass the cases they carried to the first of the bridge detail and then trot back for more. Each case crossed over, passed hand to hand to the bunch stationed on the far shore. That cut out any back-and-forth traffic on the bridge itself and the need for anyone to return empty-handed and get in the way of those carrying loads.

Apart from an occasional grunt or two, there wasn't an order given or a word said. Whoever had set up the drill had known what they were about and the women worked smoothly as though they had been carefully rehearsed.

While they were moving the lighter loads, the carbine and M-16 ammo, they had it easy enough, but when they got to the heavy rifle cartridges, the pace slowed just a bit. The cases kept right on coming, though. It was getting hotter and I wondered how long they could keep up the work without tiring, but that had been arranged. One by one the women in each gang would step out of line to rest, her gang boss coming in from the sidelines.

Over on the far side the women were taking the boxes as they came off the bridge and packing them over to the side of the track, piling them in neat stacks. As the orderly piles accumulated, it wasn't long before I heard a truck engine starting and the sounds of the vehicle backing up the trail to a point where it could turn. From there it would drive to the spot where the tanker was waiting, gas up and then make room for the next to arrive.

Up on the ridge line the watching men held their positions, barely moving but alert to what was happening below. The two

Americans were still sitting where they had been placed, exchanging a word now and then and sharing an occasional cigarette. Captivity must have taught the captain a whole lot about enlisted men they hadn't put into the curriculum at West Point. Maybe it would make a better general of him someday.

Noon came but there was no slackening in the pace. No one, least of all myself, had any desire for food and it appeared that the Vietnamese were forgoing the siesta they generally take. Both sides were anxious to finish up and separate.

As the trucks at the end of the line were emptied and backed out, the distance shortened so that the cases began to pile up until the women on the bridge could deal with them. At that point one gang on our side was switched to the other. What they were planning I had no way of knowing but it was obvious they were not going to leave the cases there long. When all but the last truck was empty I found out.

The first sign was a squealing kind of sound, high and sort of rasping, that I began to hear far up the canyon out of sight around the bend in the river. It got louder and louder, bouncing off the sheer rock walls that towered above. Pretty soon the squealing was joined by a deeper sort of grumbling rumble and what sounded like a sort of indrawn groan. It built and built and then, just as an ear-shattering howl split the air, I saw, curving around the bend, what had to be the oldest, the most battered locomotive still on its wheels anywhere in the world.

It was a narrow-gauge job, rusty and decayed, its headlight smashed, the last of its paint flaking away from the pitted metal of its slab sides, but moving right along at about ten miles an hour. Someone must have put in a hell of a lot of work on the old thing and while he hadn't wasted a minute on making the old bucket of bolts look any better, there wasn't anything wrong with the way she ran. The big drive wheels gleamed with grease and the squealing noise came not from the engine but from the corroded rails it rode on. Just behind the engine was a flatcar piled high with stacked cordwood to fuel the firebox and after that came a string of eight or ten empty cars.

Gradually the little train slowed as it reached the last sections of rail and then, with a grinding and clashing from the brakes and a loud hiss of steam, it halted. The waiting stacks of cases were precisely in position to be passed up to the cars. Without any command, some of the women clambered up to each car after stopping just long enough to get a drink from one of the water buckets carried along the line. The engineer stood mopping his forehead while the fireman dismounted and checked the cars for hotboxes, adding oil here and there.

I'd been so wrapped up watching all this that I was startled when there was a roar right behind me. The last truck was empty and the driver was starting up and getting into position to turn around and head back up the trail to where the tanker was waiting. It was just about time to make the trade-off, Miss Chi for Bostwick and Bailey.

As the truck finally got around and rumbled off, the last few cases went over the bridge and suddenly the place got a whole lot quieter. Apart from some dyspeptic gurglings from the old locomotive and the noise of the water going over the rocks at the bottom of the gorge, there wasn't a sound. The men on the cliffs above us waited, still on guard, and I just stood there watching to see what would happen next.

As far as I was concerned I'd come through with my part of the deal. The ransom had been turned over and now it was up to the other side. The only card I had left to play was Miss Chi and I really didn't know how much she was worth so I just got a good grip on her arm and held on. All I could do was to keep my eyes open and take care.

On the other side of the gorge I could see the gang of women squatting beside the stacks along the track. The two Americans were still sitting with their guard a few paces away. The sergeant who had been running the operation was walking down the long rows of cases, probably making a rough tally, and when he finished he called out an order and the women began to pass them up to the flatcars.

The work went quickly, and when about half of them were aboard the sergeant called out and Bailey got up and walked across the open space to the far side of the footbridge. He stopped right there and waited as though unwilling to trust his weight to the shaky structure. I felt Miss Chi stir a little.

176

"Are you ready, Mr. Keefe?"

It looked like the next move was mine. I picked up her suitcase in my left hand and, still keeping a good grip on her arm, I walked over to our end.

Bailey called out, "They want you to let her go now."

I shook my head. "Not until I see both of you on the bridge."

He shrugged his shoulders and I saw him say something to the sergeant. He pointed to where the other man was still being held. For a moment we seemed to have hit a stalemate. I wasn't going to let go of Miss Chi until I was certain they were going through with the deal the way I'd agreed. I sure as hell wasn't going to settle for one man and then have to repeat the whole routine to buy back the other.

Finally the sergeant nodded and I saw the other man get to his feet and start walking toward us. I couldn't tell whether he was hurt or sick but he didn't move very fast. Outwardly he looked fine even with his shaggy mop of black hair and unshaved face. He walked steadily toward the bridge, his guard with an M-1 carbine a few paces behind. When he got to where Bailey was waiting, he stopped and looked across, and I could see his glance move from me to Miss Chi.

Suddenly he smiled, the teeth white against the black of his stubble, and I felt Miss Chi tugging at my hand, twisting a little to get free. I called over to him.

"Come on across and I'll turn her loose."

"I think you'd better let her go first."

"For God's sake, man, do as I tell you. I want to make sure you're safe."

I saw him turn and say something to the man guarding him and figured that he was passing on what I'd said. They'd been calling the shots right along and now that we were so close to the finish I wasn't going to take any chance on a double cross. There were still a couple of tricks they could pull and I'd done what I could to be ready for them but as it turned out there wasn't a way in the world I could have been prepared.

It was so completely unexpected that I had to blink hard to believe what I was seeing. The man with the carbine nodded and then, without a word, he calmly handed over his weapon. The big man took it and swung it around and pointed it directly at me. "Let her go."

I guess I just froze up, unable to take it all in. Miss Chi was tugging hard now but I just hung on, hoping that somehow I might be able to make some kind of sense out of the situation. What happened next finally convinced me that I was awake and that all this wasn't just a crazy nightmare.

I saw his right hand go up the carbine and his little finger hook the slide and pull it back to bring a live round into the chamber. Slowly he raised the weapon and sighted directly at my head. When Miss Chi tugged again I released her. She snatched the suitcase from me and started across the bridge, running lightly toward the men on the other side. I saw the carbine pass back to the guard and then watched as Miss Chi launched herself into the man's arms. He swung her up, suitcase and all, and carried her toward the train, stumbling a little as she clamped her mouth to his.

Bailey stood where he had been waiting. He looked across at me and for a moment I thought he was going to say something or even possibly decide all of a sudden to join me. Finally he gave me a last look, waved his big paw of a hand, then swung around and walked quickly toward the others.

I don't know what I had in mind but without thinking I took a step forward. I didn't take another because as my foot hit the ground a shot rang out from high above me on the cliff. I heard a nasty zinging sound as the round hit a rock, raising a puff of dust and freezing me in my tracks.

Miss Chi's voice called out to me. "I think you had better remain where you are, Mr. Keefe. You will know when it is time for you to leave."

I looked up at the men on guard and then slowly turned around. There didn't seem to be any rule about that so, moving slowly, I went over to the panel truck, where Hieu and The Tiger were waiting. Neither one needed to say a thing. We had risked a hell of a lot just to make a present of a million rounds of ammo to a pair of lousy renegades.

Quickly the stacked cases on the ground dwindled and the neat rows on the train piled up. There wasn't anything we could do but sit and watch and be watched. When the last of the cases had been loaded, the women on the ground climbed up and squatted on the stacks, waiting for whatever came next.

That happened over on our side. There must have been some signal that I didn't catch but it set the men on the cliff in motion. They began picking their way down the sheer slope to the road, forming up in two columns. When the last man took his place they started forward to the bridge. There was no sign that they might make any hostile movement but then they didn't need to. They crossed the bridge one rank at a time and lined up beside the train, facing us and clearly on the alert. I saw the two Americans climb to the cab, the white man handing Miss Chi up as though she weighed no more than a five-year-old, and down the line the troops climbed aboard. They continued to keep their eyes on us, even when some took off their blue-starred caps and wiped their brows.

There was a loud clang as the firebox door slammed shut on a new charge of wood. I saw a puff of white and heard the hiss of steam as the engineer released the brake, slid the big lever over to reverse and opened his throttle.

With thirty-five tons of ammo aboard, it took just a moment for the drive wheels to get a bite on the rusty rails and then, with a sudden jerk, the train began to move, increasing its velocity as the end car took the curve and went out of sight. By the time the locomotive got to that point they were rolling right along, making pretty good speed.

Just before they reached the curve I saw the white man lift his hand above his head and, as the engine slid out of sight, I heard the loud, mocking sound of the whistle.

⫷ 21 ⫸

Senator Colville wasn't happy. The senator was downright unhappy and was anxious to find someone to share his mood. If I'd had the option I would have chosen to avoid the senator right then. Sadly I didn't.

All the way down the chain of command my superiors had employed the standard army ploy known as CYA or, to put it into English, Cover Your Ass. My tender tail was the only available target, open and undefended, for the senator's wrath to descend on. Having spent a good many years in public life and risen to his present eminence by the concentrated application of high statesmanship and low cunning, the senator had gained a lot of experience in the handling of his inferiors. Had I been only a bystander, I would doubtless have admired and benefited from seeing his technique.

He did not belong to the bone-crusher school, those who seek to obliterate by a single massive application, nor to the woodpecker type, which employs the steady and rapid attack on a single point. Instead he worked steadily and methodically, seeking out the most vulnerable points in his subject and stamping on them in turn. At the conclusion of the exercise the patient was reduced to an abject mass of slightly quivering protoplasm.

In short, Senator Colville chewed the hell out of my tail.

I felt certain that never in the many years since they had been erected had the hallowed walls of the Royal Hawaiian seen such a going-over. What made it an even more painful experience was the fact that I had to admit he was right. The operation had been loused up clear out of sight and as the man who'd been on the scene when everything went stinking, I was the logical candidate.

Tiny was in the clear. She'd been over in Bangkok, out of the line of fire, so she just sat still and watched the senator at work.

General Truong was on hand but he held his peace, probably noting the senator's technique for what he could learn while watching the bikinied tourist ladies below the window as they enjoyed the delights of Waikiki Beach. He, too, was in the clear.

His son and heir, Captain Hieu, had developed a sudden and intense interest in the pictures that the management had selected to grace the walls of the senator's suite. Still he missed little, if anything, of Senator Colville's portrayal of the famed Captain Bligh of the Royal Navy. There was no escaping the conclusion that if the senator had been given his way, I would already have been triced to the gratings while the master at arms laid on twenty-four of the best. The fact that the cat-o'-nine-tails was not included in the Uniform Code of Military Justice was the only good break I'd had.

When at last the senator began to slow down, Tiny finally remembered that in a well-run army, loyalty is something that goes both ways in the chain of command.

"Senator," she said, "let's be fair. We sent Captain Keefe on a mission that from the beginning had all the marks of a real loser. In spite of a considerable number of obstacles he managed to haul a million rounds of ammunition across a country in the middle of a real, swinging civil war. He got right to the point where he was ready to exchange the ransom for your son-in-law and his sergeant and get them home to their families.

"Now, it seems, the men don't choose to be liberated. For some reason they have decided to stay right where they are. Now that they have a million rounds of ammo for whatever fun and games they've got planned, home doesn't look so appealing.

"That means that we're up to our lower lips in one lousy situation, Senator, but I repeat, let's be fair. Who decided to pass over all those goodies? It sure wasn't Keefe. He did just as he was told and, as far as I can see, he did it damn well until Bostwick pulled the rug out from under him."

Maybe I should have been grateful to her but I hadn't forgotten that she was the reason I'd got mixed up in Operation Home Run in the first place. I didn't say a word while she stood up to Colville.

He stood there with his mouth shut while she had her say. It had been a long time, I suppose, since anyone had spoken to him that way, at least anyone in uniform. While she had him off balance she kept right on coming.

"Keefe was sent to get Bostwick and Bailey out. Everything we told him led to the belief that they wanted to come. Then all of a sudden the rules changed. Your men are the ones who changed them. Now, honestly, did you ever expect anything like that?"

She slammed the question right at him, and it took him by surprise. When he did answer it was in a voice far different than what we'd been listening to, almost as though the words were being pulled forcibly from him.

"Of course I didn't expect it. No one could have. Even with all we know of what happens to men in captivity, brainwashing and all the rest, who could even dream that such a thing might happen?

"There's only one explanation. He's out of his mind. He's got a wife and family who adore him, the respect and admiration of those he works with and every prospect of a brilliant career. Why would he toss all that away to be a guerrilla hiding out in the jungle? Since there's no logical explanation, we just have to assume that he's gone stark, raving crazy. It's a godsend the old general didn't live to see what's become of his only son." He crossed the room and dropped into a chair. "You're right. I never expected anything like this."

Quietly Tiny said, "Then how can you blame Keefe, Senator?"

I'll give him this: he swallowed his medicine like a man. He looked at me and said, "I'm sorry, Keefe. You and Captain Hieu did a damn good job. The fact that it turned out as it did is no fault of either of you. There was no way anyone could be expected to anticipate what occurred."

Tiny stood up and looked around. "Now that we've got that point settled, the question is simply one of deciding what we do now."

Colville looked up at her. "What do you mean? What is there we can do?"

"Well, for one thing, we've still got to get those two back. If they don't choose to come that's their tough luck and maybe it makes the problem a lot harder, but the fact remains that we can't let them stay where they are."

She was right as usual. There wasn't a way in the world that the U.S. Army could afford to let a fifth-generation career officer, an honor graduate of the Academy, married to the daughter of an important government figure, run around loose in the Vietnamese hills. No matter what his horoscope said, he wasn't going to go on leading a midget army of out-and-out bandits, let alone shack up with a local damsel whose hobby was homicide carried out with a sharp instrument on unsuspecting citizens. No way at all.

"Well, Colonel, if the Army wants them back that's your problem. I wash my hands of the whole damn matter."

He stood up and it looked like we'd have to get along without him, until General Truong's soft voice showed that he was there for more than mere entertainment.

"I'm sorry, Senator, but it's not quite so simple. It was only to accommodate you that we took a very considerable risk. We supplied you with what you needed and did all we could to assist your officer in making his delivery. We did it to help a valued friend who has done much to help our country. Now you say that the whole matter no longer concerns you and that you wish, as you put it, to wash your hands of the affair. I am afraid that we cannot permit that without a strong protest and our own action."

"What is it you want to do?"

"Your son-in-law and his confederates now have a million rounds of our ammunition. It is obvious that they will use it in ways that will be dangerous to our own government. To have given such a resource to a bunch of ill-led guerrillas was bad enough. Now we find that they are led by a highly trained professional soldier. Clearly we must take steps to correct the situation."

Tiny said, "What do you plan to do, General?"

Truong fanned open his palms. "We have not much choice.

There will have to be a strong reconnaissance made of the area to locate the shipment before it is too widely dispersed, and then a maximum air strike to destroy it if we can. If that does not work, then there will be nothing left but to take enough troops into the area and kill or capture these men and their leaders by direct assault."

"And do you see any possibility that we can still keep Home Run a secret?"

He shook his head. "I am afraid not. I fear that everyone connected with the matter, myself included, is going to be very embarrassed."

Tiny pressed on. "Now if there was another way, another means of destroying this Blue Star outfit, or whatever they call themselves, would you agree to delay your strike?"

He shrugged. "Naturally if such a possibility existed I would be the first to grasp it, but there is little chance of anything less than a strong force achieving a clear-cut and total success."

"And how long will it take to mount such an operation, sir?"

He thought for a moment. "I can't give you a precise answer until I have consulted with my staff in Saigon but, I can assure you, we will move as quickly as we can. Urgent though the matter is, it might be two weeks or even a little more before we could begin the operation. A plan must be drawn, troops must be found and diverted from other duties into the district in which this Blue Star, as you call them, is established. We will have to gather sufficient intelligence as well—in fact, do all we can to make sure that the outcome will be final and conclusive."

"At least two weeks, then?"

"That would be the shortest time. It might be a little longer."

"But if there was another way to get the same result you'd cooperate?"

He nodded but it was clear he didn't think there was much in her proposal.

"Would you find it useful if we could supply you with the high-level photos we got during the actual exchange?"

I guess my jaw must have dropped. It was the first I'd heard of that.

She had his full attention now. "I'll have them sent to you from our agency. In return we'd like your agreement to our trying our own approach. Your son and Captain Keefe have already shown that they know how to do things in unconventional ways. While you draw your plans and get ready, let them have a crack at it. It won't affect what you're doing and if they bring it off you'll save yourself not only the trouble but also the embarrassment of Home Run being blown. What can you lose?".

She was a real winner, our Tiny. Here she was "volunteering" me again without bothering to let me in on it. That was when my stomach went berserk and began acting like a concrete mixer with a load of oversized rocks. I looked over at Hieu to see how he was reacting to her idea. His face showed nothing but he was watching his father intently. They both had their careers riding on this horse and if it had any chance of coming up a winner they were bound to be tempted.

Truong looked at Colville. "What is your opinion, Senator? If I agree will your government go along?"

It was a tough one for Colville, too. If there was a way to bring off Home Run and keep the whole business under wraps, he had to be for it. It was that or take a chance of trying to weather a full-scale investigation when Bostwick was killed or captured by the ARVN. He had to be enough of a realist to know how slim the chances were that his career could survive that.

"Okay," he said. "I think it's a chance worth taking. I'm in."

Truong and Hieu stood up. The general spoke. "All right, Colonel. You have a minimum of two weeks. Captain Hieu will remain on assignment to your group. We will not interfere but I am afraid I cannot offer more help than that."

He beckoned to Hieu and the two of them left. I thought we'd be going as well but Tiny still had something on her mind.

"Remember, Senator, Keefe's orders will be to bring these men in. If they still don't like the idea he'll have to take what steps are necessary."

"What exactly does that mean?"

"These men are now deserters and very likely traitors as well. Desertion in the face of the enemy is a capital offense."

She had put into the politest words she could find the bald fact that Colville had been unwilling to face. He looked at me and then, almost sighing, he spoke.

"If you must, Captain. If you must."

Tiny and I were crossing the parking lot when I finally got a chance to say something.

"Why didn't you tell me about the air surveillance?"

"Easy. You had no need to know and besides, it was one way to make sure that you wouldn't keep looking up to the sky and showing your profile."

"And what's this great plan you've got for Hieu and me to romp off on?"

"I don't know, Mike, but you've got all the way back to Saigon to think up something."

⊰| 22 |⊱

For what it was worth, the whole Home Run mess had produced one bright spot. While I waited for my flight I phoned the syndicate for word on the documentary. They had already assembled a rough cut and screened it. They liked what they'd seen and wanted more, another film, and they had a suggestion I liked. It wasn't the type of thing that wins awards but it could be made into something important. Basically it went something like this:

For a century the French had kept a virtual monopoly on investments in Indochina. It was their own private bailiwick and hands off to anyone else. Ever since they'd pulled out, the fighting had caused investors to shy away from taking a chance on backing a loser, but with the possibility of peace, maybe it was time to take a new look. The Japanese were already moving in, developing a market and exploiting a prime source of good, cheap labor, natural resources and a central location in the middle of the Asian market.

There were the big rubber and tea plantations to bring back into production, the possibility of oil and metals, and a local economy starving for everything from steel to shoelaces. The French were beginning to edge back in, taking some of the choice orchestra seats, and if they didn't get moving, the Americans were going to wind up in the second balcony if they got in at all. The film was going to show them where the opportunities were, pinpoint the possibilities for development.

They didn't want a chamber of commerce puff piece, though. The syndicate wanted to be sure that I'd show the rough with the smooth. There would be big problems that any new venture would have to face and they couldn't be just brushed aside. The Vietnamese have had a couple of thousand years of doing business their own way and it isn't always the method taught at the Harvard Business School.

I wanted to do the film if there was any way I could work on it while I was trying to sort out the problem of Bostwick and his vest-pocket Blue Star army. You'd think that I already had more than I could handle with just that but I was keeping my eyes open for anything I could do for myself at the same time. I was still going to need the cover anyway and if I had a chance to do myself some good for future use, I wasn't going to fudge it.

I'd had to spend the night in Hong Kong and then catch an early-morning flight into Saigon. Hieu had come home on a military flight and when I got back to the office in the Continental Palace just before noon, I phoned and asked him to come down. Pat Brice, Potter and The Tiger, off doing a short piece on GIs who'd stayed on in Vietnam, had left Miss Binh to hold the fort. She didn't seem to be any the worse for wear after her visit with Miss Chi's friends and the bonus I'd wangled for her had done a lot to cheer her up. Now that her role in the office was out in the open, there wasn't any reason to keep up the pretense that she was just my secretary. From now on she'd be a full member of the team. When Hieu arrived she sat in while he brought me up to date.

"There hasn't been any movement reported up there as yet," he said. "It does stand to reason, though, that they'll make some kind of effort and soon. Bostwick must know that we're going to do something about him before long."

I'd thought about that, too. "My guess is that he's digging in before he tries anything. It can't be long before he's ready."

"We've been studying the reconnaissance material your agency supplied. The railroad is the interesting feature. It runs up to the top of what is actually a long, narrow plateau, a kind of no man's land between the government forces and the VC. On the east our people have built a road with a chain of fire bases that control the terrain right up to the base of the escarpment. From there on it would take mountain troops to make the climb to the top.

"Over on the other side the ground drops away less steeply, tough but climbable by good ground troops. At the base on that side the land is swampy, with a river that winds and twists along and drains the area pretty well except during the rains, when the whole place floods.

"The VC have a main supply route that goes right through there and a number of supply dumps and maintenance facilities. They patrol close in and stay away from the slopes and the plateau itself. As long as they're not attacked they stay away from making contact and keep the peace.

"Most of what we've got on the Blue Star comes from the VC. We've got an agent in place and he says the VC estimate them at about four or five hundred men and as many women. They manage to live off the country and, up to now, they just wanted to be left alone.

"Originally most of them were plantation workers who didn't like the idea of being drafted by either side. With that many of them, it just hasn't been worth the risk of taking casualties for either the VC or our local commander to sweep them up. They knew enough to keep their distance but nobody got around to telling that to Bostwick. He led his company patrol right into them and got chopped up for his trouble."

Hieu's manners were too good for him to mention that the chopping had been done by a ragtag gang of guerrillas facing trained troops. He didn't go into the matter of how and why Bostwick and Bailey had managed to make the switch from prisoners to leaders of the outfit and finally to stage the swindle for their own ransom.

"Do the VC know about the two Americans?"

He nodded. "They know the Blue Star is now led by a big European with black hair and a black man. By the way," he added, "the insignia is something new. The first time they saw it was shortly before the ransom was paid."

"So what we're facing is a homemade army with a few hundred effectives."

"Don't discount the women. You saw their discipline. Even if they aren't armed they're bound to be an active factor in their plans."

"Okay, but no matter how you look at it, they add up to little more than a single battalion. Individual weapons only, no artillery and just the railroad for transport."

"Correct up to a point. They're on their own ground and we have to assume they've built some fortifications. I would say they are at the point where they can fight on a one-for-one basis with good effect."

"In other words, they can take on a fully equipped battalion, ARVN or VC."

"For the moment. With a million rounds on hand they will be able to step up their recruiting. They will probably expand their patrol action and it should not be long before they attempt to capture heavier weapons and equipment."

I said, "Like mortars, recoilless rifles, radios, whatever they can carry?"

He didn't answer but I could see what was in his mind. The logical source of matériel for the Blue Star was the ARVN. Even the terrain made it safer for them to stay away from the VC. The longer the ARVN waited to deal with the situation, the harder it was going to be. With loyalties the way they are in that part of the world, the side that looks like a winner usually gets a lot stronger, snowball fashion. If the situation changes and somebody else looks like he's got an edge, it's easy enough to switch sides, join up with the new contender. The VC liked to think that their people were indoctrinated to the point where their loyalty couldn't be shaken. The record showed differently. Every time the VC took a licking they ran into trouble with their recruiting. I guess that's why the northerners had to get into the fight when it looked as if the ARVN and the Americans were going to win. If the Blue Star began to resemble a viable proposition they might attract a big enough following to become a real factor in the picture. Maybe even big enough to tip the balance one way or the other.

That still didn't give us any idea of what the hell we were going to do.

For starters I followed the old army rule that says when you don't know what to do, it's time to call a meeting. That way you can maybe spread the blame if the action you take goes rotten. I'd had one bad chewing on Home Run and didn't fancy another.

All of us were in on it, Hieu, Brice, Potter, The Tiger and Miss Binh, taking the notes we might need later to explain our reasoning. In other words, CYA. I laid out the setup as far as I knew it. Some things were clear from the start.

First of all, whatever we did was going to be up to us. There wasn't a prayer that we'd get any tactical help from the ARVN. The best we could hope for was an exchange of information and the understanding that unless we got into big trouble, they'd look the other way. That went for our embassy as well. They'd help out only if the operation remained under tight security. If we blew the deal they'd shed us like a dirty shirt.

There was one thing we all realized from the start. This time we would be the ones to make the first move. We'd be the ones to pick the time and the place to make our play. That was about our only advantage and we had to make the most of it. Before we'd just tagged along while Miss Chi called the tune. We could do little but react to what she did. Now the roles were reversed. If we could come up with a plan, it would be up to them to wonder what the hell was happening.

It didn't take long for each of us to contribute the little he had to say. We chewed it around, the ideas getting more and more impossible, while Miss Binh sat with her pencil and pad. In the end it turned out that while the rest of us were thinking in terms of details, she had put her mind right to the root of the problem.

"As I see it," she said, "it will take a great number of men to deal with the Blue Star. Many more men than we can assemble and move to where they must operate."

She paused for a moment as though afraid that what she was about to say might not be understood. Finally she took the bit in her teeth and went on.

"It seems to me that if we cannot get enough men of our own to defeat these guerrillas, then we must get someone to fight for us."

Hieu answered that. "Miss Binh, there can be no commitment of men or even transport from the army. They are scraping the

191

barrel as it is to assemble enough men for their own operation."

"I understand that, Captain, but I was thinking of another source."

I shook my head. "If you mean American troops, then forget it. No help there."

She still didn't give up. "All this I know, but there remains one source from which we can get enough men to attack the Blue Star."

This was getting silly. "Well, then, who do you mean, Miss Binh? There's nobody left but the Vietcong."

"Precisely," she said.

If there's any credit it's hers. It was the first idea we could really work on. There were some bugs and snags but the longer we worked, the more we could see how to make use of some and avoid the rest. Crazy though it was, we had to make it work. There just wasn't anything better.

For a start The Tiger got busy chasing up his crew of ex-Rangers. The whole bunch signed on again, not just for the money but even more for the chance to get in on the action. This time the play was going to be a lot more physical and The Tiger had orders to get every man into top shape before we kicked off. They'd get a short refresher course in the weaponry we'd use and some special training as well.

I still had plenty of the senator's folding money and I used it. Two new trucks were bought and then The Tiger's mechanics got busy making them look old enough to avoid attracting attention while still being sure that everything under the hood was top quality. If we got into a spot where we had to cut and run, I didn't want to lose my fanny because a truck decided to take a sabbatical.

Mr. Tang got an order that made even him blink. I bought a complete outfit for each of The Tiger's men—fatigues, boots, caps, ponchos, canteens, the whole works—plus a lot of extras I thought might come in handy. He had no problem filling the part of the order that called for additional weapons and ammunition plus as much high explosive and detonators as I thought we could handle. I added on a set of small transceivers and some other signal gear, lightweight rations and, in fact, whatever might be of any possible use for contingencies that could arise.

Hieu came up with a good set of maps and Tiny, over in Bangkok, got the right people to rephotograph the whole plateau and the surrounding terrain. Twenty-four hours later a Marine runner marched in with the results. I don't know how they get that kind of detail from sixty or seventy thousand feet but I was tickled to death with the results. Hieu and I spread the mosaic on the floor and knelt over it with the magnifier.

The easiest thing to locate was the railroad track. We found the spot where we'd passed over the ransom and followed the track as it wound its way up through the canyon to the top. When it hit level ground it straightened out and ran for a few miles to a scattering of buildings—a big villa, some smaller houses and a line of warehouses that probably had held the raw rubber until the train hauled it down to a place where it could be sent on its way. It seemed safe to assume that the Blue Star had its headquarters there and the ammunition would be somewhere close by. There was no sign of the locomotive or cars, which had probably been run into a warehouse to keep them out of the weather.

Around the villa what had probably once been lawns and flower gardens were now laid out in the neat rows of vegetable gardens and there were other signs that pointed to freshly dug works of some kind.

We went over the map inch by inch, Hieu identifying various features. Knowing damn well that we weren't going to get more than the single chance, we took our time. If this gimmick didn't work we'd have to pick up any marbles that were left and go home.

Once we had the high spots firmly in mind we took a good look at the surrounding area. Whether the Blue Star had picked the place by good luck or good thinking, either way it was a first-rate location. The plateau was big enough for elbow room yet small enough to defend with a limited force. There's no such thing as an impregnable position but this place met most of the requirements.

Actually it was a flat-topped ridge that ran almost twenty miles on a generally southeast-to-northwest line. At the widest point it wasn't over five or six miles wide, with sheer cliff on both sides and the plantation buildings between. At both ends of the plateau the level dropped away into a tangle of gorges and canyons with fast-running mountain streams tumbling over rocks and tangles of dead trees. Even a force with armor and siege guns would have slow going climbing to the top if a few men, well led, wanted to dispute the way.

The eastern side dropped down into the narrow buffer zone that lay beside the new ARVN road, the supply route to the troops in the highlands. Every few miles you could see a fire base, a company or so of troops well dug in to keep the road under control without attempting any offensive action. There was a small market town that was under government control, marked by a belt of well-tended fields protected by the guns of the army. Less than ten miles away were the VC.

Identifying their positions on the west side of the plateau took an expert like Hieu but even I could see the general layout. The new road they'd built was well camouflaged but it was easy enough to see that in general it followed the banks of the river that flowed in a series of curves to the south. In places the VC had shortened the route by building timber bridges across the shallows, each bridge with what Hieu said was an antiaircraft position to discourage any low-flying plane that might try to bomb or strafe the crossing. At the point where the river had come to a line opposite the widest part of the plateau it turned away, the road still running beside it and feeding the network of trails that supported the VC effort in the district as the tactical situation demanded.

According to the intelligence that Hieu received, neither side wanted to make any breach of the peace. They weren't armed or staffed for anything more than a simple holding operation, keeping their section of their supply routes open and flowing smoothly. That's where the Blue Star had found a home, smack in between the two bigger kids. As long as they didn't get in the way they were left to themselves. If it hadn't been for Bostwick and his patrol they might have stayed there forever.

Over the years the three factions had worked out some unwritten but generally accepted rules of behavior. The ARVN patrolled from the road to the foot of the escarpment on the rare occasions when they ventured out of their fire bases. Traffic on the road was allowed to move freely, at least in daylight hours. Because of the terrain the ARVN knew little of what was happening up on the plateau, rarely, if ever, sighting any of the people who lived there.

Over on the other side conditions were a little different. Partly that was because of the nature of the VC situation. The supply route there was a lot more complex. Besides the road we had seen in the aerial photos, there was a whole network of minor trails, used as demands increased or the rains rendered other routes unusable. Trucks could use the road and its bridges only during the dry season. When the rains came and the river rose out of its banks, the loads were shifted to light transport, bicycles or man-packing along the trails that stayed on the higher ground. It was there that the VC occasionally met up with the Blue Star. The parties would make visual contact at some distance and it was the rule that both sides would immediately withdraw and move back to their own ground. The presence of the two Americans had been noted and reported for several years but it had caused no change in the ground rules established under the previous management. On occasion a few women would turn up at the VC encampment to trade fresh fruit, meat or vegetables for cigarettes or other negotiables but rarely, if ever, for cash, and the assumption had been that they came from up on the plateau.

That was the situation we were getting into. Nobody wanted to fight. Not the ARVN, who had their orders to stick to their job and guard the road, leaving rougher games for the boys who were trained to play them. Not the Blue Star, at least for the time being, for they wanted to consolidate what they had and build their strength for bigger things at a later date.

Most of all not the VC. They'd put in a lot of time and effort pushing their route through the area. The bridges especially. They'd been built of materials cut and hauled mostly by man-power from a considerable distance in order to preserve the natural camouflage that screened their work from the air. If the bridges were to be attacked and destroyed it would not only choke the supply line but would put a major strain on the VC resources while they assembled men and materials to replace them. Intelligence put the VC commander's force at about fifteen hundred to two thousand effectives, supported by mortars and mountain guns, and if the bridges were attacked he'd react with every man and every gun he could muster. Only as long as he was left alone would he sit still and observe the modus vivendi.

There couldn't have been a plan much simpler than ours. All we had to do was kick the stool out from under him and make him think it was one of his neighbors.

⊰ 23 ⊱

More in hopes of changing our luck than anything else, we asked for a new operational name. I asked for Benedict but Tiny turned that down as being in bad taste and a possible reason for embarrassing questions. In the end we settled for Posse. Every night we worked on Posse, while the days were devoted to the cover. Hieu had tapped the right ministry and we were supplied with an expert guaranteed to know all the details of what was hoped might become Vietnam's economic miracle.

Professor Lien, like a lot of well-educated Vietnamese, was a Catholic, which had not interfered a bit with his youthful Marxist convictions. Born in the North, he'd been there when the French had left. Despite his two university degrees, one from the Sorbonne, he'd joined the Vietminh and had served until the peace in staff positions.

When he'd been mustered out he'd wanted a suitable job in the new government but had to settle in the end for the position of principal in a small-town lycée. Still he had high hopes for his country under the new regime and it took a while before he realized that what he'd understood of Marx wasn't quite the same thing Uncle Ho had in mind. When the directives on the new education began to arrive, he protested just long enough to realize how futile the effort was and then made his decision.

Lien gathered up his family and as many of their possessions as they could carry and headed south. They made it with a lot of luck and a good wind at their backs. No sooner did they arrive than the Bamboo Curtain came down with a crash.

197

He never referred to that time directly but it must have been rough. I'm sure that the first work he got had a lot more to do with his muscles than his two degrees. The South was packed with well-educated men who had fled from the northern version of liberation, most of them, like Lien, without resources beyond their ability to work at anything that would bring in a little rice.

Finally Lien had got a minor ministry job and that, with the two other jobs he held down at the same time, provided enough to bring him up to the poverty level. At Hieu's suggestion I proposed an honorarium for services that would make up for what he lost from his moonlighting while he worked for the syndicate.

Every morning he would arrive, settle himself at a desk in the outer office and begin to put in a day's work out of which there emerged a good shooting outline complete with notes that would be used in the narration. I worked right along with him, and I mean I worked. Tiny had made it clear that the cover had to be absolutely watertight, and Lien-tight as well. Not that there was anything wrong with him or doubtful about his trustworthiness. It was just that the day might come when we'd need him to swear that as far as he could see, we'd been doing nothing more incriminating than making a film that might be a big help to his country. Maybe it was a dirty trick to play on a nice guy like Lien but it was even tougher on me. I was trying to do two full-time jobs without letting him in on the second. We didn't even dare mention the name Posse in his presence. I'd send Lien home at five and then huddle for half the night with Hieu and The Tiger, getting reports from both. The Tiger was building some special equipment we'd be using as well as training his troops, while Hieu was gathering every last scrap of intelligence and making plans for our trip upcountry. By coincidence our first location site would be the market town near the Blue Star's plateau. By coincidence.

We never did get all the time we wanted. When Hieu came in with word that the date for the ARVN plan had been set, we had less than ten days to work with. We kicked off Posse thirty-six hours later.

We rode out to Tan Son Nhut right after daylight for the first leg of the trip. The Tiger was already at the airport, with the camera and sound equipment, for the flight to Dalat, the nearest town we could get to by air. He'd been up there and everything was supposed to be ready for us—vehicles, drivers and a place to stay in the nearest town. That is if we could get there via the friendly skies of Air Vietnam.

Even before I started up the ramp I was sweating freely but it was nothing to the gallonage I produced inside the cabin. Our fellow sufferers were largely women and kids, with a sprinkling of the local military and the usual assortment of pets and smaller livestock, pent but not silent in a variety of containers, and all doing their bit to reduce the oxygen and increase the aroma, already rich with garlic, nuoc mam and the body odors of those who eat them. With the outside temperature in the nineties and 99.9 percent humidity, we zoomed toward the pain threshold as the flight crew struggled to get revenue from every cubic inch in the battered DC-3. When at last there was not even room to add the acting company of a flea circus, the door was slammed shut and we came to a rolling boil as the pilot tried to convince his starboard engine that it really wanted to make the trip with the rest of us. We lurched across the tarmac to the runway, had a narrow miss with an F-4 coming in a shade too fast, and then were treated to five minutes of tooth-rattling as the pilot made up his mind about the wisdom of calling the whole thing off. Finally he rolled forward and onto the strip, built long enough for 747s, and used it all to coax his steed into letting go of Mother Earth. The woman in the window seat next to mine put up her rosary and an hour later we were in Dalat.

The car and the panel truck The Tiger had hired a few days before were on hand and while the others loaded up, Lien and Hieu and I went into the little café to get a cold drink. Lien, for all his Asian reserve, was all wound up and eager to get to work. He had got himself to the point where he was seeing our documentary as the force that would bring a flood of American investment dollars to unify and enrich his people.

"You see, Mr. Keefe," he explained, "everything must be planned with a number of factors in mind. When these have been defined, then we can know how to use our resources.

"First there is the need to select those things which will produce quick results. We must forgo long-range projects if only so that our people will be encouraged to go forward with good heart. After all, they are our greatest asset if they are willing to work hard, employing all their ancient and new-learned skills."

He really talked like that and he really believed in what he said.

"Too many of our people have been driven from their land and forced into the degrading life of the slums. Family ties are coming apart as our youth are forced to live by their wits and many are entering into a life of crime.

"These people do not produce for the good of all but only drain our economy. To feed them we must for the first time in our history import rice. This should not be. Now we must take these people who have been urbanized by the war and return them to the healthy and productive life on the land. One way is to offer them work in small factories near their homes where they can earn a living while their fields are once more made fertile. Hard work and hope will do far more than mere charity. We are a proud people and while we are grateful to our friends, we do not like to beg for rice."

If he'd been half as good in front of a blackboard as he was riding along in the back of the car, he must have been one hell of a teacher. As it was, I could only give him part of my attention as we drove through Dalat and south on the road out of town. I've spent some time there and I sure hated to push on without getting a chance for a good meal, but I had to settle for the view out the car window. The professor had a full head of steam now with his captive audience and I did learn a few things.

Lien claimed that the way to start things rolling was to channel foreign capital into the two basics, rubber and tea. First get the existing plantations back into production and then plant more. Both provide part-time work for men and women, tea three years after it's planted and rubber a couple more. If the investor would provide jobs, the government could provide land for the workers. The reason we were there in the highlands was to document that kind of project.

Saigon, it seemed, had come through with money for a pilot project and we'd film it as far as it had gone. I was a little excited about it myself.

The Tiger had lined us up in a nice little country hotel, not up to Holiday Inn standards but decent enough and clean. The food was good and the staff caught on quickly to our habits and quit giggling whenever we appeared. We settled in and got to work. I decided to put Lien on film and after a short bout of stage fright, he loosened up and began spouting his own brand of economic salvation like a star graduate of Oral Roberts U.

We finished the third day of shooting and rode back to town. I was just returning to my room from the shower when The Tiger came in to report.

The trucks had arrived from Saigon and we were ready to go.

Rubber doesn't do well at elevations over about two thousand feet and that's where they begin planting tea. That was the last thing Lien reminded me of before he caught the bus that would take him back to answer a summons from Saigon. For what we'd be doing next we didn't really need him. Hieu had arranged it so that Lien wouldn't be exposed to the horrid facts of Operation Posse.

The area we were driving through proved that Lien was right. The orderly rows of rubber were replaced by the shrubby tea plantations, small parties of pickers visible working among the bushes. With most of my attention on the map spread out on my lap, I didn't have a lot of time to watch them. Off to my left was the sheer rise of the cliffs that marked the border of the Blue Star's domain and a few miles farther west the VC were presumably happily doing their own thing. It was a nice, clear day, lots cooler than Saigon's normal level, a few clouds tastefully placed in the sky.

It took us almost an hour to get past the cliffs and the road we were on began crossing a number of small streams that drained away to feed the river over on the VC side of the plateau. Hieu was driving the sedan while The Tiger followed a short way back in the panel job. Hieu slowed down as we got close to our objective and when I spotted a fair-sized bridge ahead, he pulled up for a minute to make sure we had the road to ourselves before he swung left and followed a trail along the small river that the bridge crossed. I looked back and saw The Tiger turn in behind us and follow along until we were out of sight of the highway. The trucks were there, the ex-Rangers sitting and waiting for us in the shade.

Hieu braked and The Tiger halted right behind him. I waved to him to go ahead with it. He called out to his squad leaders and in a minute the truck doors were open and the cargo began coming out. With only a couple of hours of light left, we had a lot to do.

First thing was to get busy and assemble the rafts. I'll be the first to admit that they wouldn't take any prizes at a boat show but they would do the work. They were nothing more than empty steel drums lashed together inside a bamboo framework, with a plywood deck and a steering oar or pole at the stern. I wouldn't want to shoot Lachine Rapids on one but they weren't going to be called on to do that.

We made it by dark, with time for some food and a last check on equipment. The rafts were in the water, the supplies aboard, both trucks were gone, following the panel truck and The Tiger to the next point on their route. I had one more short argument with Pat Brice before he gave in and drove the sedan away. He couldn't see why he had to miss the party when John Potter was coming along. There was still a lot left for him to handle and if I did take him he'd do little more than occupy space and maybe get in the way and get hurt. The way we were set up, every man had a slot to fill and there just weren't any reserves or supernumeraries to work with. Finally he got in the sedan and drove off in the last of the daylight, and as the sound of his engine died in the distance, the silence settled down like a curtain. We'd passed the point of no return. For better or for worse, Operation Posse was committed.

There's a lot of twilight up in the hills and that evening seemed to be extra long. We'd reviewed the map and the plan so many times that I was beginning to worry that perhaps we'd gone too far and overtrained. Hieu was as antsy as I was and I saw him talking with each of the men who would ride on his raft just as I had with mine. Potter had checked his supplies, making sure that everything was right where he could put his hands on it even in the dark. I don't know where he'd got it but someone in Saigon had sold or lent him a riot gun and he kept hefting it to find the

202

best balance point when he opened up with it. Finally I checked my watch and gave the signal to put out the fires and board the rafts. Hieu and I stood on the bank as the men climbed down and took their places.

Everything considered, the rafts themselves were a success. With a dozen men and their equipment plus the other supplies on each, they rode well, high enough to keep everyone's feet dry and stable enough as long as nobody made any violent movements. If it all went according to plan, they'd get us where we were going and out again. If they didn't, it wouldn't be because the rafts lacked fresh paint and shiny brasswork. That you can leave to the weekend yachtsmen.

When everyone was in place, Hieu and I climbed down and stepped aboard, each of us at the stern of his raft. The steersmen cast off and then rammed their poles against the bank to shove us out to where the current could start us moving downstream. I saw the branches overhead begin to move away and another shove of the poles took the two rafts along, still tied together until it was time to separate.

⊰|24|⊱

There wasn't anything very special about the plan, no fancy capework or real attempt to do major damage. All we wanted to do was stir the hornets up and get them mad so they'd start stinging anybody they could get at. We'd need only enough light to see what we were doing and to let them get an occasional quick look at us. Quick mainly so they wouldn't have time to open fire. Just a nice hit-and-run attack with lots of noise.

We rode the rafts down to the point where it met the main river and then I signaled to swing in to the shore. We landed the two shore parties and then got busy on the last few details. Potter and Hieu began arming the bridle charges—pairs of floating bundles with a detonator and a block of high explosive. A light piece of rope connected the pairs so that if they were dropped just upstream of a bridge pier they'd catch and swing together before the time fuse blew them. There really wasn't any reason to expect they'd do much damage but they were bound to call attention to the fact that somebody must be after the bridges.

Shortly before dawn, I hopped ashore and looked over the troops. They were quiet but you could see they were all geared up for the festivities. The blue stars on their caps looked right and so did the chevrons The Tiger had awarded to his NCOs. To my eye they looked like a bunch of Bostwick's troops and of course that was just what we had in mind. The half light just before dawn would help, too.

Hieu called softly to me. His charges were ready and Potter indicated that he was set also. I got back aboard the raft and gestured to the shore parties. Time to go. Hieu's raft was cast loose and he went sailing off to catch the current in the main river and then work over to take the channel on the right. If everything timed out everybody would be in position and ready to go when his initial charge signaled the kickoff. That would be the cue for the first shore party to start working along close to the river and opening up on any target they could spot. It would also tell me to get moving along the left-hand channel, hitting the bridges there and letting the VC get a good look at Potter and at me. Finally the second shore party would set out, using the higher ground away from the river and trying to look like the main body of a big force. That was the whole plan and it was taking every man we had. If it didn't work it wouldn't be because we hadn't tried.

We had a couple of minutes to wait and Potter and I squatted down on the raft. There was just one man at the stern with a pole to guide the thing and another at the front end to keep an eye on the river ahead. I pulled the shaggy black wig out of my pocket and tugged it over my head. It had a musty kind of smell but it would make me look enough like Bostwick, particularly in a bad light and in the heat of the attack. It was getting lighter now and I started to worry that something might have happened to Hieu. If he delayed much longer it would be bright enough to expose us. Then it came, a big, bass-drum kind of detonation, made louder by the stillness it broke. Without a word the man at the stern cast off, rammed his pole into the bank and shoved. The current caught us and we were on our way.

Off to the left the crackling of small-arms fire showed that the first shore team was in action and trying to call attention to itself. The raft was in the main river now, the man at the stern still poling. There were long streamers of mist draped just above the surface, making it hard to see very far, and I began to worry that we might miss our channel and get into the one Hieu had taken, where everybody was wide awake. We were rounding a long, sweeping bend where the river had cut away at the bank when we saw the left-hand channel. The man up forward rammed his pole over the side and we just cleared the point and got on the right road.

The bend continued and then, through the mist, I saw the first bridge. It was just a rough timber affair, made of trees cut right in the neighborhood, crossing the river in two spans held up by log piers in the water. There was bound to be a guard there but he wasn't in sight from the raft. Potter bent down and armed the first pair of charges and just before we passed beneath the bridge he tossed them. As we went under the span I could hear the sound of feet running on the planks. The man at the front end of the raft heard it, too, and he swung his weapon up one-handed and opened fire. There was the thud of lead slamming into the timber and then a burst of flame as I swung up my own weapon and fired, full automatic, for the best effect. I saw a pair of startled faces and a glimpse of a machine gun on the bank, its crew struggling to depress the barrel to fire down at us. We were about fifty feet out into the clear when the charges blew, one after the other, raising a column of water that showered down on the soldiers shooting from the bridge. The man at the stern dropped his weapon and heaved against the bottom with his pole and we went around another bend and out of sight.

There was still plenty of noise from the shore where the first team was staying pretty much parallel with our course down the river and from the rear I heard the second squad doing their bit to add to the confusion. I closed my eyes for a moment, trying to call up the aerial photos I'd studied so hard and long. In the confusion and with the mist, it was difficult to estimate just how far it was to the next bridge, but then I got a break.

The ack-ack team at the bridge must have got a little confused about where the attack was coming from. They opened up with the heavy machine gun and a stream of tracers arched up into the sky, marking the spot for us. They were so busy, in fact, that they never saw us below them. The charges were armed and we were under the bridge before they spotted us. One hero started firing with a pistol and a round actually reached the raft, raising a few splinters but nothing else.

By luck the second charges had hit just right. Maybe this bridge hadn't been built as well as the first, but in any case, when they blew there was a moment's pause and then the entire center of the bridge went, collapsing the span into the river.

Along the whole stretch of river we could hear the crackling of small-arms fire as our two shore parties blazed away and the confused defenders replied, shooting blindly in their attempts to locate the attackers. The sustained rattle of machine guns was punctuated by a deeper pair of bass-drum effects as the bridle charges blew, one after another, followed by the wrenching noise of the superstructures slowly collapsing into the stream. By the time our raft had passed the third of our bridges the whole VC camp was alive and shooting, even those clear back upstream where we had launched the first attack.

We had got by the first two bridges without any problem but at the third everyone was wide awake. When we went under the span someone spotted us and opened up on the raft, raising a shower of splintered bamboo until the charges blew and threw him from his feet. There had been a dull booming sound from beneath the deck as a stray round slammed into one of our empty drums but the raft continued to float well up in the water, riding the current around the bend that took us out of sight.

For a minute or so we got a brief respite where the river straightened out for a few hundred yards before making its next swinging curve.

It was getting lighter now and as we approached the next bridge we could see a sandbag emplacement for an antiaircraft heavy machine gun, and its crew struggling to depress the barrel and fire down at us. Potter was on one knee and I saw him swing his riot gun up, pause a moment to aim, and squeeze off a round. There was an ear-shattering *blam* as the gun recoiled from its charge of heavy buckshot, then a bright flash on shore as the ammunition of the machine gun exploded. We tossed the last of our charges and I grabbed for my M-16. We went under the bridge and I fired almost blindly at the first man I saw kneeling above us on the shore. I wasn't trying for any fancy sharpshooting but just let go with the full clip before reversing the magazines and looking for a fresh target.

The man at the stern was poling hard, rocking the raft and making it almost impossible to take aim had there been any target to shoot at, but at the rate we were moving the range opened quickly and then we were in the clear.

Off to my right I heard Hieu's last charge go off and I yelled to our bow man to pole toward the right bank and the point where the two channels joined up. Just before we reached it the other raft emerged and its steersman struggled to head it in our direction. They were a shade too far ahead to lay alongside us but the man rammed his pole into the bottom, braking their raft and allowing ours to come up on the left. Hieu tossed over a line and Potter scrambled for it and tied off. Together the two rafts picked up speed as the channel narrowed to pass close under the cliffs ahead on our left.

There was a grove of trees there and I knew from the aerial photos that it marked the place where the road left the river and changed direction away from the plateau. Under the trees I could just make out ten or fifteen trucks, probably waiting for full daylight to resume their trip. The drivers were milling around, trying to crank up and get away from the sounds of firing, making no attempt to defend the place but hell-bent to get loose. Potter and I began firing, mostly for the morale value but, low as we were, without doing much damage until, from across the river on our left, a volley rang out.

It was our shore party, joined up now and waiting for us to arrive. One man with a grenade launcher was using his head. He raised the weapon and, ignoring the drivers, fired directly at the nearest truck. There was a loud crumping sound as the grenade detonated and a second as the fuel tank went in a ball of flame and black, greasy smoke. The rest of the men followed suit and by the time we had poled the rafts to the place where they were waiting a couple of other trucks were aflame, fuel and cargo contributing smoke to blanket the scene. Potter snatched at a low-hanging branch and held on long enough to let the men scramble aboard and then, with a powerful thrust, shoved the rafts free. The polers dug in and then the current caught us and we went flying past the point where the road and the river separated, out of range of the last defenders. Our fire stopped and the men lay back to catch their breath, smiling at the sounds of firing still coming from the camp upstream.

I looked them over quickly and counted noses. We hadn't lost a man and the few who had been hit were making it under their own power. Behind us I could see a tall column of smoke still rising but there was no sign of close pursuit. It wouldn't be long before they got sorted out, though, and launched their counterattack. We had to dispose of the rafts and start making tracks.

There were still a couple more miles to cover on the river and Potter opened the first-aid kit and did what he could for the wounded men to make them fit to travel the rest of the way to safety.

Hieu was watching the channel up ahead. The dawn breeze was snatching at the streamers of mist and improving visibility. When he saw the river begin to widen and swing to the right away from the high ground, he signaled to the polers to slow the rafts. A few hundred yards farther and we saw the place we were headed for, a marshy tangle of trees and shrubs standing in the shallows along the bank on our left. The polers got the rafts pointed right into the place and as we went under the low branches some of the men jumped into the water. A couple of minutes' tugging and hauling got the rafts far enough back to be invisible from the banks. I took a last look around to make sure we had everything, checked my weapon, then stepped off into the water and headed ashore.

The men didn't need any orders to follow right along behind us. In five minutes we were all on dry land, closed up and making good time. The VC had had plenty of chances to get a good look at us and by now their commander knew that a big European and a black man had led a bunch wearing blue stars in a raid on his position, breaking the unofficial truce and begging for rapid punishment. If he knew his business he'd take steps to get right out and take care of it.

For the first half hour I set a pretty good pace to get clear of the area and on our way while I watched the terrain ahead, trying to remember the aerial photos and pick the best route. We were moving through a stretch of big hardwoods, the ground dry and firm. I kept working my way to the left, to get as close to the cliffs as I could and still have good footing. It wasn't a pace we could keep up for long and I began to look for a place where we could take a breather without danger of being surprised. We had just crossed a little stream that came tumbling down over a slippery, rocky bottom and on the far side I saw a good place. There was a big curtain of vines hanging from the bigger trees on the bank and a few seconds' work with a machete made an opening through which we could pass. The men ducked in and then dropped to the ground, too beat to smoke or talk. I stayed in the open, squatting at the stream bank, using my binoculars to look back for any sign of pursuit. By now the VC commander and his staff would have made sense of the reports they'd received and got something moving. Even a child could have seen the route we were following through the camp, with the burning trucks clearly marking the last place we'd hit. Somewhere beyond that point he knew he'd find us if he could send his patrols out quickly enough to get more information. His problem was to narrow the search by determining the available routes and trying to move his men into position to block our escape to what I hoped he thought was the base up on the plateau.

Even with the binoculars there wasn't a whole lot I could see through the trees. Finally I let the glasses drop to my chest and scrambled through the gap in the vines. I dropped to the soft ground and someone handed me an open canteen. The others were still breathing hard after the breakneck trip through the camp and the forced-march pace we'd set on the rising ground. I fought down the temptation to stay in that nice, secure little spot, let the pursuit go past and then take the chance to get to our destination.

There was one thing I knew I had to be careful about. I had to assume that the VC commander was as smart as I was. He was bound to be suspicious as hell right off the bat because the whole attack had been such a crazy stunt to pull. If the masquerade had worked, he would be wondering why the Blue Star had suddenly decided to break the truce. He was sure to speculate on whether the whole thing hadn't been just a ruse to draw his counterattack into an elaborate trap of some kind. He'd move as carefully as he could, watching to see what we'd do next. What might convince him would be our route leading to one of the trails up to the top of the plateau. If he needed information to establish that, then it was my job to supply it.

Much as I wanted to just lie there and rest, there wasn't any time for mere pleasure. I lay flat on my back, sucking in all the air I could hold and counting slowly to fifty, and then made myself get up. I called to Potter and Hieu and told them in a few words what I had in mind. We gathered up what weapons could be spared and all the extra ammunition we could carry, then pulled back the vines and took off. The others had orders to wait until they heard the sound of firing on the slopes above and then proceed alone for the rendezvous. They were to stay out of sight, even if it slowed them up, and under no circumstances try to help us. We'd be on our own.

Our route lay up the slope, away from the one the rest would take. At first we stayed pretty close together, scouting the ground ahead for the best place to set up shop. It took a little time to find a spot with a good open field of fire yet enough concealment for us to be able to withdraw without taking any curtain calls after the performance. Finally we fanned out a bit to cover more ground and it was Potter who turned up what we were looking for. It took only a minute to agree on what we'd do and then Hieu moved back down the slope about fifty yards while we started setting the stage.

Right at the base of the vine-draped cliff was a litter of big rocks, slabs that had fallen from above to land at all kinds of crazy angles. Most of them were big chunks about the size of a car or truck, the kind of layered sandstone that tends to split into big flat sheets. Potter and I dug in, piling up the smaller pieces into little strongpoints, three for each of us, about ten feet apart. We placed a weapon at each, loaded and ready to fire, while Hieu was busy getting his own setup ready, using the materials at hand.

It was hard work and, with the sun rising, I was sweating by the time I had things the way I wanted them. I took a moment to rest, feeling the warmth of the sun on my face and fighting the urge to close my eyes for a quick cat nap. There was still work to do if we were going to carry this off and not get caught in our own mousetrap.

From my prone position there wasn't much to be seen of the slopes below, where we could expect our company to come into sight. I let Potter know what I was going to do and then got up and began to climb even higher, clambering over the slabs and

211

trying to keep my balance when a couple of them teetered under me. I kept checking back over my shoulder but it was several minutes before I got to a place where I could see the sun glinting on the river far below. I settled my tail where I wouldn't have a rock stabbing me and unslung my binoculars. With both elbows propped on my knees, I held the glasses steady on the river, scanning what I could see of it for the slightest movement. From there I switched to the open ground, searching for any sign at all. It didn't take long to find something.

There was a quick flash of light and I focused in on it, to see someone doing just what I was, a man in a sun helmet, his own binoculars sweeping back and forth. I held my position just long enough to see him zero in on me and then slid down, waving wildly in both directions, yelling at Hieu and Potter to start the show. John raised himself to full height and fired his riot gun, making sure that while he was aiming in Hieu's direction he didn't do any real damage. The sound of the heavy ten-gauge echoed and reverberated from the cliff and as Potter dropped behind a rock Hieu rose up and fired a short burst before dropping back and scuttling, under cover, to another position and another type of weapon. Now it was my turn to get into the act. I showed myself and fired a few rounds and for the next couple of minutes we did as nice a rendition of a hot fire fight as Hollywood could stage. If it was working as we wanted it to, then the observer would have to conclude that there were at least a dozen men engaged, the rear guard of the Blue Star fighting off some VC trying to cut them off from the route to the top.

We kept popping up and firing, Hieu occasionally doing a stirring rendition of a man being hit, then falling into a place where he could crawl, unseen, to another firing point. While I fired I did some quick calculation. I tried to be careful since if I missed my estimate by very much, we might wind up letting the audience get too close.

I'd timed our climb up and based on that I thought I could predict how long it would take the comrade captain down there to get his men on the scene, deploy them and open fire. We had to maintain the act long enough to have him coming up at top speed and still leave just enough time to slide out and make our escape. The VC would be looking for us to go for a trail to the top and, with any luck, we'd be able to take off to the south, across the slope to our rendezvous with The Tiger and the rest of the men.

To tell you the truth, I goofed.

The VC knew the terrain a lot better than I, probably because it was part of his regular patrolling area. His men were still fresh, too, and they made it up to the scene a hell of a lot faster than I'd figured.

Anyway, he came right along fast and the next thing I knew, his forward element was in sight about a hundred and fifty yards away down the slope. I yelled to Hieu to warn him that we'd let them get too close and, if we were going to get out of there, we'd have to make a fast change in plan. That meant only one thing. We'd have to run like hell and hope to God we could make it before they could catch us.

Hieu didn't see it that way. He got up and let them see him and began firing off to his left, completely away from where Potter and I were lying. He repeated his getting-hit act and wiggled to another place and got up to fire again, away from us. There was a shout from the men below and I saw Hieu turn as though he were seeing them for the first time and was glad for the help. He pointed off to his left and started yelling in Vietnamese as the first squad came in sight. They stopped dead in their tracks, clearly wondering how some of their own people had got so far ahead. Hieu kept yelling and pointing, finally taking a few steps in that direction and then lifting his weapon and firing a burst. I tried to help out by firing from cover, shooting at the rock above so that the rounds would ricochet and sing where they hit.

Hieu yelled a third time and then, as I fired, he "died" again. That got the squad moving and they formed a ragged skirmish line, crouched down and began to trot in the direction Hieu had indicated. The second squad, just coming into sight below, saw the first bunch moving and they swung out and formed a second line on the flank.

Right about then, just like in anybody's army, some idiot opened fire at a monkey or a falling leaf or maybe a shadow and that was all it took to get the whole outfit involved. In a few

213

seconds I heard the sounds of firing all the way down the line and it kept up smartly as the men moved into the trees and out of sight.

We didn't hang around for them to discover their mistake. We kept down and worked our way across the slope, heading south and using the big rocks for cover until we got into the brushy growth toward the base. The distance between us and the patrol grew but we kept moving, even picking the pace up a little when the sound of the "battle" ended. How long it would take the VC captain to figure out what had happened was anybody's guess. So was the question of what he'd do next.

I had my second wind and we were all moving along at a fair speed when I pulled up and raised my hand to keep the others quiet. They heard it, too, a new sound, several miles away at least, and different in tone from the snapping and cracking of small arms. We all knew what it was and Hieu put it into words.

"They've made contact," he said.

He had to be right. The VC had come far enough up the slope to come in contact with Bostwick's outposts. When they'd opened up with small arms the VC had brought up their heavier stuff and we were hearing it now. This was the authoritative sound of mortars and rockets or even recoilless light artillery. They would sit back out of the range of the Blue Star weapons and begin pounding their way up, reducing each strongpoint that tried to resist. As long as we heard those sounds we'd know that Bostwick was still holding out. When they stopped it would mean that either the VC had reached the top or that Bostwick had beaten off the attack. It didn't make much difference either way.

The VC couldn't take the risk that after a good spanking he might not come back again. They'd bring up more force until he was finally dislodged. That would be when Bostwick and Miss Chi and Bailey and anyone else still able to move started to pull back along the top of the plateau. They'd take what they could carry and retreat until—

Until they ran into us.

⊰ 25 ⊱

Potter and the men who'd followed him around the bend in the canyon wall were gone only a few minutes and when they came trotting back I'd done everything I could think of to get ready. He called out that he was all set and I waved him and the others up to their positions. I took a last look around to make sure that we were well hidden to all but helicopters or eagles. Even I, knowing where my men were hidden, couldn't spot a thing and finally I climbed up to where I could get the best view of the whole layout. All we needed now was patience. Patience and lots of luck.

Not everything you learn in the Army comes from the manuals. One thing you realize right away is to relieve yourself any time you get the chance because it may be quite a while before you get another. The same thing goes for eating, not only for the obvious reasons but also because it makes the time pass quicker. I'd already taken care of the first item and once I got settled in I dug out a carton of C ration and opened it. I used the little block of smokeless fuel on a handy rock and when the gravy started to bubble I ate slowly to use up more time. Finally I sat back and tried to take stock.

So far we hadn't done too badly. Thanks to Miss Binh's good idea and the hard work everyone had put into pulling it off, we were in fair shape. There was a vote of thanks due the VC as well. They'd stuck right with the plan, coming in on cue just as though they'd been rehearsing for weeks. So far all those who'd come out for Posse were still with the program, even the wounded still able to keep up and pull their weight.

The Tiger had been waiting at the rendezvous with our trucks. Our main body had moved a little more slowly than the three of us from the rear guard and they'd arrived only a few minutes before we pulled in. We loaded up and The Tiger did a fast end run around the south end of the plateau to the place where the wine bottle signal had been hung. We drove almost all the way to the bridge, unloaded and then let The Tiger take the trucks back up the trail to where they could be hidden from sight.

Next I took a minute to get everybody together to make sure they all knew what I had in mind. Then I crossed the swaying bridge and got to work. Once I made sure that any outpost that may have been there had been withdrawn to get into the big fight, we had the place to do with as we wished. There were still sounds of firing off to the northwest but the pace seemed to be slackening and perhaps even getting a bit closer. I kept looking over my shoulder toward the big outcrop the track curved around before it went out of sight. The first of our visitors would show up right there and I wanted to have everything ready for their reception.

That was the reason I'd taken the ten best men we had and placed them carefully, interlacing their fields of fire to cover every inch of ground. Potter was just below me with his own special gear and while he looked fully relaxed even on the sharp rocks I knew he was alert and primed to act on command.

Hieu was over on the other side with another squad, ready to give us what fire support we might need and to handle anyone who might make it across. Our last line was out of sight up the trail, where The Tiger and three men were hidden. If anyone got that far he was to be allowed to go his way in peace unless, of course, he was so bad-mannered as to start shooting.

Tactically we were in good shape, making the most of our assets and exploiting the terrain the way you're taught. Logistically it wasn't quite so rosy. The big problem was ammunition. After delivering enough to Bostwick to take care of twenty or thirty Latin American revolutions, we found that we were running low ourselves. The trip through the VC camp and the phony battle had taken almost every round we'd carried and all we had left now was what The Tiger had on the trucks. It wasn't any secret. All our people knew the situation and we didn't have to tell them to take it easy and if they had to fire to be sure and make it count.

The sun was directly overhead now, shining straight into the canyon, heating the stone and reflecting down from the rock walls above us. Far below I could hear the sound of the water foaming over the rocks and, cold though I knew it was, it was almost irresistible, hot as I was. Mostly to take my mind off it, I listened carefully to the sounds coming from the northwest. Over the pleasant sounds of the river the gunfire was a barbaric snarling, out of place and offensive to the ear.

There was no longer any doubt that it had come a lot closer. In the narrow canyon there was no way to guess just how far off they were but one thing was apparent. What I heard was almost all small-arms fire without the underscoring sounds of anything bigger. To me it meant just one thing. The VC were on top and were holding their heavy stuff for fear of hitting their own men, close as they'd come to the retreating Blue Star. It also told me that if he wasn't already on his way, then it wouldn't be long before Bostwick would head for his escape hatch, the bridge that was swaying slightly down below me.

Potter was reading the signs, too. I saw him stir and turn to look up at me. Toothpick in place, he smiled and stuck up two fingers in the old Churchill "V" sign. We both turned toward the curve in time to see what happened next.

Rising into the sky was a rolling tower of grayish, oily smoke. Up at the plantation, one side or the other had fired the warehouses, igniting what stock of rubber still remained along with the buildings themselves. The rising air caught and tore at the smoke, pulling away long streamers of it, and in a few minutes the acrid smell was carried to us on the wind. It couldn't be long now and I rechecked my weapon and saw Potter do the same. Whoever our first callers might be, we were ready.

The first bunch that came around the bend wasn't really what I'd been expecting. There were about twenty-five of them, women and children, loaded down with string bags and straw baskets filled with the tangle of things that people snatch up when they've got only minutes or less to save their necks. Most had

217

carrying sticks and when they got to the bridge there was some milling around until they could get sorted out enough to form a single file and begin to cross. There was no sign of a weapon and I couldn't see any reason at all why they shouldn't be allowed to go their way in peace. The sooner they cleared out, the smaller the chance that they might get in the way when the boys started playing their rough games. We just let them pass on through without even knowing that they'd been watched.

I could see that some of the smaller kids were scared pretty badly when they set foot on the walkway and felt the bridge tremble under them but not one of them cried or protested as they clutched the ropes and let their mamas urge them on.

Finally the last of them made it across and they streamed off up the trail past Hieu's positions to wherever they thought they could find a haven along with a few million others in their country. The only remarkable thing was that not a sound had been heard, not from the women or even from the tiniest of the babies. The Vietnamese are real experts in the refugee business, particularly the women and kids. They've had a couple thousand years' experience. The only difference I saw in this bunch was that they were all younger women and kids. No old folks at all.

There was a little lull and then traffic began to pick up. A few minutes after the first party had crossed the bridge and gone out of sight, I spotted a man poking his head out from behind the outcrop. He took plenty of time for a good look around and then started out down the track, closely followed by four or five others. They all had the star on their caps and were armed with U.S. weapons. They didn't waste any time about getting out. They'd already made their judgment on the probable future of the Blue Star and had got to the action phase of the exercise. In less time than it takes to tell, they had crossed and gone out of sight up the trail. There was no sound of firing so I had to assume that if The Tiger hadn't stopped and disarmed them, he'd just let them go on their way, arms and all. In any case, they were out of the action and no longer a factor for anyone.

For the next half hour that was the pattern. Small groups of men, women and kids filtering past in hopes of making it to the valley beyond. The smell of burning rubber grew stronger and the sounds of firing grew closer and more sporadic. The smoke was now beginning to blanket the whole area, not enough to dim the blazing sunlight but sufficiently to show that the fire was spreading, blazing out of control. When I saw a new column of smoke rising I thought at first it was still another building, some other kind of structure, which produced thick black smoke filled with flecks of red that sailed up along with the rest. It wasn't until I saw it stir and begin to move toward us that I woke up to what it really was.

That smoke was coming from a wood fire under forced draft; the red flecks, burning embers carried aloft on the smoke from the logs in the firebox. Somebody had got steam up in the old kettle and they were on their way.

Judging by the size of the smoke column, they didn't have far to come and when it arrived we were going to have to do a lot more than just sit on our cans and watch the parade go by. If that train was the VIP special we would finally have to take a hand in the proceedings. I checked the double clip in my M-16 and tried to get my blood back to its normal routes and my breathing even and regular. With the moment of truth right on top of us, I was nervous as a china shop owner when a bull strolls in. I tried my old stunt of counting to myself, making bets on what number I'd reach when the action began. I lost the first five or six but finally I won. At eighty-five I heard the sounds of the old locomotive getting pretty near.

It was coming slowly, probably not much faster than a man can walk, the sound of its wheels like that of a platoon of pigs being driven through the narrow gorge. I lifted my rifle and aimed at the point where the locomotive would first be seen but just as I was sure it would appear, the sound of the wheels on the rails stopped and all I could hear was the snorting of the boiler as the fire built up steam. Whoever was running things wanted a little more information before he poked his nose out.

This time I saw a man in the ditch that lined the track on one side, working his way along the ground in the standard way the U.S. Army has been teaching ever since it was chasing Geronimo. This guy kept his head well down, his nose almost scraping the rocky surface, his rifle cradled in his arms. Through a narrow gap in my rock wall I could see his blue star and chevrons as he wiggled forward a few feet at a time, advancing and then pausing to take a look around.

When he got forward far enough to take a clear look at the bridge, he paused for what must have been a full minute, looking left and right for any sign of trouble. He was listening as well, his head cocked to one side, as I held my breath in fear that if I even moved that much I might dislodge a pebble big enough to give the whole thing away as it went rattling down to where he lay.

He knew his business and he didn't rush into anything but waited patiently, his senses tuned up so high that I could almost feel the tension myself. Finally he was satisfied. He got to his feet and took one last look before he turned and waved back to the train, then he stepped off the tracks and waited.

After a moment's delay the wheels begin to screech as the brake was released, the gear lever shifted and the throttle opened with a loud hissing—built-up steam going to the cylinders. There was the clank of the firebox door being slammed shut on a new charge of logs and then the headlight came into view as the train edged forward.

I knew right away that it was the same one I'd last seen when it had hooted at me and then rolled away with Bostwick, Bailey, Miss Chi and the thousand cases of ransom. There just couldn't be two like that on the whole face of the earth. It came grinding around the curve, not looking a bit better but still healthy enough to haul itself and the same string of flatcars and its tender loaded with logs. There were a few minor hemorrhages where thin jets of steam were hissing but, by and large, it did the job.

Bostwick had apparently chosen to leave the ammo right where it was, preferring to keep his big asset mobile and not take a chance on being cut off from it when he might need it most. There were a few gaps in the neat rows, probably where stock had been drawn for use in the fight with the VC, but it couldn't have been more than a few thousand rounds. It takes a lot of shooting to burn a million cartridges and most of it was still there, along with what I guessed was the remainder of the Blue Star army. They must have taken a hell of a good licking from the VC.

From where I was I couldn't make an accurate head count but

there weren't more than fifty or sixty effectives, just about all of them NCOs, and probably the hard core of the outfit. Most likely the rank and file had been the first to either die or cut and run, like the few men who had already passed our way, when the VC had brought up the heavy stuff.

Just about every man had a woman and a kid or two with him, squatting on the ammo cases with the belongings they had salvaged. Some of the men had been hit and crudely bandaged but there weren't any real litter cases. Those who hadn't caught the train must have been left behind to whatever fate the VC might think appropriate. Probably those they could patch up would find themselves doing the same old thing in a new army with new NCOs yelling the same old things at them. The rest didn't have to worry about the future.

So far there had been no sign of either American or of Miss Chi. At first I thought they might all be riding first class in the engine cab and as the train came steaming along to where the rails ended at the brink of the gorge, I watched to see who would dismount. There was another shriek as the engineer set the brake and the train skidded a foot or so as it came to a stop, breathing heavily and leaking a little steam. I saw Bailey jump down from the cab and just as he landed John Potter leaned forward and twisted the handle of the detonator he held.

There was a single giant report that boomed and bounded from wall to wall and then a great crashing and roaring as the charge we'd planted wrenched great masses of rock loose from the wall and sent it crashing down on the tracks and into the river, carrying rails, roadbed and all away and blocking the way back to the top of the plateau.

A huge, choking cloud of rock dust came swirling around us, blinding those on the train and hiding them for a minute from our view. As an explosion it was a real four-star winner and all the credit goes to Potter. Until you've seen it with your own eyes there is no way to describe what an expert can do with a few hundred pounds of fresh dynamite when it's properly placed in soft rock. John had used every last stick of what I'd bought from Mr. Tang. That first real big slammer had torn right into the rock, then had come the roaring as the slide began and finally it dropped down to a series of smaller crashes as the rocks tried to get reorganized under the new arrangement. They were still bumping and scraping when the smaller pieces, which had gone straight up, got the word about Sir Isaac Newton's law and decided to come back to earth to fall on the just and the unjust alike, the people down on the cars and those of us on the slopes above.

I got my arms over my head and tried to protect the softer spots in my skull but I did catch a glimpse of Potter beaming up at me through the dust and falling gravel, his toothpick cocked at a jaunty angle. That was when I found I couldn't hear. All sorts of things were going on down below that my brain told me should make some kind of sound but nothing was getting through to me.

It was weird, like an old silent movie. It took a moment to realize what had happened. In that narrow cleft in the spine of the mountain, the blast had been magnified to a point where our eardrums had just gone dead. How long it was going to take before we could hear again I didn't know but I did know one thing:

The people down below couldn't hear any better than we could.

Bailey was waving his arms around like a wild man. Finally the man he was trying to communicate with got the message and I saw him run to the bend and peer through the dust at the work our charge had done. When he came running back with his report he didn't need words. A good bit of the mountain was now lying on top of the tracks, with most of them gone for good in the river. The only thing that could get through now would have to make it on foot, whether it was a goat or a man.

As soon as the rocks had stopped falling the people on the cars had begun piling off, milling around while they tried to snatch up their bundles and the smaller kids. Slowly my hearing began to return and I could make out Bailey yelling over the rest of them, trying to get things coordinated. His NCOs weren't much help, each one giving his own version of what Bailey was trying to order. There was a general drift toward the bridge, which was still rocking violently after the blast, and the whole scene looked like the legendary Chinese Fire Drill the old drill sergeants like to use for horrible comparisons with scenes of total disorder. At last Bailey got the word through to his men. The people began to form a ragged line along the tracks, some of them bleeding from cuts inflicted by the falling rock. Gradually he got things calmed down and by the time my hearing was back to normal he had them in some kind of order.

I saw him stop long enough to look back up the canyon but whether it was for some sign of Bostwick or for the VC there was no way to know. Right at the moment Bailey was the man in charge and, no matter what, he was a trained NCO and he was still thinking a good straight line. He didn't have much in the way of options and damn little time to compare their merits. The question he had to be debating was whether he should stay where he was and try to make a stand or whether to get what was left of his force to hell and gone over the bridge and out to the valley beyond, where he could get enough time to lick his wounds and regroup. It didn't take more than a few seconds to make up his mind.

If he stopped long enough to give Bostwick a chance to get through to him, he was taking a bigger chance than any sane man would. He couldn't go back the way he'd come, not with the VC still coming on hard and strong, ready to wipe out what was left of the Blue Star.

He couldn't stay where he was with only the fragile bridge to escape over. There was no way for him to know just who had set the charge in the rock that had just blown and I don't guess he was taking much time to worry about it.

I heard him bark out the Vietnamese order to fall in and saw the men form a double line facing their women and kids. Then he gave the command to face right and I knew I had to quit being a spectator and get myself into the act. There wasn't time to come up with anything catchy for use by biographers who someday may write the life of Mike Keefe.

I stood up and yelled, "Okay, everybody. Hold it!"

⊰ 26 ⊱

Why should I deny it? It was one hell of a moment. I'd have given a year's pay to have a camera turning on that scene so I could have a film to show my grandchildren, which they could pass on to theirs.

"Now look, kids. There's Grandpa right up there on the side of the cliff with his rifle. Listen now, listen. How about that? 'Hold it!' Grandpa says, and now look at all those people. They're just standing there frozen. They don't know what the hell to do."

"But why didn't those men just up and shoot old Grandpa?"

"Shut up, Orville, and listen now."

I hope Orivlle, or whatever the little stinker's name is, does ask that question; it was what I was asking myself when I made my grandstand play. My own guess is that they didn't start right in shooting and zap me right where I stood because they were dumfounded at the idea of anybody doing something that stupid. That and the sounds of weapons being cocked on both sides of the gorge. For them the smart thing was to cool it and let the situation develop a little.

Bailey was the first to get his wits back but before he could start anything going I yelled at him to lay his weapon on the ground and back away from it. Hieu from his place yelled out the same thing in Vietnamese, telling the men to get as far as they could from the train and the women and kids to stay put. When all that was sorted out, Potter and I left our perches and slid down to the level ground. The rest of our men stayed put, covering us in case of trouble.

I edged along, keeping my back protected, to where I could cover the men, my rifle up and on full automatic.

"What now?" Hieu yelled over to me.

"Tell the women to cross first with the kids. If we separate them from their men maybe they'll be easier to handle."

He yelled out something and he didn't have to say it twice. The whole gaggle of women and kids started forming into a ragged line and moving across the bridge. As soon as the first of them were over Hieu yelled again, not letting them pile up while they waited for the men. Instead they trotted right along and in a minute or two I could hear The Tiger's voice in the distance as he urged them on. The men shifted nervously from foot to foot, glancing up now and then, trying, I guess, to figure out just how many of us there were. They had that funny hunched-up look men get when somebody is holding a loaded weapon on them, almost as though they were trying to make themselves smaller targets in case we started shooting. With the VC right behind them, there was only one idea and that was to get the hell over to the far side of the gorge and make tracks.

That was their problem, though. I had my own and one of them was standing off to one side a little. I worked my way along the rocks until I was standing just above him.

"Sergeant Bailey."

The time he'd spent up there in the hills hadn't wiped out the reflexes he'd learned in his years with the Army. His shoulders came back as he popped to attention and he sounded off, "Yes, sir."

"I'm Captain Keefe. You're under my orders now and here's the first one. You stay nice and cool and don't make any sudden moves."

"Does that mean I'm under arrest?"

"Arrest? Hell, no. If I arrest you I've got to read you your rights and let you call a lawyer. Frankly I don't know the words and I haven't got that kind of time. Let's just put it this way. You just do as you're told. Otherwise you might suffer some kind of permanent injury. Okay?"

He nodded and I asked, "Where's your buddy?"

"I don't know, Captain. I saw him about an hour back and then

225

we got separated. He said to get the engine fired up and start moving back. Most of the people had left already and he and that Miss Chi were trying to get some kind of a rear guard organized. I suppose he figured it was going to take a little time to get everybody over the bridge to where they could split up and fan out."

"You think they'll be coming this way?"

"I guess so. It's the only way out."

So there it was. If I was going to get Bostwick it would have to be right there. I didn't mind that so much except that when he finally arrived he was sure to have a lot of nasty people on his tail. To grab him before they did was going to require a nice touch.

The women and kids were all across now and Hieu had the men going. They didn't need any prodding, either. They went right along, trotting to catch up with their families when they got off the shaky catwalk. When the last of them were over I waved my men down from their perches and, with Potter to keep an eye on him, I sent Bailey over. He didn't show any signs of wanting to make a getaway but I didn't want him underfoot for what was going to happen next.

From somewhere back up the line there was another burst of firing. It was all small arms, which meant that they were too close to use mortars or any kind of heavy stuff. If I was going to do anything I had to make up my mind fast.

The Tiger's men were beginning to show signs of wanting to get going. None of them liked the idea of being pinned down on the same side of the gorge with Victor Charlie and I can't say I blamed them. I gestured to them to gather up the weapons dropped by the Blue Star crowd and get across, and they didn't stand around to discuss it. I wouldn't need any help for what I had to do and they could cover me just as well from the high ground on the far side.

Judging from the number of men we'd disarmed plus the casualties they must have taken in the fighting, there couldn't be much left of the Blue Star. The rear guard wasn't going to be able to do a hell of a lot to slow down the attack and I could be looking for them to drop in anytime. I had enough people to take care of Bostwick but I didn't have a chance against a well-organized VC unit. They were sure to win the whole pot, including a nice windfall of ammunition. The first thing on my agenda was doing something about the load on the train.

Except for the few missing cases, it was just about the way it had looked when Bostwick had gone happily off with it the day we'd made the delivery. There was still some steam up and every so often the safety valve would let out a snort to relieve the pressure in the boiler. A steady column of smoke was rising from the battered stack and I could hear the crackling of the logs burning in the firebox. A good-sized stack of firewood lay on the tender just in case you might want to take a long trip but I'd pretty well ruled that out when we'd blown the charges a few yards away. It was another case of "all dressed up and no place to go."

The way it looked, if I wanted to get rid of all that stuff I didn't have a whole lot to work with. For one thing, it was going to have to be done in the next few minutes, and there was another small consideration. I had no plans to go up with it. If I was going to have to blow the whole shebang, I preferred not to be on the premises.

Now even if you don't know a damn thing about ammunition or any high explosives, you can understand that it's not the simplest thing in the world to get shut of. If you do it by the book you don't try. You get on the phone and make an appointment with your friendly neighborhood team of demolition experts. You just pass your problem along to them and let them take over.

They come around and pick up your old ammo, or bombs or whatever, and then truck them to a place they've got for the purpose. Usually it's a big open area of maybe a couple of hundred acres where nobody lives. They make a large pile of everything and here and there in the stack they plant some small charges. When all of them have been wired up, they pass the word around the area that they're going to make a lot of noise at a scheduled time. That's so when the whole mess blows no one will think that perhaps World War III has commenced.

When it gets close to time for the big event, the whole disposal team goes into a nice safe shelter they've got. They count noses to make sure that nobody's been left outside and then they hook up their electric detonator.

As a rule they like to schedule it for noon. Right on the dot of twelve they close the circuit and the whole mess blows and everyone for about ten miles around can set his watch. The team waits a bit just to make sure there are no late starters and then they pack up and go home for a hot lunch and your problem's been solved.

I didn't have the time to send for a demo team and wait around until they arrived. Even if I'd been an expert myself, and I wasn't, there was neither time nor equipment to do the job by the book. I'd have to work with what I had on hand and that was nothing but the elderly train standing there gurgling and burping, the safety valve letting off the excess pressure with a periodic snort. Like any kid who's grown up in a jerkwater town, I did know a little about them.

For one thing, they run on tracks. Once you get them going, all you have to do is sit back and make sure there's nothing up ahead that's using your rails.

The specimen I had was steam-powered, of course. If you wanted to ride you had to burn coal or logs or anything that would make steam in the boiler. When the pressure got high enough you moved the big lever to forward drive and opened the throttle to let the steam get to the cylinders, pushing them against the drive wheels. You could back up by shifting the lever. Either way, as long as you kept up the pressure you kept going. To stop you closed the throttle and used the brake. If you wanted to leave shortly you kept the fire going and the pressure up. If you lost pressure you'd have to build it up again: more fire—more steam —more power to move. Simple.

I climbed up to the cab and looked around, trying to identify everything before I got to work. It was your basic, standard model. The steam pressure gauge showed enough to get her moving and I put her in reverse, loosened the brake and opened the throttle slowly. There was a series of hunching sounds as the couplings closed and I let the train roll back until the last car was right at the bend and braked there. I'd gone back about fifty yards from the point where the track ended at the brink of the gorge and that was going to have to do.

The next move was to get rid of the pressure in the boiler, or of as much as I could. I found the right thing to pull and there was a loud hissing and a cloud of vapor. As it lifted I saw the pressure gauge needle drop to the bottom of the dial. Until the pressure built up again the engine wasn't going anywhere.

Without pressure and with the throttle closed, I moved the lever to the forward position and reset the brake so that it would just hold the wheels until the steam pressure would be high enough to free them. I stepped back to check everything and then opened the firebox door just as Potter climbed up beside me. He took one look and figured out for himself what I was doing. He put down his riot gun and went straight for the tender. I got into position at the firebox, and as fast as John heaved the logs into the cab, I chucked them into the firebox.

The wood was good and dry and, with the open fire door making a strong draft, they caught quickly. A steady stream of smoke and flying embers rose from the stack as log after log ignited and contributed its share. I crammed the last possible piece in and slammed the door, swinging around to watch the pressure gauge needle start to edge upward. Even after I'd vented all the steam it wouldn't take long before there was pressure enough to get the engine moving. What I had to avoid was letting it start without enough pressure to do what I needed. That was the job for the brake. All it had to do was hold until it gave way, under enough pressure to let the train go with plenty of power. One other thing. It had to hold long enough to let us get off the premises with time to save our skins.

I waved to John to get going and he grabbed his gun and headed out. I crossed my fingers and opened the throttle wide and then ran like hell for the bridge. Potter had already found a good spot behind some fallen rocks on the other side and I dropped down beside him and looked across at the engine.

If you didn't know better you'd probably think it was a nice peaceful scene. The locomotive was putting out a pleasant cloud of smoke but there was no outward sign of what was going on inside. The steam was beginning to build, little squirts were emerging at a couple of small leaks, but the bulk of the pressure was starting to course through the open throttle to the cylinders, held now only by the lightly set brakes.

Of course if you didn't know about all those things I'd taken the trouble to arrange, you probably wouldn't give it a second look and just go right past the train and the locomotive and make tracks for the bridge just beyond where the tracks ended and get across to the other side before the nasty people behind you caught up and tried to start an argument.

With a spare minute you might even consider chopping through the big ropes that held the bridge up if you had a machete handy the way Miss Chi did when we saw her come into view at the bend. It was in a scabbard swinging at her right hip, back far enough not to interfere with the carbine in her hands. I heard a scattering of shots that couldn't have been more than a couple of hundred yards away and then right behind Miss Chi appeared the cause of all our trouble.

He must have been coming along hard for quite a while but he didn't head right for the bridge. Instead he stopped at the bend and looked back. Miss Chi must have called to him because I saw him shake his head and wave her on before lifting his rifle and firing at some target out of our sight. I could see his shoulders heaving as he fought for breath while he emptied the clip before finally turning away and limping heavily after her. There was a slash of bright red against his black hair and a red stain on his left thigh but he kept coming even while he was reversing his magazine to bring up a fresh load. I saw Miss Chi run back to him and watched as he leaned on her shoulder. That helped and he made a little better time. I let them get almost to the bridge before I stood up.

"Hold it right there. Drop the weapons and come over one at a time."

The two of them stopped in their tracks, looking around to see where I was. They showed no signs of being about to drop their rifle and carbine and finally I yelled again.

This time he spotted me and for a split second I thought he might open fire. If he had any such thought he gave it up when

Potter stood and raised the riot gun and aimed it directly at them. Even at that range the heavy buckshot would have torn them to bits.

Close as they were now I got a really good look at him, unshaven and grimy, holding himself together with what could only have been sheer will power.

"Come on, man. They're right behind you. Drop the weapons and get over here."

I didn't seem to be getting through to him and, for a moment, I thought he was going to shoot at me. Instead of dropping his rifle, he swung around on his good leg and looked back. What he saw got him moving.

He dropped to his belly and, with Miss Chi at his side, he began a rapid fire at the men clambering over the rocks and moving down the track in short rushes. A few of them tried to get some cover behind the train wheels until somebody with more brains than the rest saw what was loaded on the cars. Behind me I heard The Tiger's troops laying down a fire cover and at my side Hieu and Potter opened up as well. I could hear Bailey yelling something and finally I made it out. He wanted to get into the fight as well. There was an M-16 in the truck and I called to him to get it.

All this time I was yelling at the pair over on the other side. If they stayed down and moved evasively there was a chance for them to make it.

"Come on, we're covering you. Come on, Bostwick. Come on."

Finally I got through to him. He looked around and saw me waving and then he struggled to his knees and the two of them began to crawl toward the bridge. They had only about twenty-five yards to cover when there was a sudden wrenching groan from the old locomotive. The pressure in the boiler was way up and the cylinders were starting to buck against the brakes. The strain was becoming more than the old brakes could hold and it would be only seconds before the wheels would struggle free of them and the whole rig would start to roll. Even from our distance we could see the ancient engine beginning to shake.

There was a final roaring groan and then down the track she started. I yelled again, "Come on, Bostwick. Get up and run." He was attempting to get to his feet, holding onto the woman, who was trying to lift his weight all by herself. Half supporting, half dragging him, she was striving to cover the last few remaining yards when the attackers woke up. They began to fire at us, and I felt a sudden sting when a flying rock fragment tore a scratch across the back of my hand.

I took a split second to look at the train. It was moving faster now, the wheels shrieking like banshees on the rails, a dense cloud of smoke and burning embers billowing from the stack. There wasn't anything more we could do and I yelled to the men around me. We dropped behind the rock for whatever cover we could get. I heard the train wheels suddenly begin to rumble as the locomotive left the track, the drive wheels still forcing it along over the rocky ground, and then there was the sound of masses of metal being wrenched apart as it went over the edge, pulling the whole string of loaded cars behind it into the gorge.

With one piercing roar the boiler blew, sending a cloud of steam into the air, and then the ammunition began to go in a whole string of detonations. I clung to the earth as a rain of rock and wood and bits of steel fell around us, covering my head for whatever protection I might get from my bare arms. The air was filled with the bitter smell of cordite as the fire spread to the wooden cases and then to the ammunition, cordite mixed with steam and wood smoke and the billows of pulverized rock that eddied around us. Underlying the sharp, snapping explosions of the high explosives were the deeper bass sounds from the rocky sides of the gorge, echoing and reverberating between the close-set walls, and the dull rumbling of masses of rock being torn from the backbone of the mountain to go hurtling down to the bottom.

Finally it ended. The last of the ammunition must have been blown and the last of the rocks torn free. The only sound was the crackling of the flames that were consuming what was left of the wooden cases. Slowly I got to my feet and looked around. The bridge was gone along with about ten feet of the lip of the gorge on the other side. That was just about where the pair of them had been when I saw them last. There was no sign of the attackers, nothing, in fact, but the rusty rails that led back to where the rocks had fallen on them.

When I could get my feet to work, I walked over to the brink and peered down. The gorge was filled with a tangled mass, the remains of the locomotive and the cars. Most of it was buried in the rock that had fallen and the whole business had compacted into a giant dam that filled the stream bed almost to the top. The water had ceased to run and already was beginning to rise until it could find a way over the top.

I turned away, my stomach churning. Bailey was there looking at me with a funny expression on his face.

"Captain, can I ask a question?"

"Sure, Bailey. What do you want to know?"

"Sir, you called him Bostwick, didn't you?"

"Sure. Why not? That was his name, wasn't it?"

He shook his head. "No, sir. Captain Bostwick is dead. Has been for three years. He was the first one to get hit when they overran us."

⊰ 27 ⊱

There hadn't been any need to hurry but nobody really wanted to do anything but get going and home as soon as possible. With only three vehicles we made good time and it wasn't until late afternoon that I called a halt and we made camp for the night. Between the letdown after all the tension and the wound on my hand, I was beginning to feel a little fuzzy around the edges. The Tiger put a fresh dressing on me and did what he could for the others who'd been hit or banged up during the day. Considering the amount of damage they'd done, we'd come off pretty well. The Tiger and his crippled commandos had done a hell of a job and I had every intention of going to bat for them when we got back to Saigon.

I was sitting beside the fire with Hieu, waiting for the water to boil for tea, when Potter came over.

"Captain, what do you want to do about Bailey?"

That was something I still hadn't given any thought to. On the road Potter and Bailey had been back in one of the cargo trucks and I'd chased the problem out of my mind until I could talk to the man. There wasn't any point in putting it off any longer so I told Potter to bring him over. I could get his story while we ate.

He still looked a little battered but he'd done what he could to get himself cleaned up. The blue star had been ripped from his cap and he came over to where we were sitting, looking like any good soldier reporting to his superior. I saw him hesitate for just a moment before he finally made up his mind and saluted. A man under arrest doesn't have the right to salute and he still wasn't sure of his status. I returned it and told him to get comfortable. He found a place to sit but he wasn't very relaxed. Someone had given him a cigarette and he asked if he could smoke. I just nodded and he got a twig from the fire and lit up. That seemed to help and so did a pull at the brandy bottle I had in the truck. He wiped the neck and pushed in the cork before he put it at my side and settled back.

If I was ever going to get the whole story it was going to be right now. The most important thing was not to scare him into clamming up.

"Do you want to talk about it, Bailey?"

He took a deep breath and said, "I guess so. What do you want to know, sir?"

"Tell me about Bostwick first. What happened to the captain?"

"Well, like I said, he was the first one to go down. We'd stopped for a break and then they hit. I tried to get to the radio but they moved in so fast I never had a chance. A couple of the men went down and then he yelled at me."

"Who did?"

He jerked his thumb in the direction from which we'd come. "Him. When the old first sergeant was charged they'd moved him up until a new one could join. He'd been the next senior NCO and he took over."

"What was it he yelled?"

"Well, he had his hands in the air and he saw me still on my feet. He said, 'Surrender, Bailey, and all your troubles are over.'"

"What did he mean by that?"

"I guess he meant that with all the trouble I was in, it would be a lot better to be a prisoner right there than in Leavenworth with a dishonorable discharge. That way my pay would go on and my family would be taken care of until I got back. Maybe by that time the trouble would have been forgotten and everything would be okay."

"What kind of trouble were you in, Bailey?"

He gave me a funny look. "You know what I mean, sir. He told me about it that morning before we went out to the choppers. He said that Captain Bostwick had been asking a lot of questions and that he had me figured for fraggin' that lieutenant. A couple of guys were willing to swear that I'd done it and the captain had already put in for my court-martial."

"Did you do it, Bailey?"

He shook his head vigorously. "No, sir. No way. But I didn't have any way to prove it. It would have been their word against mine and if two or three of them got together and said I was the one, I wasn't going to have much of a chance." He looked down into the fire. "I guess I'll get my court-martial now."

"I don't know what for, Bailey. I've been through every last thing in your file and there's nothing in it to hook you in with the fragging. The men who did it were tried and convicted and they're in the U.S. Disciplinary Barracks right now."

He looked up, staring intently at me as he struggled to accept what I'd told him.

"Okay, Bailey, go on with what happened. You say he told you to surrender and that all your troubles would be over?"

"Yes, sir. I dropped my weapon and stuck up my hands and then they were all over us. One of them grabbed me and shoved me around a little, then another one came up and they led me off a ways and made me sit down. They didn't hit me or anything but they took my wallet and my cigarettes and I understood that I had to sit still and behave.

"I could hear firing off to where the other people were and then it got quiet and the headman came back and I could see they were getting ready to pull out. I was starting to sweat by then. They didn't look like anything more than a bunch of bandits and there was no way of knowing if they were going to bother with us as prisoners or just zap us and go on their way."

"I wonder what made them decide to let you live."

"Maybe it was what he did. They took me back to where the captain's body was and he was still there. He still had his hands up but now he was wearing the captain's jacket and cap and I saw he had taken the rings, too. I guess he figured he'd get better treatment if they thought he was an officer.

"He shouted to me to call him Captain Bostwick but they didn't let him say any more. The headman just pointed the way and we got moving.

236

"We must have marched about four hours or so until we got back to the old plantation. They gave us some rice and locked us up and next morning that Miss Chi came for us. They took us up to the main house and asked us some questions."

"Who did?"

"Well, mostly it was Miss Chi. The big boss didn't speak much English and anyway he didn't seem to give much of a damn. Looked to me like all he did around there was lay up and smoke that pipe of his, and I don't mean he was usin' tobacco either. Miss Chi, she ran the works.

"Well, she kept looking at what she thought was Captain Bostwick like somebody who's just bought a new stud bull and has a lot of hopes for him. She looked me over pretty good, too, but anybody could see that he was the candidate she was goin' to vote for.

"That night we heard a couple of shots and next morning they turned us loose. He was moved in with Miss Chi and the new management took over." He shook his head sadly. "For a while we had it pretty good until they started gettin' greedy."

"How did that happen?"

"I suppose it was when we heard about Captain Bostwick's wife and mine goin' to the White House to get our medals. I'd listen to Armed Forces news every night on the radio and I told him about it. That's when they got the idea. By that time Miss Chi knew who he really was. She said we might be able to fool Mrs. Bostwick but his father, the general, would be pretty hard to convince, but even before I heard that he died they decided to try it."

"They moved pretty fast, didn't they?"

"Well, they were all set to go. They sent that lawyer or whatever he was right along. I don't know much about that part. They weren't telling me any more than they had to."

"Why not, Bailey?"

"I suppose it was because they knew that I was still hopin' to get home someday. He didn't give a damn, though. He just thought it was funny as hell, everybody thinkin' that Bostwick was still alive."

237

"You know that there was a court-martial waiting for him, don't you?"

He shrugged. "It figures." He frowned and then shook his head. "You know, sir, I've been trying but somehow I can't remember his real name."

"It's probably just as well, Bailey."

⊰ 28 ⊱

We were back in the room that looked out over The Plain. Apart from the few men at work cutting the grass and a few cars passing Trophy Point, there wasn't much activity. It was midsummer, the low point in the Academy year. The cadets and faculty were mostly on leave while the incoming class was off at camp going through the basic training they call Beast Barracks.

After the heat in the cemetery, the room was almost chilly but I accepted the cold drink I was offered and took a seat.

There hadn't been much of a ceremony. The few people present had barely filled the front pews of the cemetery chapel, all of them in uniform except for Anne Bostwick and her father. We were sitting across the aisle and I couldn't see her face until she turned to watch the flag-draped casket being brought down the aisle.

She was pale but, from what I could see, had herself under control. I saw her father reach over and touch her hand and she looked back at him and then faced forward. She had got past the sight of the casket and I guess she was steeling herself for what was yet to come.

The service was short, only the essential minimum prescribed by regulation. I had just a few minutes to look around the old chapel, its walls covered with memorial plaques, lit by the light coming through the windows. When it was over we walked the few yards to the open grave beside the spot where Duke's father had been laid just a few months before. It was the last space in the row, right against the wall of the small cemetery, beside the

239

graves of the other Bostwicks. It didn't really matter. There weren't going to be any more.

The last of the line was buried without the caisson, the black horse, the firing party and the train of mourners in dress blues. A bugler blew Taps and then the folded flag was brought to Anne Bostwick. She looked down at the neat triangle in the officer's hands, then touched it lightly with one gloved hand and turned away and walked slowly but steadily toward the line of parked cars. The rest of us followed behind, unwilling to intrude on her private grief. The uniformed chauffeur had the door of the long black limousine open for her but she didn't enter the car.

Instead she turned and looked back at the grave as the rest of us filed past. She paid no attention to the others, but as Tiny and I approached she took a half step toward us and I could see that there was something she wanted to say. When she'd seen us last it was with hope of seeing her husband again. She had been told no details of his death, only the bare fact and that his body would be buried at the Point. What inferences she had drawn couldn't have been very much.

Tiny and I stopped when we reached her and waited quietly. Her eyes were dry but red-rimmed. She was trying to speak, to do the right thing as she had been trained. We stood that way for a moment and then I reached out and touched her arm. As I stepped back Tiny bent quickly and kissed her lightly on the cheek and then we left her. As we walked out of the cemetery I could hear the mechanism that was lowering what was left of Duke Bostwick into his grave, his class ring and his wedding ring in the casket as his widow had asked.

When our driver dropped us at the mansion the others were already there. After we had been served, our host excused himself and Tiny and I were left alone with Colville. It didn't take him long to say what he had on his mind.

"I haven't been given a copy of your report, Captain, and I don't intend to ask for one. It's enough to know that the man you went to ransom was not my son-in-law but an impostor. For whatever comfort we can get from it, we know that Duke is now in his own grave where he wanted to be buried, here at the Point.

"I'm afraid that what you did cannot be recognized officially. There will be no mention of the matter in your records and no decoration or other commendation from the Army. For myself, I've sent a letter to the Secretary and that will be all that can be done to commend you for a fine job well done."

There wasn't anything I could say. I'd done my best carrying through what I'd hired out for and for that kind of work you don't get much in the way of fancy hardware to put on your chest.

"There is one thing," he went on, "that you'd like to hear. The Vietnamese have asked if they might offer some discreet recognition of your services. Something in the way of one of their better orders."

I was pretty sure that General Truong was sleeping better and that he'd remember that his son had a lot to do with solving his problem. Without Hieu and his veterans, we never could have made it.

I said, "If you see the general I hope you'll thank him for me, Senator, and maybe you'll mention my sergeant, John Potter."

He nodded. "Now there's one other matter. I've seen the two films you made while you weren't otherwise engaged. My people think very highly of them and they'd like to know whether you might be interested in joining the Colville Syndicate if you decide to leave the service."

He went on for a minute with a lot of details about salary and benefits and the retirement plan and stock options but I didn't really take it all in. In the end I said I'd wait to hear from the syndicate office and finally managed to get away.

Naturally we couldn't talk in the car but when we got back to the hotel I had worked up a good head of steam. I put it to Tiny right off.

"You knew damn well that the man running the Blue Star wasn't Bostwick."

She took her time lighting a cigarette and then nodded. "Not at first, though. I took a little convincing. When we got those proofs I didn't have any doubts. The lab did a giant blowup of the white man's face and we could see that somebody had put Bostwick's ID photo on the other man's body."

"Then will you please explain why you let us all risk our collective asses to get back a pair of common deserters?"

"First of all, because they weren't just another pair of deserters. Not in the opinion of a lot of people important enough to demand that action be taken. By the time I was sure that the man they were offering wasn't Bostwick at all, it was too late to call things off. Home Run was committed, and we had to see it through. More important than *who* was there was *what* was there. There were two American servicemen involved. The Army wanted them back. The Army got them back. Mission accomplished."

"Now that Bailey's back, what's going to happen to him?"

"Not a damn thing. He was a bona fide captive and when you came for him he came right along without a peep. Unofficially, I figure he was conned and if he used bad judgment in falling for it that's not a court-martial offense. Anyway, he had all that time to serve with the Blue Star and I don't guess that was much better than a tour in a military prison.

"I got his promotion back-dated and he'll have a nice piece of money coming. Maybe that wife of his will leave some of it unspent."

"From the records, she can get through a whole lot."

"Not where they're going. His orders are for Alaska."

"And the other man? The one who died back there. What about him?"

"You know what I did. I had the grave opened and Bostwick's body taken out for reburial at the Point. Then I had them rebury the empty coffin and reset the headstone. Unless somebody has a reason to dig it up, the matter is finished."

"All the loose ends policed up and nice and tidy."

She didn't answer that and there wasn't anything left to say on the subject. The small bandage on the back of my hand was all I had to remind me of Home Run and that would be gone in a few days. Probably I wouldn't even have a scar.

Tiny finished her cigarette and then went over to gaze out at the city. Without looking at me, she asked, "What are you going to do about Colville's offer?"

I hadn't given it any thought because I'd made up my mind

while he was still making it. If I took it I'd never know whether he had made it from some feeling of obligation and I sure didn't want it that way. There was no sense telling that to Tiny so I just said, "It depends on what kind of a night I have."

GLOSSARY

Some of the terms used in *The Chinese Fire Drill* may be unfamiliar to those not blessed with an opportunity to be present during the last days of the Republic of Vietnam. For their benefit the following is appended:

ao dai (ow zai). The traditional dress of Vietnamese women, consisting of a flowing, floor-length gown with high neck and long sleeves, slit at both sides to the waist to reveal baggy pajama pants. A group of schoolgirls wearing this ensemble in a moderate breeze produces a most pleasant sight.

ARVN (are-vin). Acronym for Army, Republic of Vietnam, but, as a rule, applied to all forces of the nation.

BOQ. Bachelor Officers' Quarters. In Vietnam, as in any area where married officers serve without the consolation of having their families present to greet them after a hard day, it refers to any establishment for housing officers.

BEQ. Similar to above, but provided for use by senior enlisted men, in contrast to tents or barracks.

Cao Dai (cow-dye). A major religious sect in Vietnam, which at one time maintained its own, autonomous army.

Control Commission. The body created by the signatories of the Paris agreement to supervise the scrupulous observance of the terms of the cease-fire by all concerned. Its effectiveness was on a par with what might be expected if the Keystone Kops were to assume the duties of the entire New York City Police Department.

CP. Command Post. The point, fixed or mobile, from which a unit commander controls his troops.

DMZ. Demilitarized Zone. The strip of territory that was to have kept the partisans of both North and South Vietnam from making faces at each other and provoking possible physical retaliation. Unfortunately, this version of the French *cordon sanitaire* ended at the Laotian border, where the local authorities went blind while the northerners dutifully made their way around the obstacle on their way to bring the blessings of Ho Chi Minhism to their neighbors.

DPOE. The Defense Photo Operations Executive, the cover organization to which Mike Keefe and his men have been assigned.

frag, *v.* From "fragmentation grenade," known to the British as a "Mills bomb" and to the Prohibition era as a "pineapple." In Vietnam it provided a means by which disgruntled men might express their disapproval of certain officers and senior enlisted men. Usually fatal.

MAC-V. Military Assistance Command—Vietnam. The mini-Pentagon which exercised overall operational control of U.S. forces. Many felt them to be a major factor in the success of the American effort.

number one. GI slang brought from Japan. Understood by all to denote the very best of anything. Number ten meant the worst.

nuoc mam. The sauce concocted of fermented fish and other exotica with which the Vietnamese flavor most foods. Once the user gets past the odor, he often becomes addicted to the stuff, which is really quite tasty.

NVA. North Vietnam Army, the acronym by which the regular troops of the invasion were differentiated from the Vietcong.

P. GI abbreviation of piaster, the Vietnamese monetary unit.

R and R. Rest and recreation. The program which gave combat troops a five-day special leave in areas as far distant from Vietnam as Hawaii.

Since the whole country was deemed a combat area, this goodie was shared by even those who never heard a shot fired in anger.

sappers. The specially trained NVA and VC troops who went through barbed wire and other defenses with awesome ease to sow destruction, usually with high explosives.

spook. Any type of intelligence or counterintelligence personnel. Spooks come in an assortment of sizes, shapes and colors. Some openly wear the uniform insignia of their organization. Others limit themselves to guilty looks and may be identified by the vehemence of their denials. The good ones look like you and me.

Victor Charlie. The letters V and C as used in the military spoken alphabet. To those with firsthand knowledge of Charlie, the term is generally used with considerable respect and even admiration.

White Mice. The Vietnamese National Police, from their white caps and shirts and their bad habit of taking informal leave in the face of danger during the early days of the troubles. During the 1968 Tet offensive, they did much to redeem their position by showing considerable fortitude under fire.